The New Ze

The New Zealanders

Maurice Shadbolt

David Ling Publishing Limited
P.O. Box 34-601
Birkenhead, Auckland 10

Distributed in New Zealand by Lothian Books

The New Zealanders
This edition first published 1993

ISBN 0-908990-05-7

First published 1959 London by Victor Gollancz
Reprinted Victor Gollancz (twice) 1960
Reprinted Atheneum New York 1961
Reprinted Whitcombe & Tombs New Zealand 1974
Reprinted Whitcoulls New Zealand 1976
Reprinted Hodder & Stoughton New Zealand 1986
This revised edition © 1993 Maurice Shadbolt

Design by Biggles & Co.

The front cover shows a detail from
Land and Family, acrylic on board,
1979, by Nigel Brown.

Photograph of the author by Sean Shadbolt.

Printed in New Zealand

For Gill

Cloud riders, companion
Shakers of morning all,
Rope coiled on saddle horn
At the Sun's funeral,
Sleep in the blind canyon
Of a dream's rock...

Wave walkers, at the edge
Of dark...

James K. Baxter

...here in this far-pitched perilous hostile place
this solitary hard-assaulted spot
fixed at the friendless outer edge of space.

R.A.K. Mason

Contents

Author's Note

REASING these stories, for the first time in more than thirty years, I now
see what I was about, which I didn't altogether when I wrote them in
the middle 1950s and Victor Gollancz published them in book form in 1959.
I *was* aware that I was in rehearsal for the novel which would be published,
more than a decade later, as *Strangers and Journeys*. Three or four stories
in this volume may be found in later form in that novel. (My first, though
the fourth published.) One or two preview other novels, novellas and stories.
Does that, however, justify a new version of *The New Zealanders* in 1993?
I confess to mixed feelings. But publishers have persuaded me to keep the
stories in print, on and off, for more than three decades; I have to presume
that they know their business best.

Certainly what *is* happening in these pages, sometimes innocently, is a
young writer locating his legacy; finding his times, place and people. He even
appears, on occasion, to be resuming Katherine Mansfield's kamikaze
mission — 'to make our still undiscovered country leap into the eyes of the
Old World'. An exile much as Mansfield when I put this book together, I
had notions of a similar nature. Some might say that the country's large burst
of literary energy in the 1970s and 1980s, and now the 1990s, means that
mission is now immaterial; that New Zealand is no longer undiscovered by
literature. Perhaps Mansfield's athletic agenda was never more than an
expatriate fantasy anyway. New Zealanders now write with seldom more
than a nod in the direction of the Old World.

The rest of the tale is told in my memoir *One of Ben's, A New Zealand
Medley* (1993). *The New Zealanders* might now be seen as a supplement
to that memoir. Where there are gaps in the memoir, this book bridges them.
The reverse is also true. *One of Ben's* accounts for the person whose first
book was *The New Zealanders*.

Charitable critics have suggested that I was testifying to the experience
of my confused generation of New Zealanders, or proto-New Zealanders.
Possibly I was. I was certainly serving my apprenticeship in public. I might
now wish the stories different; I might now wish them better. On the other

hand I no longer feel accountable. The person who wrote them is now a stranger. I am not even sure I remember the milieu from which his stories came. New Zealand in the 1950s, isolated and conformist, austere and puritan and tepidly colonial, was not an inspiring sight. From the vantage point of the lively 1990s it *is* a different country: a lost and half-forgotten land. For all its flaws its soil was fertile. Historian-poet Keith Sinclair goes so far as to argue that the New Zealand intellect and imagination came alive in that dour decade. (If so, it owes not a little to Sinclair himself. His *History of New Zealand*, appearing towards its end, was to suggest what we were, and who.)

So there is a more utilitarian reason for republication. Little of New Zealand's 1950s lives on in the literary record. If *The New Zealanders* and its most conspicuous sequel *Strangers and Journeys* did not exist, there might be even fewer fragments of my generation on file. The arrangement of these stories suggests that I was conscious of the record as I put the book together. The eleven stories are divided in three parts: the first draws on rural and small-town New Zealand, the second on urban society, or such of urban society as existed in New Zealand in the 1950s; the third is tinged with the colour of the larger world. I appear to have been burying a time capsule for some bookish archaeologist.

There have been a number of corrections and cuts meant to make this edition leaner and more lucid, and more the book it might have been in 1959. Since its substance was later annexed by a dozen or more books, I see no large sin in editing my twenty-six-year-old self. There will be no more meddling. This edition of *The New Zealanders* will be the last.

M.S. *April 21, 1993*

Wave Walkers

THE WOMAN'S STORY

IT always seemed important to Mother that I should remember England, and for a long while I never understood why. After all, I had been not quite four years old when we left; such things as might have printed themselves on my mind were tattered by time and distance. And, for Mother's purposes, they were almost entirely irrelevant. I mean, for example, such a shred of memory as the one I have of myself peering with intense curiosity at the skin of ice on a large puddle; I was very young at the time, and so I have always presumed that scene set in an English winter. Or such a memory as that of a summer wind stroking the long grass of a yellow field, a field of a certain colour and texture, squared by neat hedges, that I cannot remember having seen in New Zealand; so that memory too must belong to an earlier time.

'But Bridget, darling,' Mother would insist, 'surely you must remember more?'

With her prompting, and my own desire to please, I could sometimes conjure up other things to tell her. And afterwards I could never really be sure if I actually remembered what I told her; or whether I had only constructed it from her own vivid stories, and from the pictures in the books about England which she fed me from my earliest years in New Zealand. I would describe the narrow little street in Ealing where we once lived; the line of shops at the corner; the red pillar-box; the shady green in front of the public library where I took my first faltering steps; the old church where I was christened; and the wide common, with its periphery of rich green trees, where she sometimes walked me in summer. Since it was also important to remember such other items as the lilac which bloomed in our small garden, the walks we had taken at Kew through the long days while Mother waited for the call to New Zealand, the cottage where we stayed with her grandmother in Somerset (perhaps that is where my memory of the yellow field, of strange colour and texture, has its origin), I remembered all these too. And such real memories as I might have had of England became inextricable from the elaborate fictions I created and recited, like catechism, for Mother's peace of mind. And now, when I try to jettison those fictions, all I am left with is a skin of ice, and a yellow field.

Mother was pleased that I could remember such a great deal. 'And you were so young too!' she would say. 'It's remarkable that you can remember so much of home. It shows the impression it made on you, doesn't it? You mustn't ever forget those things, darling. But, then, how could you?'

Indeed, how could I? It was important to her that there was at least one person in her world with whom she could share memories of home; for England was always home. And so my pretence was kept alive from week to week, month to month, year to year; and Mother's persistence had, of course, precisely the effect intended. I grew to awareness rejecting as alien our scrubby backblocks farm, the thick bush of tall kauri, rimu and kaihikatea strung with creeper and supplejack, the mangroved tidal creek, the dusty wooden schoolhouse, the cabbage trees in the playground, the bare coastline where wild surf whitened the rocks. And not only as alien; as somehow unwholesome too. England—the narrow street, the red pillar-box, the green and common, the lilacs, and the tall-towered church—was home. It was tamed, known, and entirely wholesome. New Zealand was a burden to be shouldered, like her marriage to Father. Long before I had the words to fit my inner knowledge, I sensed that their love—and love I presume it had been—had dwindled to a loyalty spiced with casual affection; and then to a habit sprung from necessity. For with the death of the slow years, Mother's links with home became more and more tenuous. Her parents died; her elder brother, in the army, was killed quelling a riot in India. There was still a sister alive, married to a factory manager in Birmingham; but there was no longer a house in Ealing, or a cottage in Somerset.

She met Father in the last year of the first war. He was young then and (I imagine) a sturdy colonial, tanned with sun, still suffering (though he had since fought in the trenches in France) intermittently from a wound he received when he landed with the Anzacs at Gallipoli. He was introduced to the linen and silver of the family dining-room one Sunday; and over the soup, the roast beef and the Yorkshire pudding, and the Sunday trifle, produced an excess of politeness to cover agonies of shyness. He was a junior officer, a lieutenant, promoted from the ranks after heavy casualties in his company; and, in peacetime, a farmer. So naturally the conversation at that quiet dinner-table—with the summer garden tranquil beyond the curtained window—turned about the probable result of the new Allied offensive; about the possibility of the war ending; and about peacetime, and the life of a farmer in New Zealand.

'Things are very different there,' he told the family, without exaggeration.

Afterwards he and Mother walked sedately in the tiny garden. They talked shyly. She was an attractive girl, pale-skinned, dark-haired, and brown-eyed; she was slender, alert, quick in movement and rapid in speech, though she often expressed herself rather too awkwardly when uncertain or excited. She was, like all of her kind, proper in dress and precise in manner. Yet doubtless Father never saw her as one of a kind; but as one set apart, and perfect.

At all events, when the war ended and he returned to New Zealand, he corresponded with Mother for three or four years. His handwriting was always huge and clumsy, with curiously-formed letters and indecipherable words; I imagine it was no different then. Mother, of course, had other suitors; polite and nicely spoken young men sprung variously from English middle-class life who sat at perfect ease in the drawing-room while the clumsily addressed letters from across the sea rustled through the front door. Why she accepted none of these young men has always been beyond her capacity for explanation. Perhaps Father's letters carried some magic of the exotic, the unknown; though I cannot really believe Mother was a great romantic. Perhaps it was just that she did not see Father merely as a sturdy, brown young man of the colonial kind; but also as one set apart, and perfect.

His devotion won; he proposed by letter, and was accepted. And he announced his intention of travelling to England for the marriage. This naturally pleased Mother's parents (strange how I think and speak of them always as 'Mother's parents'; but never, now, as my flesh and blood, my English grandparents) who had feared Father might expect Mother to travel alone to New Zealand for the wedding. It also created a most favourable impression since, like many middle-class people of poor fortune, they spoke with diffidence and reluctance about money, and had been rather too circumspect about enquiring into Father's financial circumstances; they were now able to presume, without caution, that a man who owned a farm, a man who could afford to travel on such a vast scale, must indeed be one of good means. As it happened, they could not have been more wrong.

The ownership of Father's farm was originally shared with three of his brothers. One died on the beach at Gallipoli; another, the youngest, who managed the farm during the war, died in the influenza epidemic afterwards. The third tired of farming on his return from the war, married a city girl, and went to work as a labourer on the Auckland waterfront. Father was left alone on the farm with hungry pastures and a sadly depleted dairy herd. He chopped and burnt through the second-growth of scrub and fern which had been eating, year by year, at the pasture; and fired and flayed his way into new acres of bushland. But results were slow: the cream-cheques were never large; money was always short. When he made the decision to come to England he took out a moderately large mortgage on the farm, persuaded his brother off the waterfront to look after the herd for six months, and departed for England with a dark suit and little money over and above his return fare.

After the wedding he explained, with perfect good sense, his situation to Mother. He did not, of course, detail his financial miseries. He said merely that the farm was not yet ready for a woman. It would be better if she stayed in England for a little while longer until it was ready. Meanwhile he would send money regularly. Mother agreed to this arrangement, since there seemed little alternative, and they presented the plan to her parents as a *fait accompli*. They accepted it with mixed feelings: on the one hand they were pleased that they would not lose their daughter so soon; on the other, the procedure—after all, it was a big thing, expecting Mother to travel so far alone seemed rather irregular. Nevertheless they still did not enquire into Father's circumstances: his reasons seemed quite sound. In any case it would have been far too late for that.

Father returned; a little afterwards I was born, sickly and premature. Mother waited: I grew stronger. The money arrived, each month, from New Zealand. Father worked to get the farm ready (whether 'ready' meant suitable, and livable, for a woman, or just a paying proposition, I have never discovered) but of course it was never really ready. It was all he could do to send off the money to England every month. Finally, in desperation, he took out a second mortgage on the farm to pay Mother's fare to New Zealand. Clutching me, Mother embarked at Southampton full of new fears and hesitations. She wept; her parents wept. I wept for no precise reason, and was curious.

But Mother's nightmare journey (at least that was the very conventional way she always described it) only really began when our ship docked at Auckland. Father was not there to meet us. Instead, he sent his brother, the waterfront worker, with a message. It is difficult to know which shocked Mother most: the fact of Father not meeting her, or the fact of his brother being a labourer. There had been recent heavy floods, and Father was having difficulties with the farm. It proved impossible to leave it in the care of a neighbour, as he had hoped, so that he might travel down to Auckland to meet the ship. So there was his brother, hands and hair still whitish from unloading a phosphate ship that morning, to meet us. He put us on the train north, since Mother wished to leave immediately for the farm, and sent off a telegram to Father. The journey was long and slow; our carriage was one of two second-class carriages attached to the rear of a goods train, and filled, to Mother's surprise and alarm, with Maoris—tattooed, pipe-smoking old women, and loud young men with cases of beer. Mother remembered quite distinctly that one of the young men held an uncapped bottle directly under her nose, offering a drink. The old women clucked and the young ones became drunk and noisy. They had all been to a large tangi near Auckland, and now they were returning to their tribal country. It was a humid summer, and the inside of the carriage was hot and sticky; the landscape jolted past, losing its green complexion for the bleached, brown colours of the summer north. We survived to the end of the train journey, where the bus-ride began. The bus was ramshackle and bumped over stony, uneven roads. We were finally deposited in the shambling little river-town which Mother came to know so well and hate so much; wooden and sprawling, the old houses were scattered along a bush-laced finger of land, and its shops, about the crazy-shaped jetty, were stilted out over the water. The town stood near the end of a long harbour; on each side, creeks fed through grey mud-flats and thick forests of mangroves. For Mother, as we stood upon the jetty waiting for Father to appear, we might well have been looking out, across that wild and lonely landscape, at the end of the world. But I cannot imagine that she displayed any emotion, certainly not to the lazy-voiced inhabitants of the town, the Maoris squatting in the shade of pepper trees, or the roll-trousered launchmen and half-caste fishermen lounging and yarning about the jetty. Her kind had been tested by worse than this before; and survived.

Father appeared, at length, in the launch of a neighbour. His trousers, Mother remembered (she always had a fine eye for certain detail), were milk-stained and patched; he wore gumboots and a torn flannel shirt. Possibly there was some mild display of affection on the jetty that day—after all, it was nearly five years now since they had last seen each other, and Father had never seen me before—but the memory escapes me, and in any case it was not the kind of detail Mother was inclined to remember. We were introduced to the neighbour, a broad-featured Maori in a wide-brimmed hat, a Mr Patera; our trunks were loaded, and the town and jetty dwindled into the distance behind as the launch puttered up-river, zagging back and forward to avoid the shallows left by the out-going tide and sliding under steep banks hung with obstinate bush. The wake of the launch sent small waves hissing over the glistening mud and through the tangled roots of the mangroves. I must have been delighted and excited by the new sights; for I can remember, very clearly, Mother telling me to contain myself. Eventually the engine-sound ceased and, in sudden queer silence among the sounds of cicadas and bush birds, we glided up to a fern-fringed jetty, a rickety structure made of twisted manuka trunks. In those days there was no road to the farm; the only access was by way of launch and horse. The trunks were lashed to a konaki, which Mother discovered was the Maori word for a horse-drawn wooden sled; Father helped Mother side-saddle on to a placid natured horse, and sat me forward on the saddle of his own. Mr Patera followed behind with the konaki. In this way we travelled a mile back into the hills, along a horse-beaten track, and the long journey, really begun that summer so many years before when Father and Mother first walked together in an English garden, was at an end.

Paint peeled from the house; broken windows were covered with sacking (again Mother's memory for detail comes to my assistance). The corrugated iron roof was bright with rust; the guttering in some places had come adrift altogether, and rattled in the wind. Still, the place, a pioneer structure, had a fine solidity about it; it stood, aloof and strong and independent of the landscape, planted down on a rise in the lee of a great hill. Norfolk pines stood to the front of it; a grove of cabbage trees, at the rear, screened off the milking-shed and the hay-barn. The long verandah, with its convoluted mock-iron cornices, overlooked the valley, the widening and winding tidal creek running shining to the sea, and the hazy blue hills shouldering tall bush to the skyline.

But Mother would naturally have been more concerned with viewing the interior of the house. And the interior, she always said, altogether beggared description; so I must take her word for it. Apart from Mrs Patera, who in kindly and neighbourly fashion had sometimes come to tidy and clean for the lonely man on the farm, the place had not seen a woman for years. First with the four brothers, and then with Father alone, it had been an exclusively bachelor domain. But there and then, in the chaos and filth, among the broken sticks of furniture, she set about making a home.

She forgave Father in the end, of course. For he had, as she said, not an ounce of deceit in him; he was a fine man, even if rather limited. It simply hadn't occurred to him that she might expect to find the farm, the house, any different. And, she added generously, he always meant things for the best; after all, he had tried, quite wrongly, to save her from it as long as he could.

She forgave Father; but not the country. How could she forgive the country for being so utterly, so inexplicably, different from that which she had expected? No, it was the country itself which had deceived and betrayed her; there could be no forgiveness. And when she said Father was limited, she meant simply that Father failed to share her anger at the cruel trick played on her. 'You know,' she would tell me, 'your Father has no real affection for England at all. None at all. He might as well never have been there.' This actually, so far as Mother was concerned, was his greatest limitation.

So the strangeness of soil, water and light in time bred a sickness of despair in her. Her life became an unwilling, lonely pilgrimage over a terrain littered with stunted hopes and forlorn memories. Even I, to whom she could confide, was lost to her on those days when Father mounted me, with my neat lunch-packet secure inside my school-bag, on the konaki beside the cream-cans and took me, with the cans, down to our jetty, there to await the cream-launch which carried me down to the little riverside school. It was of course shock enough to have to lose me at all: it was even greater when she realized I should have to share a tiny schoolroom and a solitary teacher with some thirty other Maori, half-caste, and pakeha children. 'How can she learn there?' she would demand of Father. 'Under those circumstances?'

'My school was no different,' he replied cryptically. 'I learnt.'

'And besides,' Mother said, 'they all go barefoot.'

'So?' Father said. 'Do they keep their brains in their feet?'

'I should like,' she would often repeat, 'to see Bridget go home to finish her education.'

'Yes, dear,' Father would say, rising, methodically hitching his trousers, and finding something to occupy him in another part of the house.

There were neighbours. The nearest were the Pateras: they could be reached on foot. They were members of an old well-known Maori family, descendants of the chief Hone Heke who had repeatedly chopped down the British flagstaff at the new colony's capital of Kororareka, in the Bay of Islands. Mr Patera was a man of raw speech, rough gestures, and quite marvellous natural intelligence; his talent for invention, his affection for even the simplest piece of machinery, was exceeded only by his talent for producing and entertaining a houseful of children, and his affection for his wife. Mrs Patera herself was an astonishingly delicate woman, of slight bone and thin flesh; through years of child-bearing and work, she had somehow managed to retain the impression that she must once have been a singularly handsome woman. She had received a good education, and could quite well have won a prominent place for herself somewhere in the European world, or even in the twilight world of Maori politics; but, instead, she accepted young Kiwi Patera, and was taken to spend her life above the placid tidal creek. Children seemed compensation enough for whatever she had lost, if indeed she had lost anything; though in her middle years, as if stirred by conscience, she began to play an active part in tribal affairs, and her voice was heard with respect by the elders.

Kiwi, in the hard years after the war, became Father's closest friend; it was entirely natural that I should become friendly with the Patera children.

But relations between Mother and Mrs Patera were never natural. Mother could not conceal an overwhelming self-consciousness when with a Maori; and the fact that Mrs Patera was both educated and intelligent only seemed to aggravate her feelings. It was almost as if some incipiently hostile part of herself was announcing: it is all wrong; they should not be like this; this man should not speak so casually to my husband; these children should not play so freely with my child; this woman should not sit so much at ease in my house. When she first met Kiwi, that day we arrived on the town jetty, she misunderstood the nature of the introduction and assumed he was a labourer of Father's and therefore had not shaken the friendly hand he offered. It was a handshake of a kind, with a man, with a country, she was never to make.

Then there was Mrs Benjamin. If Mother found a real friend at all, it was Mrs Benjamin. She was of the third generation of a famous pioneer family, and lived, with her taciturn husband and sullen children, in a large and prosperous white homestead near the town. The homestead was quite famous in itself; and was often visited by those who wished to find an authentic colonial atmosphere. Its interior was still cluttered with heavy polished furniture, and decked with pioneer knick-knacks; in that sombre, rather gloomy place, only the people had changed in the past hundred years. Mrs Benjamin had never been to England; yet she spoke with an artificial, sometimes comic, English accent, and received *The Tatler* and *The London Illustrated* regularly. She liked Mother to talk about England. 'This, of course,' she would confide to Mother, 'is a second-rate country, my dear.' It was enough to win Mother's affection; enough even to overcome her aversion to Catholics, for Mrs Benjamin, though not a very devout Catholic herself, liked to make much of the fact that an ancestor of hers had been present at one of the first Catholic masses celebrated in New Zealand.

The Benjamins visited us on Sunday afternoons. Their large, brightly-painted launch would be tied up at our jetty; Father and Tom Benjamin, who did not really like each other, would be wandering about the farm, talking in a desultory fashion; and, from a sense of duty, I would be playing with Millicent Benjamin, a sulky, rather fragile child, while Mother entertained Mrs Benjamin in the drawing-room.

'I hope, of course, to be able to send Bridget back to England to finish her education,' Mother would tell her. And if Mrs Benjamin found any incongruity in this thin, pale woman on a poor farm (it was the depression then, and Father's mortgages were causing him sleepless nights) speaking of sending her child overseas for education, she certainly did not show it; another point, of course, in her favour.

'That is the ideal, naturally,' she said. 'I mean there would be so much for her there. So much that she would never find here. Everything here is so, well, so—' (a pause and then, for want of another, the tired old word would be paraded once more) '—so absolutely second-rate.' But Mrs Benjamin had more realism about her own children. 'I simply couldn't bear to lose Millicent,' she sighed. 'I mean even the thought that she might go down to Auckland university worries me. But then Millicent isn't really a terribly scholarly child, you know. Your Bridget has the advantage there.'

'Well,' Mother said modestly. 'I only do my best, you know. I supplement whatever Bridget learns at school as best I can. Every little helps, I imagine.'

'Of course, dear. You're really a quite, quite remarkable woman. To manage it among—well, among all this.' And the flattery would be spread with an all-inclusive but entirely genteel sweep of the arm. 'It's quite remarkable.'

Then there were the people of the town and the farms along the creek.

'They're buried here,' Mrs Benjamin would say. 'Simply buried. And so cut off from everything.' She meant, of course, that they did not receive *The Tatler* or *The London Illustrated;* but only the *Herald* and the *Weekly News* from Auckland. 'And the most terrible thing about it is that they just don't seem to care.' There would be, perhaps, a brief but meaningful silence while Mother and Mrs Benjamin meditated on the idlers and drifters about the pub and the jetty, who ventured away from the town only on fishing expeditions to the harbour heads.

'Now take the Larkins,' Mrs Benjamin added. 'There *is* a peculiar family for you. Well-educated too, I might say. But what is the difference between them and the Maoris? I ask you, dear.' The Larkins had a farm on the creek not far away from us. It was once quite large in size, but second growth and aspiring new bush had effortlessly found its way back down the upper slopes while the useful pasture diminished. Like his father before him, Cecil Larkin, a freethinker, was less interested in large-scale farming than in the business of quiet living. Luxuriant sub-tropical growth rioted about their creeper-entwined old bungalow down above the creek; olive, fig, and uncertain banana trees grew crankily in the gardens. The children ran as wild as the bush which encroached on them. 'But there you are, dear. The blood will out. Cecil Larkin's mother was a Potoki, you know. A half-caste. It's what I always say. Mix the races, and the seed goes bad.'

Then there were the Maoris themselves.

'Of course they're very different from us,' Mrs Benjamin said.

'Yes,' Mother answered; she could never show great enthusiasm for this subject.

'They have, well, different—different outlooks on things.'

'Yes,' Mother said.

'Morally, I mean.' Mrs Benjamin began working hard to ignite a spark of interest.

'I can imagine that,' Mother said. 'After all, they've not long been in touch with civilization, have they?' She was prepared, despite the vague promise of spice, to let the subject rest there; but Mrs. Benjamin was clearly determined to pursue it.

'I mean we have to be tolerant,' she said. 'Their minds work differently.'

'I imagine they do.'

'I mean it's common knowledge about what happens at the pa when there's a big hui. There's always too much liquor there, and the boys and girls mix freely. Really, if you were to think about it, you just wouldn't credit that it's a hundred years since the missionaries first came.'

'No,' Mother said. There was a silence.

'But,' added Mrs Benjamin, 'there are other things—other things that aren't such common knowledge.' 'Oh?' 'Other things—well, you could only call them unnatural things.'

This time there was a quite definite silence.

'Mind you,' Mrs Benjamin went on, 'I shouldn't normally breathe a word of this outside the Church. But I do happen to know that often when priests are coming to work among the Maoris they're given, well, certain advice. To prepare them for what they might hear in confession, you see.' She paused. 'I mean if they come out with it in confession, they must know it's wrong, mustn't they?'

'I imagine they must,' said Mother coolly.

'But there you are, dear. They're only savages, really. It only goes to show. They know quite well now the difference between right and wrong, and yet they're still not prepared to observe common decency. I mean if you were to think about it, it'd make your flesh creep. You wouldn't credit it in this day and age. Older women taking young ones and initiating them—'

At this point Mother must have observed, through the french windows, Millicent and me sitting within earshot, dangling our legs over the verandah rail; and gestured for silence. For when Millicent and I re-entered the drawing-room they were talking about something else altogether.

Friendship with Millicent was urged on me: I disliked her. My real friend was always Mere Patera. Mere was a tall, slender, fast-growing girl, striking in appearance, and two years older than myself. She, alone of all her football-crazy brothers and dreamy sisters, seemed to inherit her mother's aptitude for learning; for she always headed her class at school, and her mother and her teachers early foresaw the day when Mere would go to Teachers' Training College at Auckland. For she showed ability both to acquire knowledge and to impart it; in her last year at the little riverside primary school, she often helped the sole teacher with his infant classes. But our friendship was not based on learning, at least not on the schoolroom kind; in any case, probably because the conflict between home and school confused me, I was not a scholar of particular promise even if I did read, hungrily and redeemingly, books of haphazard and erratic choice (even Father's tracts on the monetary theory of Douglas Social Credit, which attracted him in the worst period of the depression, did not escape my attention).

Our friendship, at the beginning, was a casual thing, as casual as the lives of the people of that town through whose dusty streets we dawdled on Saturday afternoons (when we went down the creek for a movie matinee); but it grew with us. Mere was not only clever, but beautiful; and, for some reason I have never properly understood attractive girls, in adolescence anyway, invariably seem to acquire plain girl friends. I was the plain friend, an awkward, rather plumpish ugly duckling; and we walked together, her brown beauty shown to advantage beside my pale drabness of figure and feature. By this time she had finished with the riverside school; each morning she continued her journey on the cream-launch all the way down-creek to the high school in the town, where again she began to head her classes. I was lonely then, without her in the schoolhouse and playground, and I counted the months to the time when I should begin to travel with her to the high school.

It seems now that my life, from the age of four to seventeen, lacked any sense of permanence. It was all a kind of giant holiday until the real business of life, in England, began. Perhaps that was why I thought I could afford not to take school too seriously: it was the mood Mother encouraged in me. One day, not far distant, I should return to the country where I properly belonged. I shared in her fantasy. I took it as something natural, inevitable. And Mother, pleased, could regard with amused tolerance my affections for the farm, the animals, my surroundings; and for Mere.

'But a girl like yourself can never really feel at home here,' she said. 'I know you will love England.'

I used to talk of it with Mere.

'But when you go to England,' she said once, 'what will you do?'

It was the end of a warm summer day; we lay on a grassy cliff-top overlooking a huge expanse of twilit sea. In the school holidays we often excursioned, on horseback, to a coastal farm belonging to her uncle, where we spent lazy days before returning. All this particular day we had spent some distance from the farmhouse, by a quiet and sheltered tidal lagoon, shut off from the roar of the Tasman by barriers of rock and hills of sand. We collected mussels and pipis in flax kits, swam naked in the heat of noon, picnicked in the shade of a crimson-blooming pohutukawa grove, and sunbathed the afternoon away. In the cool of dusk we were making our way slowly home along the crumpled, crumbling coastline, pausing to rest now and then.

'Yes,' she repeated, plucking at blades of grass when I was silent. 'What will you do?'

'Well,' I said, 'I expect I shall study and learn and—'

'But I mean,' she said, 'afterwards.'

'Well,' I said uncertainly, 'I expect I shall travel about a bit. Mother wants me to see as much of England as I can.'

'But you can't do that all the time,' Mere pointed out sensibly. 'You going to live there? You going to work there?'

I was slow answering. Mother had never been very explicit on those points. 'I expect I shall,' I said.

She was puzzled. 'Won't you get lonely? Won't you want to come home?'

'But England is my home,' I said.

'What you talking about? Home is where your folks are. That's what I always thought.' She paused. 'What about your Mum, anyhow? What about her when she hasn't got you, eh?'

'I expect she'll come and see me,' I said. 'For holidays and things.'

'For holidays and things?' echoed Mere incredulously. 'But England's a long way. It costs money to go there. A lot of money.' Even Mere had the imagination necessary to see that. 'I reckon your Mum must really be pretty rich, that's all.'

But she made no impression; my fancy had already darted away. 'Perhaps you can come too, for a trip,' I said.

'And stay with me,' I added grandly. 'I shall have a house in Kensington.'

Mere laughed. We picked up our kits of mussels and pipis, and went on our way again.

It was during that same long summer that we first talked about Ed Larkin. Ed was the youngest of the Larkin boys. The others had gone away to get education, had found manhood, worked for a while, and sooner or later seemed to tire of the city, for they returned, one after the other, to the tranquil Polynesian life of the farm. They farmed after a fashion, fished, played football, drank beer, went to country dances, and dissected Social Credit and talked Communism with their father on Sundays. Ed was young, vigorous, and studious, a contrast to his lethargic brothers; that summer he finished high school, and was preparing to begin a law course at Auckland university. Ed was always friendly with the Pateras; in childhood he often squatted, along with the other children and myself, around Kiwi Patera and listened to his stories. With the pride and self-knowledge of adolescence, he grew a little aloof and away from us all while he attended high school. But at school dances, that final year, he began to notice Mere again. They often danced together, and once he took Mere outside to sit some distance from the hall, on a hill looking down on the town and the interwoven tidal rivers. If they kissed and petted, Mere never told me; she only told me how they sat there together not speaking, arm around arm, watching the scattered lights and shimmering water in the blue evening.

'I think maybe I love him,' Mere said, as we lay once more upon our favourite high cliff-top above red rocks, yellow sand, and blue sea.

And so we talked of Ed Larkin.

Ed was tall and stringy, fair-haired and brown-faced. He wore glasses sometimes, mostly when he read, which gave him a scholarly appearance. He was captain of the high school's first fifteen in his final year, and played cricket for the town side as a star spin bowler. In the weeks before he went away to Auckland Mere and I often used to watch him play; we admired the casual way he polished the ball against his shirt and spun it from hand to hand before he flicked back his hair and made his slow, ambling run up to the wicket. We could not foresee the time when the ball which curled so slowly, so accurately, through the air would become instead a grenade; or the time when one such grenade, inexpert in construction, would blow off his hands and most of his head on some Middle Eastern battlefield. It was midsummer, warm and blue, and the players were white on a green field, the beer passed about in the shade of the pavilion, and families lunched in and about the marquee down under the willows by the river; and there were mild bursts of applause for Ed Larkin when he took another wicket.

Ed came back for vacations in May and August. Once or twice he took Mere to country dances, but always they were along with a crowd. By this time, however, Mere was generally acknowledged as Ed's girl. All this happened at a remove from me, since I was still only fifteen and in my second year at high school, and there would be plenty of time, in Mother's view, for dances when I was older. To find out about Ed I had to question Mere. He was dissatisfied with university, and at Christmas he returned to announce that he despised law as a profession, and was now going down to the South Island, to study medicine at Otago university. He took Mere out again, though not regularly, during that Christmas vacation; and the Saturday night before he left for Otago he kissed her goodbye. I had difficulty persuading Mere to admit that he had; for she was growing more and more reticent about Ed.

That year Mere should have gone away herself, to Training College at Auckland, but some difficulty over admission decided her to leave it till the next year, and to spend the intervening time helping her mother on the farm. Ed was too far away now to return for mid-year vacations; Mere wrote several letters to him and received one in reply, written about the middle of the second term. He said he was well and liked Dunedin. He hoped Mere was well.

That was the year I first remember people talking about men called Mussolini and Hitler; and about another, more obscure, called Franco. But only Father, who told Kiwi Patera that international bankers were plotting a new war, and the Larkin family became really excited about what was happening on the other side of the world. The eldest of the Larkin boys, who had been a member of the Communist Party in Auckland after the unemployed riots in 1932, left his family island of quiet in uproar when he went to fight in Spain. Mrs Benjamin, who thought Franco a Christian gentleman, thereafter avoided the Larkins, whom she always thought subversive anyway.

It was the year I turned sixteen, and Mere eighteen. My birthday was notable only for the reason that for the first time I saw fit to argue with Mother about being forced to invite Millicent Benjamin to my party. Mere's party was notable because of Mere. Kiwi Patera, deciding that this, her first adult party deserved special celebration, called in relatives and friends from miles around. The party was in early December; and the summer was already warm.

Father took me; Mother pleaded a headache, and remained at home. We broke through whooping children and pushed through an overflow of guests to get into the house; then Kiwi took us, and steered us to Mere. She was dressed in a gay Mexican skirt, gaudy colours woven on black, and a crisp white blouse; a simple silver necklet lay against her dark skin. Wineglass in hand, she stood erect and contained, with the assurance of a woman, among a crush of young men. She made me aware of my own inadequacy, made me feel my own incoherence of poise and gesture. I almost fled. But as soon as she saw us she broke away from her admirers.

Kiwi led Father to the keg; and I was left, bewildered, with this new, dazzling creature. She took me aside and told me gleefully that Ed had finished his exams, and was on his way north for the vacation; in fact, he was expected that day, but so far there was no sign of him. The Larkins were all at the party; but they had left a note at the homestead in case he should arrive.

The old Patera house shuddered with noise and movement; the floorboards creaked and bent under the slamming feet of the dancers. The Potoki boys hammered the piano and banged the drums; Keith Larkin played the saxophone. Kiwi rolled in new kegs from outside. People were still arriving from the other side of town: the newcomers drank to Mere. She was caught, dance after dance, by eager young men. I sipped cautiously at beer, and found it bitter. And about midnight, long after Mother had instructed Father to bring me home, Ed Larkin appeared, still dusty and red-eyed from travel. His appearance was quiet, almost unnoticed. He already had a glass of beer in his hand when I first saw him standing quietly in the doorway; he was looking across the room at Mere. Eyes brilliant, hair cascading, she was giving herself entirely to the dance, to the discovered rhythm of her body. Probably I was the only person in that room to notice Ed. He was changed. He seemed older, taller; he wore an open-neck check shirt and a zip-up jacket. The expression on his face seemed to me odd; but only because then I knew too little about people to recognize it. He stood there watching, waiting, altogether patient and sure of himself; and when the time came, when the music paused, he moved across the room to Mere.

At three in the morning guests were beginning to depart; launches were throbbing on the creek, and horses thudded off into the night. Father belatedly remembered his promise to Mother. 'Time to go, girlie,' he said, fetching my coat from a darkened room where one of the Potoki boys had pitched a girl, in unequivocal fashion, upon the bed. At the front door we found Kiwi dismayed. Mere was not there to say goodbye to her guests. No one knew where she had gone. Someone had seen her on the verandah with Ed Larkin not long after midnight; then she vanished.

I heard later that they did not re-appear until breakfast time, when they came walking down from the hills hand in hand, as if an early morning stroll were, for them, as natural as the day. I say that I heard advisedly, for it was not Mere who told me; I did not see much of her that summer. She was rarely home when I called. And not once did we ride out, as we always had in summers before, to her uncle's farm on the coast. She was with Ed Larkin.

I also heard, in the way one heard things along the creek, that Ed and Mere were near to being engaged. Towards the end of the school holidays Mother prevailed upon me to accept Mrs Benjamin's invitation to holiday with Millicent at a cottage in the Bay of Islands. Millicent, lipsticked and perfumed, dragged me out on expeditions to attract teen-age boys also on holiday. When I returned Mere had already gone to begin her studies at Auckland Training College. After I was home a day or two Ed left for Dunedin. No one knew anything about an engagement.

That was the beginning of the year of Munich; but, so far as I was concerned, it was the year I finished high school and, above all, the year I learned the truth.

I was not, after all, going to England.

'You might as well know it,' Father said angrily one day in the middle of the year when I had ridden out with him to mend some boundary fences. 'Your mother's been filling your head with a lot of damn nonsense for years.'

He calmed quickly. I felt the anger had been more directed at himself than at anyone, or anything. 'She doesn't like to admit that she's beaten,' he added quietly.

But it was Father who had been beaten. The land had sapped him, thinned him to dry, lean middle-age; the farm, he realized now, would never be the one he wanted. Already erosion had claimed the land he had taken from the bush in the four frantic years after the war. The pastures were still not rich, but sparse and hungry. The farm would never run a large herd. Always there would be the monthly struggle on small cream-cheques.

'You'll have to face it,' he said. 'The damn idea's always been impossible.'

'Then why,' I cried, 'haven't you ever said anything?'

He finished working the wire-strainer, and surveyed the line of the fence. 'Because,' he said, 'I wanted her to have something— even if it was only a dream of something she couldn't have.' He finished with the fence, and we walked back to the horses. 'And once I thought it mightn't be so impossible myself,' he added.

'There's never been much for her here, you know,' he said. 'I've often thought it was a mistake, bringing her—' He checked himself suddenly; and, tight-lipped, swung up into the saddle. It was too difficult to quickly dismiss twenty years, and a marriage.

'Anyway,' he said, 'forget it.'

The hills were bleak that day, I remember, and the sun was watery in a grey sky. The creek was swollen and ran a muddy brown. I felt shrunken and defeated, at one with the misery of the winter landscape; I seemed cheated of myself, of all the sixteen years of my life. Everything had been taken, suddenly, and nothing given back.

It was some time before I could bring myself to talk to Mother. I expected a painful scene. Instead she was so calm, so philosophical, that I was too astonished to be angry. After all, she had months, years, to prepare herself for this eventuality; and, moreover, an excellent excuse was near at hand. 'It's probably all for the best, dear,' she said. 'There might be a war, you know. While things are uncertain it's better that you stay here.'

Sitting on our verandah idle, emptied of myself, I watched the slow change of the seasons, saw the colours of spring begin to freshen the hills. At school I worked without effort, and sat matriculation. I knew I had done satisfactorily; well enough to have passed. But it seemed pointless: it did not concern me, one way or the other. I was oddly friendless too. Millicent came and went, prattling about what she intended to do when she went to Auckland next year. She was in love with the son of a Waikato racehorse owner. There was a letter from Mere. She did not mention Ed, but this was not significant, since she had been secretive about him a long while now. I replied to say that I too might be going to Auckland next year; I would stay with my uncle, the watersider, and if Mother and Father could manage it, I would study at university. I wrote these things down coldly, as if they were facts about another person, not myself.

I was aware of the strangeness, the lassitude that spent itself in vague yearnings; I wandered through bush lit with rata flower, and meditated by the creek. Change had overtaken me mysteriously; my childish plumpness was gone. But even that seemed not my responsibility.

I had no boy friend. But at the end-of-year school dance there was a boy who seems, in memory, strangely faceless; he danced with me, and I allowed him to lead me outside. We drove in his car to the top of the hill above the town, and parked off the road. I remembered how Ed and Mere had escaped from the dance in the same way, to look down at the lights and the silvery water. I wondered what Mere had felt then; for I felt nothing.

He was very nervous. He offered me wine. He held me clumsily and kissed me. It all seemed an awkward business. I was afraid of crumpling my frock, and smearing my lipstick.

I feel absolutely nothing, I told myself. And we drove back to the dance.

Summer came, and with it Mere. But I had hardly time to see her before I was whisked off to Auckland for Christmas. Mother had judged the time convenient to discuss my future stay in the city with my uncle, who had just acquired a pleasant beach cottage at Takapuna. Kiwi and his sons looked after the herd while we were away. Mere, I gathered, had enjoyed her first year at Training College; again she did not mention Ed. But I still presumed this was because they were to be engaged soon.

Father returned to the farm first. Mother and I followed, two days before New Year. The first morning home I walked over to the Patera farm; though the sun was not yet high in the sky, the day was thick with heat. I met Mere emerging from the house. She had a towel slung over her shoulder. 'I'm going to cool off,' she said. 'Coming?' She went back into the house and fetched another towel. We walked to the back of the farm, to a place where a fresh-water creek spilt down terraces of rock to form deep pools of dawdling water; it was a pretty place, set about with bush and fern, and clamorous with bellbirds. As we undressed Mere asked how I'd enjoyed Auckland. I asked, more pointedly, how she'd enjoyed Christmas, since I knew Ed had been back some time.

'Oh,' she said vaguely, 'it was all right.'

We were lying naked now, like two long lazing sunlit fish, near the surface of the water, rolling gently, from side to side, in the cool sway of the circling currents, so that now and then our flanks and our shoulders touched. The sky was vivid, the air motionless. The drooping leaves of the nikau palms sprinkled a confetti of sunlight on the fern and moss of the banks above us.

'Have you seen much of Ed?' I said finally.

'I expect I'll be seeing him tomorrow night,' she said. 'At the barbecue. You'll be coming, won't you, Bridie?'

'Yes,' I said. It was only afterwards I realized she had not answered my question.

She slid away from me, turned sideways, and wriggled to her feet. Water showering from her dark skin, she waded up to the waterfall at the end of the pool; she stood there erect and smiling, the diamonds of spray glittering down her. She seemed very cheerful. She looked down at me.

'You've grown up, Bridie,' she said. 'You've got a good figure now.' She laughed softly, as if the thought had just come to her. 'You got a boy friend yet?'

'Not really.' I still found the memory of that clumsy night in the car an ugly thing.

She laughed, that soft laugh again, and splashed down beside me. Her long hair fanned loose and silky in the water, flowing across my shoulder.

'What is it like,' I asked cautiously, 'when boys kiss you, and things?'

'Oh,' she said. 'It's funny.'

'Sometimes I wish I knew. Sometimes I don't think I'll ever know.'

She agitated the water gently with her long legs. 'Oh,' she said. 'You'll know all right. You wait till you get to the city. All the boys will be after you there. Wait and see.'

'Were they after you?'

'They would have been. If I'd let them.'

'Didn't you because of Ed?'

'Yes,' she said, reticent again.

'Anyhow,' I said quickly, to end the silence, 'I don't think they'll be after me.'

'Why?' she said. 'You scared, Bridie? Why shouldn't they be after you?' She touched me lightly on the breast with a tentative finger, and withdrew it quickly. 'You're pretty, Bridie. And you mustn't ever be scared. Ever.'

In the hot day, floating weightless on the cool water, I felt, in place of apathy, a curious excitement begin to stir my body. Mere was crooning softly to herself; her eyes were closed. A new listless breeze rattled the nikaus; a chittering fantail flickered in and out of sunlight.

Then I was afraid. I slipped from the water and began to towel myself. Mere, eyes open in surprise, followed. We talked again.

'So,' she said, 'you're not going to England now.'

'No.'

'And you're not the English girl any more.'

'I don't suppose so.'

'Don't look so sad,' she said. 'Is it very terrible, being a New Zealander like me?'

'I don't know.'

'How do you mean you don't know?'

'Well,' I said miserably, 'I don't really know what it feels like yet.'

'Then you better hurry, eh?' she laughed.

We dressed and walked downhill, hand in hand, along a narrow bush track. It was time for me to go home for dinner. We said goodbye and arranged to meet and go to the New Year barbecue together. I was surprised that Ed wasn't taking her, but I said nothing. After all, their arrangements always did seem casual; there was nothing unusual about him promising to meet her there.

The barbecue was held on a sandy spit about a mile, by water, from the place where the town met the tidal creeks; there the creeks became sea, and the sea swelled out to the harbour heads. It was chosen first because it was a respectable distance from town, and beer could be sold there illegally and the local policeman kept pacified; and second because it was actually a very pleasant place.

The moon was rising as we arrived, and there were fires lit all along the beach, under the pohutukawas. Parties with rugs and beer and guitars were strewn in the gay yellow light. Here and there sucking pigs turned, crackling, over glowing pits. There was even a crude dance-floor erected for the night a little back from the beach. There were parties spread there too, in the shadowy light, on the sparse grass, among the lupins and the dunes.

Mere and I wove in and out around the fires, saying hello. We met some of her cousins who had come down from an up-river timber mill, and who insisted we sit with them a while. They were rowdy, good-natured boys. When we declined their beer they triumphantly produced some sherry from a Dalmatian vineyard which they had kept aside for just this possibility. We sang with them and they took us to dance.

'Why you no with t'at pakeha fullar Ed tonight?' one of the boys asked Mere, throwing an affectionate arm around her. 'What's a matter? Don' you like him no more, eh?'

'When you goen to be te big-time schoolteacher?' asked another. 'When you goen to start given all te kids te whack, eh?'

'One and one are two,' a couple started to chant. 'Two an two are four...'

'One an one are three!' cried another. 'You don' know your sums, ehoa. Don' you know t'at one an one makes te little one. Ehoa, you don' know nothing at all.' He guffawed.

'I don' t'ink you like t'at pakeha fullar no more, eh?' said the first. 'I t'ink you like t'is fullar best, eh?' He tightened his arm around her possessively.

'I like everyone best,' Mere said non-committally, her eyes dancing mischievously in the firelight.

'You better watch out, ehoa, or she be given you te whack.'

'How you know, boy? How you don' know he might like Mere given him te wackety-whack. Oho, maybe he like te wackety-whack from Mere. I wouldn't mind her given *me* te wackety-whack.'

There was no sign of Ed. That was when I knew something wrong. It was getting late, after eleven, when I at last had a chance to ask Mere, 'What time did Ed say he'd be here?'

'He didn't say,' she answered vaguely.

'But he's coming?'

'I expect he is,' she said, even more vaguely.

'How do you mean—you expect?' At that moment I felt an urgent desire to shake her, to shake away her slowness and stupidity about a thing of such importance.

'He's been with his family ever since he got back,' she said finally.

So that was the truth of it, I saw suddenly; she hadn't seen him at all. She had been confidently waiting out the days for him to come to her once more, in his casual fashion. Only this time he hadn't come. I was silent. There was nothing to say.

In a little while I wandered off and found Keith Larkin on the dance-floor, where he was playing the saxophone. 'Ed?' he said. He looked at me curiously. 'He was here early, but then he shot off back to town in the launch. Had to meet someone off the night bus. Why? You want to see him or something?'

'No,' I said. 'It's nothing.'

It wasn't long after that when I heard the launch. Its wake was phosphorescent in the moonlight. Presently the engine quieted, it drifted a while, and then an anchor splashed. A dinghy slid out from the shadow of the launch, and I saw Ed was rowing a passenger ashore. Mere, beside me, had grown very still and quiet. The dinghy beached some distance from us: the two people, Ed and his passenger, were hidden behind one of the fires.

I turned to Mere urgently. 'Hadn't you better go and see him?'

'I expect I'll see him in a little while,' she said placidly.

She began to annoy me again. There was a lot of noise coming from that part of the beach where the dinghy had been drawn up. I heard Ed's name shouted several times.

'For heaven's sake,' I cried. 'You haven't seen him for a year. And you just want to sit there.' But she said nothing. If he came, her mild face seemed to say, he came; if he didn't, he didn't. She was not the girl who had floated beside me in the pool yesterday, and told me to be unafraid.

I became impatient. The noise drifted off towards the dance-floor. I went angrily across the sand, away from Mere. Looking back, I saw her half-risen to her feet. Confused, shamefaced suddenly, she followed, tripping and sliding in the sand in her haste to catch up with me. She clung to my arm as we went up to the dance-floor. The crowd was thick there. Then I felt her grip tighten on my arm: she saw Ed first. He stood in the centre of a laughing group. His shirt was unbuttoned down his chest, his trousers were rolled above his bare ankles, and his hair was awry. He swayed on his feet: he was very drunk. People shook his hand, slapped him on the back. He smiled slow-wittedly as he accepted their congratulations.

I saw the reason why Mere might wait, and Ed never come back.

The girl was dressed in a tight black sweater and dark slacks. She was short and blonde, not particularly pretty. She had an affected voice and a hoarse laugh. Holding a glass of beer in one hand and a cigarette in the other, she seemed entirely at ease; on the third finger of her left hand an engagement ring glittered. She was talking to Ed's brother, the one who had been to Spain.

'I've been so keen to meet you,' she said. 'Ever since Ed first told me about you. I was terribly thrilled when he told me I'd meet you along with the family when I came up for New Year. Of course I've always been too busy passing exams to be in the Party myself, but I was all on your side over the Spain business. I imagine you must find all this rather limited after all the excitement you had over there. Tell me, do you think there's going to be a war?'

'There's always been one,' he said shortly. 'Some way or other. Can I get you another beer?'

I didn't like her: I didn't like her, or her tight sweater, or her zipped slacks, or the way she held her beer and her cigarette with such ease. She was a stranger, a foreigner speaking a foreign language.

People were still jollying Ed, shaking his hand, slapping his back. Before Mere could slip away unseen, one of the Potoki boys saw her.

'Hey, Ed!' he cried drunkenly. 'Come an say hullo to Mere. You mus' say hullo to Mere.' Mere, still clutching me, backed away. The Potoki boy led Ed towards her. The crowd became very silent: they wheeled about, forming a long passageway of staring faces. At the other end of it the short, blonde girl in slacks looked on with curiosity. Ed shambled up to Mere and looked at her. In the silence someone giggled. I saw a faint fluttering at the corner of Mere's mouth.

'Hullo, Mere,' Ed said at last. His eyes were quite dead.

Then he backed away, ending the tension, grinning amiably and calling for another drink. Someone announced from the dance platform that it was just thirty minutes to midnight. I went back to our place on the beach blindly, stumbling on the lupins, not daring to look at Mere. The boys, oblivious to what had happened, were scattered about the fire, eating pork and drinking more beer. They must have thought we had escaped them, for they received us with jubilation. Prancing about us, they gave us wine, urged us to dance. I emptied most of my wine on the sand; Mere drank hers. Her eyes were perfectly clear, and startlingly bright; too bright. Whenever I looked at her, she only smiled and raised her glass. She drank more, and let the boys spin her round in wild dances. Her hair tangled down her face, and her blouse became undone at the top. She was barefoot now, and her red skirt and white petticoat swirled about her legs. The circle had grown about our fire; there was a chanting, a twirling, a clapping of hands. The bare feet stomped the sand, and Mere was flung from partner to partner. Sometimes she was lost in shadow; then she emerged, high-stepping and erect, head snapped back and body thrust forward, colours flashing in the light of the dying fire. Always there were new arms to receive her, new partners to spin her onwards.

Then it was midnight, and the dance was joined: it became confusion. We danced till we were exhausted; until, dropping coupled to the sand, the boys claimed their New Year kisses. I picked myself up, retrieved my dignity, and saw Mere still dancing. When she fell, at last, there were willing arms to receive her; and again she was thrown, hot and full-lipped, from partner to partner, this time enacting with each a parody of passion. I was bewildered and a little horrified.

From the platform above the beach voices still proclaimed the birth of the year: it was nineteen thirty-nine.

And then Mere was suddenly in my arms, and weeping.

We were given a ride home in a launch which belonged to a young married couple who lived at the top of the creek. We left early, soon after midnight, and the lights and singing were lost across the shining water. It was not cold, yet Mere still shivered against me as we held to each other at the back of the launch. The wine, and a sadness for Mere, still sang in my head. Perhaps too there was a faint premonition of the time when we would watch the boys swing, bayonets flashing, down streamer-strewn streets towards the grey ships. For our youth was ending even more quickly than we knew: fires of another kind would greet the years ahead.

The launch nudged up the creek, waves washing the wiry mangroves in the moonlight. The Patera jetty came into sight, around a turning. Mere stiffened. 'No,' she whispered. 'I don't want to go home.' She was afraid of being alone. The solution seemed perfectly simple. 'Come home with me,' I said. She held to me gratefully, forlorn and strangely flimsy, as I called to our friends to keep on going, past the Patera jetty; to our own. Little distance separated the two jetties: soon I was helping Mere up on to the rickety landing, and we were waving goodbye as the launch chattered away up the creek.

We turned and walked towards the homestead, through the silvered bush, and over the blonde grass; the nikau palms and cabbage-tree groves stood vivid in the night. The moon was cold and high. Everything glistened, faintly luminous, and larger than life. We walked slowly, resting now and then, over a world become oddly unfamiliar, unreal. Animals stood frozen and statuesque in the drenching white light; cicadas sang thinly; a morepork called from up the creek.

We crept across the creaking verandah and through the french windows into my room. Quietly we undressed and slipped into my bed while the world lived in the pale fire of the moon. Mere lay quiet, breathing evenly. She no longer wept; she seemed almost to have become herself again. But something—the deadness of Ed's eyes, Mere's dance, the voices calling, the fires vanishing across the sea—had disturbed me, and left an ache of disquiet: it was my turn for tears. The sobs rose huge in my throat. I wept for no reason and every reason. For Ed gone, for England gone, for years betrayed. Mere's arms slid around me.

'What is it?' she whispered.

She took my face between her hands. 'What is it?' she repeated. 'What is it, quiet one?'

But it was no use. The storm had come at last: the storm, and the shelter of Mere's arms.

Awakening was a slow sliding upwards through liquid layers of web-thin sleep, a tender surfacing in a strangely new world. I could hear birds singing in the bush. I loosened Mere's arms and slid from the bed gently, so as not to disturb her. Then I padded across the floor to the open windows and found morning. I felt perfectly calm; and bruised with wonder.

It was the hour before dawn, the hour before the first sunrise of the year. The turning earth unrolled a pastel sky. The moon, and the transparent night, were gone; fresh colours lit the land. A stranger to myself, I had a longing to walk barefoot, clean-limbed, through green forest where clear waters fell: to tread banks of moss dappled with new sunlight: to bed in silver fern with the slender fronds tickling my cheeks: to sleep flesh to flesh with the warm earth.

When the moment of revelation overtook me, I felt faint, and I reached out, to the side of the window, and held myself steady.

I should never go to England.

I should never go to England; and I was glad.

And I was no longer afraid.

At first I thought I only imagined it: but then I heard, across the calm morning, a launch idling up the creek, guitars strumming, and voices singing. The Potoki boys were returning home from the barbecue. As their launch passed below the farm, the distant voices rose in Maori harmony.

I turned slowly from the window and walked across the room, as if in a dream in which all that was old and known—all the paraphernalia of my seventeen years, the pictures, the books, the clothes, the brushes arranged before the mirror—had risen vivid and marvellously strange. Pausing, standing in the centre of the floor, I felt my heart in its cage of cooled flesh. Everything swam, settled, solidified again.

I went to the bed. Mere was still asleep, her arm curled limp where my body was printed on the sheet. I bent towards her and lifted her arm and kissed her on the cheek. She stirred and murmured but did not waken.

Then I lay beside her and waited for day.

AFTER THE DEPRESSION

T HE night had come and almost gone again; now, when the rough
sweep of his large hand gashed the mist of the carriage window, he
was able to see, beyond steep yellow clay-cuttings crested with damp green
bush, the brightening grey of the morning sky. His view was obscured for
a moment as steam from the engine, shredding and spinning, gusted past
the window. But he had seen enough: he sighed, stretched, yawned, and sat
back in his seat.

The guard, his cap awry, picked his way through the swaying second-
class carriage, carefully avoiding the pillows, heads and legs which jutted
into the narrow, dirty aisle. He called the name of the next station, a one-
minute stop. His voice in the dim, sleeping carriage was loud, without
apology for intrusion. There was an angry mutter from one awakened
passenger; but the rest, apart from the tall man stiff in his seat, stirred
sleepily, adjusted their pillows, and slept again. The guard left the carriage,
slamming the door after him: and once more there was only the sound of
iron wheels racketing on uneven rails, and teacups and saucers rattling
beneath the seats.

The tall man, who had sat sleepless through the night, gashed the healed
mist of the window again. But his view of the dawn sky was gone; in its
place was a swift, gloomy blur of thick bush tangling close to the track. Weak
spots of light flickered on his face: a face with a coarse, grainy quality; the
spare flesh bleak and unhealthy. The features, though, were firm, the
eyebrows dark and heavy, the eyes sharp blue, the nose slightly hooked, the
lips dry and pale; there was a faint blackish stubble on his thin, pointed chin.
He wore a tight black suit that had probably been too small even when it
was purchased from a cheap ready-made store six years before; it was frayed
at the cuffs and food-stained on the lapels. His thick, broken-nailed fingers
and flattened thumbs had by degrees loosened his brown, imitation-silk tie:
it hung askew, proclaiming its unfamiliarity with his sinewy neck. The top
button of his shirt was undone, and the twisted collar grubby with travel.

He occupied a double seat, his back to the engine. He hesitated a moment before waking the woman and child who slept in the seat opposite.

The woman was upright, her head against the window: a woollen jersey packed between the window and her head served to cushion her from the monotonous violence of the train's motion. Her face was young and pale, verging on plumpness; it quivered with the movement, and her mouth had fallen open. The lapels of her shabby grey coat were drawn up to cover her white throat. Her figure was short and mannish, and her dumpy legs barely touched the floor. The child, cocooned in a faded tartan blanket, slept with his head against her thigh. He had the fresh, sexless face of a three-year-old; the features girlish and delicate, like those of the woman. A cream beret had slipped to the back of the head, releasing a small cascade of uncut crinkly blonde hair, streaked with brown.

The man reached forward, finally, and touched the woman gently on the arm. She woke with a jerk, her eyes fluttering open: finding herself in the gloomy, jolting carriage, she was, for a moment, bewildered. Then she saw the man and smiled sleepily.

'Nearly there,' he said. 'We're nearly there.'

'There?' said the woman, vaguely. 'Already?'

'It's morning,' he said. 'Look out the window.'

'Ian,' the woman whispered. 'Ian, wake up.'

The child woke and murmured. The woman stood, replaced the lapels of her coat, shook out wrinkles, and bent to the child. Uncovering him, she folded the blanket and put it away.

The train, hammering along a flat stretch of track now, had begun to slow. Whispering soothingly, the woman fastened shoes on the child; the man removed luggage from the rack above their heads. There was a hoarse whistle: the train shuddered with a prolonged clashing of couplings, and was still.

The three descended from the stuffy warmth of the carriage into the chill of a sunless, misty morning; they were the only passengers to leave the train. His thick dark coat flapping obstinately about his legs, the man carried two heavy suitcases alongside the stationary, hissing carriages. The woman followed, carrying a small case in one hand, and guiding the slow child with the other. Their feet made crunching sounds on the raw gravel.

The station consisted of a square, broken patch of concrete, a set of hand-operated signals; and a dully reddish waiting-room, an uninhabited box of feeble yellow light. The buildings of the settlement around were dark and obscure in the mist.

'It's early yet,' the man observed, as he set down the suitcases in the waiting-room. 'We can wait here.'

The room smelt of soot and urine. They sat on hard wooden seats, the child's feet dangling above the filthy, paper-strewn floor. The woman blanketed the child and drew the coat-lapels over her throat again. The man sat hunched forward, his large veiny hands dangling fidgety between his knees: he looked at his hands, turning them over for inspection, as if seeking some answer there.

'It'll be all right this time,' he said at last. 'I know it will.'

The woman was silent.

'I got a good feeling about it,' he said, still looking at his hands.

The woman remained silent. The child was again asleep against her thigh. The man became annoyed with looking at his hands, and suddenly thrust them deep into the pockets of his coat. He discovered, as if by accident, a tin of tobacco and began, laboriously, to make a thin cigarette.

The engine whistled: the shrill, imperious sound echoed and re-echoed against hills hidden in the mist. There was a renewed hissing and lurching, and a long line of unlit carriage windows steamed past the waiting-room.

A solitary railway employee, walking homeward, looked into the room. He was puffy-eyed; and under his railway uniform a pyjama-top showed. 'Anything I can do for you people?' he asked.

The man looked up. His eyes were sharp and hostile. 'We're just waiting here,' he said aggressively. 'No law against waiting, is there? That's what this place is here for, isn't it?'

The railwayman was startled. He blinked. 'Don't get me wrong, mate. Just wondering if I could help, that's all.'

'You can't,' the man said.

'Strike me dead,' the railwayman said. 'No need to bite me head off, mate.' He retreated, still astonished, and strode off; his feet crackled away into the quiet, grey morning. They were alone again.

'He was only trying to be helpful,' the woman suggested timidly. 'You could of been nicer to him.'

'Helpful?' The man laughed. 'Nicer?' He stopped laughing suddenly. 'I pick his sort a mile. Bloody snoopers everywhere.'

The woman shrank from him. The child stirred and murmured.

'Sorry,' the man said. He seemed dismayed. 'You're right. I don't know.' He shook his head. 'There wasn't no need for me to go crook like that. I'm just a bit jumpy about everything. I didn't sleep. I suppose he might of been all right.' He drew hard on his cigarette, but it had burnt out. He threw it away in disgust, then reached in his pocket, took out a soiled paper bag, and tore it open. There were three stale-looking refreshment room sandwiches inside. He offered them to the woman. 'You hungry?'

'We can wait a while,' she said. 'You eat.'

'I'm not hungry neither.'

The woman looked sick with tiredness; she touched his arm hesitantly. 'Where are we?' she asked softly. 'Do we have to go far?

'This place here's a timber-milling outfit,' he said, pointing out the door to where mist still curtained the landscape. 'The mine's a couple of miles or so from here There's a road down to the mine, and a railway track. Don't know how the loco runs from here down to the mine. That's what we got to find out.'

'You could of asked that man then,' the woman pointed out cautiously. 'He could of told you how the loco runs.'

The man sighed. 'I could of,' he agreed. 'I just wasn't thinking. When I seen him come along I was thinking other things.'

The woman seemed altogether satisfied by his reply, by his admission that he had been wrong. It was an event of a rare kind, and she could afford satisfaction. He sat forward, looking out the door, thinking his other things again.

The light outside was now quite bright. The mist, retreating from the settlement, fled up the sunlit flanks of the hills. In the waiting-room, the child slept against the woman, and the woman against the man; the man was awake. He at last reached for a sandwich and began to eat it slowly and thoughtfully. His movement woke the woman, then the child.

She took the child to a tap outside the waiting-room and washed his face with a dampened handkerchief. Then she set the beret squarely on his head and led him back into the room. She took a bottle from her case and poured some cream-flecked milk into a peanut-butter jar that now saw service of a different kind. She gave the child the milk and a sandwich. There was one sandwich left. She looked at her husband, then at the child; and her hand darted out, as if of its own volition, and carried the sandwich quickly to her mouth. She ate almost guiltily.

The man stood. 'I'll find out what time the loco runs down to the mine,' he announced. He went out of the room, across the tracks, and into the settlement, walking with an abrupt, jerky stride. Presently he returned.

'There's a loco comes up about ten,' he said. 'It don't go back again till about one. That's five hours yet.'

'We can wait,' the woman said patiently; she fingered back her limp hair.

'Wait?' he said. 'I'm sick and tired of waiting. It drives you up the wall. We can walk to the mine. It's not far.'

'Walk?' the woman said faintly.

'All right?' he said briskly, but gave her no time to answer. He took up the two large suitcases. 'Let's go.'

They walked over the tracks and through the settlement. Along a single stony road, pooled with rainwater, there was a store and post office combined in an ungainly wooden building with unpainted weatherboards; one or two early-morning loungers watched the three strangers go past. Further along there was a string of old houses, knotting at the end into a cluster of ramshackle single men's huts. The timber mill, which stood at the end of the settlement, was already alive with grinding, tearing noises.

'Hell-holes, them places,' the man observed.

'They couldn't be much worse than mines,' the woman said; but he didn't seem to hear.

An articulated timber-truck, unloaded and jerking, rumbled past, splattering them with mud. The man spat after it. 'Could of given us a lift,' he said.

'He mightn't of been going the same way as us,' the woman observed.

'How does he know till he's asked us?' he demanded. He spat again, at nothing in particular this time.

'Anyhow,' she said, 'there wouldn't of been room for the three of us in it. Not in the cab.' She was right in defending the driver; she knew she was right. But this time, she knew also, he would not admit it. So she added appeasingly, 'It doesn't matter much, does it? You said it wasn't far.'

'No. It's not far.'

They walked in silence. His pace, even with the two heavy suitcases weighting him, was too brisk for her and the child. Soon he was several yards ahead.

'Wait,' she called, her voice mild with an old despair.

He sat on his cases and waited. She expected irritation in his face, but found only concern. 'I'm sorry,' he said. 'I keep forgetting him.' He pointed to the child. 'Let's have a rest.'

The child's face was still sleepy, and bewildered; the woman sat him on her case. 'Where we going?' he said.

'I told you before, sonny,' the woman said, sighing. 'We're going to a new place.' She was tired of the question.

'Why?'

'Shush, Ian,' she said with annoyance. Then, repenting, she straightened the cream beret on the small head.

'Why?' the child repeated.

'Because,' she said, raising her eyes in appeal to the man. 'Because Daddy's taking us.'

'Why Daddy taking us?'

The woman didn't answer: she didn't look at the man. He knelt beside the child; the child surveyed him gravely. 'We're going to a new place because it'll be a better place,' he said simply. 'That's why.'

The sun warmed the pale sky, lighting a landscape stripped and harsh. On the upper slopes of the hills, where limestone outcrops stood gaunt against the sky, were long-dead trees, tangled and whitened, and giant ulcers of erosion scabbed with weeping crusts of clay and papa; on lower ground lank wire fences straggled about small, pine-sheltered farmhouses. The pasture was a dead green colour, and loose-bellied cows grazed. The road unwound slowly, a thin strip of clay and bluish metal edged with ti-tree and gorse. They came, at length, to a crossroad, and a signpost which said: FERNDALE MINE 2½ M.

'I thought you said it wasn't far,' the woman protested.

The man didn't argue. 'It was a bit further than I thought, that's all.'

'We should of waited. We should of waited for a loco.'

The man seemed to agree. 'I just wanted to get there. I just don't like hanging round.' He paused. 'I didn't think it'd of been so far. I'm sorry.'

She was placated; she nodded, as if she too well understood his impatience. 'I don't like hanging round neither,' she said. 'But we should of waited.'

They came to a rise. The man, walking ahead, met the rise first. He stopped and set down his suitcases. 'There she is,' he said, pointing as the woman and child came up beside him.

The mining settlement discoloured the end of a tawny valley; the hills around were lacerated with black weals. Two groups of buildings made the settlement, one group large and dark and tightly gathered, the other small and white and more scattered. The large dark buildings belonged to the mine; the small white ones, a little distance removed, were the miners' homes. Above and beyond the valley were hills tall and blue and remote.

'What that?' the child said.

'That's where we're going,' replied the man. He said it almost with pride, sitting on a suitcase and rolling a cigarette. 'Might as well have a rest now,' he announced. 'It looks pretty good to me.'

Sitting beside him, the woman looked down the valley with a pensive expression. He touched her playfully under the chin, tilting up her face. 'What do you think, mother?' he said. 'Look good to you?'

'Any place,' she said. 'Any place looks good.'

'I think you'll like it here. I just got a feeling.'

'I'd like it anywhere. It doesn't matter where. Just as long as it's somewhere.' She continued to look thoughtfully down valley.

'I don't want to go,' the child said. 'I want to go back.'

'We can't go back,' said the woman, softly. 'We can't ever go back.' She didn't look away from the distant settlement.

'Why?'

She didn't seem to hear.

'Why?'

'Shut up,' she hissed suddenly, jerking her eyes to the child. Astonished, he began to whimper; she softened. 'Shush, Ian,' she whispered. 'We're going to a new place. A nice new place.' She pointed. 'See?'

But the child couldn't see; his eyes were filled with tears. 'My feet are hurty,' he complained.

The man picked up his suitcases. 'Let's go,' he said jubilantly. He set off with a jaunty stride, humming a tune.

The sun grew hot in an empty sky. A few hundred yards down the road they came to an old wooden bridge which spanned a clear, glittering stream. Upstream a little they could see a sandy place, like a miniature beach, strung around with toi-toi and flax, and shady with willows.

They made a halt on the bridge. 'It's a pretty place,' the woman murmured. 'A pretty place.'

'That'll be nice in summer,' said the man, pointing across the glittering water to the place of sand and shade. 'We could have picnics there. And swim. And eat our lunch under the willows.'

'Yes,' said the woman doubtfully. She had heard all this before. But there had never been picnics.

Their halts along the last stretch of road became more frequent. The child whimpered with hurting feet while the woman became tired and ill-tempered. The man, however, only seemed to increase his pace as they neared the settlement.

It was late in the morning when they came to it. The white miners' homes, attractive from a distance, were now small square boxes, crudely built and ugly, crammed together as closely as houses in a city suburb; they looked as if huddled for protection in the bare valley under the colourless sky. Each had a black strip of garden and a green patch of lawn.

The man nodded towards one of the homes. No curtains showed in the window; no smoke wisped from the chimney. The lawn was long-grassed and unkempt, and weeds grew in the garden. 'That one's empty,' he said. 'That might be the one we get.'

The woman looked at the place wistfully.

'Like it?' he said.

'There'll be a lot of work to do,' she said. 'I expect the inside's a mess. And the garden.'

'I knew it was going to be good,' he said with satisfaction, spitting on his parched palms and gripping the suitcases again. 'I knew it was going to be pretty good here. I had a feeling we was going to like it.'

This too she had heard before. Reluctantly, she turned her eyes from the house, took the child's hand, and followed the man.

Beyond the store and post office they found the settlement's most imposing structure, the mine office; a squat grey building. 'Wait here,' directed the man. 'I don't think I'll be long.'

The woman and child sat outside while the man went into the office. She removed the child's shoes and massaged the small, blistered feet. 'We'll be all right soon,' she said.

'Why?'

'I know,' she answered, confidently.

The reception office was a small, gloomy room. Beyond a dark counter were two desks. At one a grey-haired woman sat typing. At the other was a clerk, a slight mousy man of about fifty. He had a shiny bald head with a slender periphery of silver hair; steel-rimmed glasses sat on a thin, bony nose. His face was dried-up and humourless. He worked in a limp black smoking jacket. Just beyond him was a door displaying the sign Mine Manager.

The clerk looked up from his papers, apparently to ascertain that the visitor was of not much account, and then bent to them again. His pen scratched briefly, and he rose without haste, fastidiously flicked a spot of dust from his papers, and minced slowly to the counter.

'Yes?' he said. 'Anything I can do for you?'

'I'm here about a job. I wrote a letter—'

'The name?'

'Morrison's the name. William Morrison.'

The clerk screwed on the top of his fountain pen; he began to twirl the pen slowly in his fingers. 'Ah, yes, Mister Morrison,' he said. 'I remember.' His expression was pained; the pen twirled.

'It's all right, isn't it?' the man said. 'You said in your letter—'

'There were two letters actually, Mister Morrison.'

'Two letters? I only got one. You said there was a job for me here.'

'It's apparent you couldn't have received our second letter. We only posted it two days or so ago. We hardly expected you would turn up here so soon. You see, there was some mistake.' The clerk smiled blandly.

'Mistake?' His voice trembled. 'What do you mean a mistake?'

'About the job. An error in the office here. Really most unfortunate. What it amounts to is that there isn't a job here for you at all.'

'But you said—'

'As I explained, Mister Morrison, there was a mistake. We tried to tell you in our second letter. Unfortunately you set off before that letter arrived.' The pen still twirled between nervous fingers. 'The whole thing is really most unfortunate.' He shook his head. 'I'm so sorry.'

The man's eyes flickered, and were suddenly sharp. He slammed his fist on the counter. 'Don't lie to me,' he snapped.

'Really, Mister Morrison. Please.' The clerk retreated from the counter; he gave a small, despairing shrug.

'I don't want none of your bloody lies.'

The grey-haired woman, startled, looked up from her typewriter. The clerk appeared to wither before the prospect of further violence of language. 'Please, Mister Morrison. Please. There's a lady present.'

'Tell me the truth,' the man demanded.

'I'm afraid I don't understand,' said the clerk weakly. 'I've explained all there is to explain.'

'Let me see the manager.' The man pointed to the door beyond the clerk's desk. 'Maybe he'll have some truth.' He went round the end of the counter, but the clerk blocked his way.

'He's a busy man. He wouldn't want to be disturbed. He really—'

Shoved aside, the clerk fell back against the woman with the typewriter. She gave a cry, and saved her typewriter.

Without knocking, the man pushed open the door of the manager's office. This room was bright after the gloom of the other, too bright. He could not see at first. Sunlight fed through a long window in the opposite wall, silhouetting the desk and its occupant. The walls were cream-coloured, and there was now a thick green carpet beneath his feet. This room was not only brighter; it was luxurious by comparison. There were leathercovered chairs and light-varnished filing cabinets.

'My name's Morrison,' he announced.

He could see the occupant of the desk now, as he rose slowly to his feet, removing his thick tortoise-shell glasses. A short stocky man, moon-faced, in a pepper-and-salt suit; a gold watch-chain was looped across his waistcoat. He was a man with every appearance of assurance. He looked mildly puzzled.

'I beg your pardon?' he said.

'I said my name's Morrison. William Morrison. I want to know why I can't have a job here. After you people said I could have one. And I don't want none of your bloody lies.'

'A job?' the manager said. He resumed his seat and began, methodically, to clean his glasses with a white handkerchief.

'The job you people promised me. Now your bum boy out in the office tells me I can't have it. I want to know why.'

'Why?' the manager repeated. He seemed amused. 'You want to know why?' He coughed significantly, and added, 'There was a mistake. No doubt you've been told that.'

'I told you I don't want no lies. I'm sick of these kind of lies.'

The manager replaced his glasses and studied the man before him. The glasses seemed to give him added assurance.

'Well, Morrison,' he began casually, 'if you must know—'

The clerk put his head cautiously around the door. 'I tried to stop him coming in,' he started to apologize.

'Get out,' the man said. 'Leave us alone.'

The manager appeared to agree: he too irritably waved the clerk out. The head vanished and the door closed softly.

The manager straightened a file on his desk and closed it. 'Now,' he said slowly, fingering his lower lip. 'Your name is Morrison. William Morrison.'

'That's right. And I'm proud of it.'

'I daresay, Morrison. I daresay.' He slipped the file into a wire basket and drew out another one. The item he wanted was near the top of this file. He coughed before he spoke again. 'You're the Morrison who was gaoled for sedition three years ago, aren't you? You seem to get around quite a lot. And everywhere you've been there seems to have been trouble. Strange how trouble follows you around, isn't it?'

'I'm not ashamed of it. None of it. I've never caused no trouble. It's you people make the trouble. No, I'm not ashamed of nothing.'

The manager coughed tactfully. 'That, of course, is no concern of mine, Morrison. My concern is that we don't have trouble here, or trouble-makers. Up till now we've been free of trouble. The management's on excellent terms with the men. We wouldn't like any change. We want to keep things pleasant here.'

'Keep them down, you mean. I know your kind. I suppose you run the union too, eh?'

'I don't want to hear speeches. Speech-making might be part of your business. Listening to them is not part of mine.'

'You won't get away with this. You can't victimize—'

'No one, to my knowledge, is being victimized. No one is being discharged from employment here. There was just a mistake, as I told you. In any case, I'm sure if I discussed this thing with the men they would certainly prefer to be without your company.'

'Or else,' the man said with sarcasm. 'I know your stunts.'

'They would,' the manager repeated, 'certainly prefer to be without your company.' With an expression of innocence, he held up his hands. 'The clerical error which led us to advise you that we had a job offering is, of course, most regrettable.' He laid his hands flat on the desk, as if to signify he was finished with the subject.

'Bloody lies.'

'If you persist in seeing things in that light, Morrison, then of course there is simply nothing I can do about it.'

'If everything's so sweet here, what are you scared of? Eh?' He didn't give the manager time for reply. 'You know as well as I do. This place is known right up and down the country as rotten, isn't it? That's why.'

'If it's as bad as you say,' said the manager calmly, 'why did you come here, Morrison? Why don't you,' he added deliberately, 'go to Russia?'

'You really want to know. Because I don't like the likes of you. Because I got a kid I want to bring up decent here. Because I'm not a Russian.'

'Just as well for you,' observed the manager. 'They'd shoot you.'

'And you.'

'I've a considerable amount of work to do today,' the manager said abruptly. 'I'm sure we could have a most interesting discussion some other time.'

'Like hell. Scared, aren't you? All your kind.'

'If you'll excuse me, Morrison.' The manager opened a new file. 'I have work to do.'

'Take a good look around you sometime.' The man pointed out the window. The colliery workings, the mine shaft, blackened sheds, rakes of coal-trucks shunting, were all visible against scarred hillside. 'One day that's not going to belong to you. Or any of your kind. One day this country will belong to the people who sweated into it.'

'Get out,' the manager said.

He strode out of the mine office into the street; a door slammed behind him. He went past the woman and child, as if he had not seen them. The woman ran after him and caught at his sleeve.

'Where you going?' she said. 'It's all right, isn't it?'

He stopped to look at her; but his face was remote and expressionless. He hesitated, turned, and walked silently back to the suitcases. He lifted the sitting child aside, and took up the two large cases again.

'It's all right, isn't it?' the woman said, still plucking at his sleeve. He shook her away and began to walk. She picked up her small case, took the child's hand, and hurried after the man. 'Where we going?' she pleaded. 'It's all right, isn't it? There's nothing wrong? You got the job, didn't you?'

He stopped walking and let the cases fall heavily. 'No,' he said. 'They knew. They found out.'

Her eyes trembled. 'But the letter,' she said. 'The letter. They said you could have—'

'They must of found out after they sent the letter.' He was not looking at the woman now. 'They said it was a mistake. All a mistake. Bloody liars.'

Her shoulders quivered; the child began to whimper in sympathy. The man took her by the arm. 'Stop it,' he said. 'Not here.' He looked up and down the deserted street, but there seemed, at that moment, no onlookers. 'Not here,' he repeated.

'Where we going?' she whispered. 'Now?'

He avoided the question. 'We'll wait,' he said. 'Until the men come up from the pit. The day needn't be wasted.'

The woman gave her attention to the child. 'Shush, Ian,' she said. 'He's hungry,' she appealed to the man.

He wasn't listening: he had taken a letter from his inside suit pocket and was shredding it. 'Liars,' he said, more quietly now. A light breeze fluttered the torn paper from his hands; it whisked a little distance along the street and then lay still. 'Well?' he said at last. 'What are you waiting for? You can get something to eat from the store, can't you?'

In the late afternoon a low siren moaned: echoes circled the valley. Thick wire rope strained against turning winches: the cage from the pit screeched and rattled to the surface. Presently men emerged, dusty and blackened, in scarves and helmets, with eyes negro-white, through the colliery gate. They carried lamps and lunch-boxes and blinked against the bitter sunlight.

On one side of the gate they saw the short woman, drab and pale, with a child and some suitcases; on the other, the tall gaunt man in evangelical black. They were distributing leaflets with huge, exclamatory headings. The woman gave out her leaflets almost apologetically; the man was confident, entirely without apology, and called friendly slogans to the miners as they passed. 'The truth,' he said. 'Get the truth, comrades.'

Puzzled, most of the miners accepted the strange, rustling sheets of paper with urgent words; though some, as if fearing infection from a malady which they themselves could not properly define, side-stepped the outstretched hand, the humourless slogan, and hurried away. Some accepted only to repent, crumpling and discarding the leaflets as they walked with quickened step towards the safety of their homes. One or two stopped to talk briefly with the gaunt man in black; one pressed money into his hand. And then they were gone, all of them, into their square ugly homes with strips of garden and patches of lawn: the streets were empty again.

The man, moving slowly now, gathered up the remaining leaflets and packed them into a suitcase glutted with pamphlets, books, and other leaflets.

'How we going to get back to the station?' the woman said, as though waking from deep, dreamless sleep. 'Can we catch a loco?'

'Walk,' said the man. 'The way we came. There's no loco back now. It's too late in the day.'

'Walk?' the woman said.

They walked. The sinking sun coppered the land; the valley was still and quiet, dry and dead. The road had whitened, and their footwear grew dusty.

'Where we going?' the child said.

'Shush,' said the woman. 'Daddy's taking us.'

The sun sank; the valley was shadowed. In the east the clouds were pale and curdled; in the west they were gold and pink.

'Why?' said the child.

Dusk smoked from the land. When they reached the rise in the road from which they had first seen into the valley, they paused and looked back. An island of weak lights had grown under a lone star. The child was tripping and crying.

'Why Daddy taking us?'

'Shush,' said the woman, patiently.

The man set down his suitcases and took up the child. 'He's tired,' he said. 'Poor kid.'

'Why?' the child said, stubbornly.

THE STRANGERS

1

THE sun of a hot summer cooled in lightening blue skies. Along the trees of the front driveway the leaves withered and twisted into their autumn colours. Sudden breezes showered them down, chasing them across the grass; afterwards, in the calm, their browns and reds and golds speckled our paddocks brightly.

Sometimes, feeling the new chill in the air as I walked back to the house after putting the cows to pasture for the night, I would see the yellow light from the kitchen window slant out into the blue twilight, and I would consider, almost with surprise, how tightly the nights were gathering about the days: I was still young, and had yet to learn by heart the farmer's story of changing seasons, birth and death, growth and decay; of the fluent dance of natural things.

And with our household milk slopping noisily inside the billy which swung from my hand, I would hurry to get inside. Already the dusk song of birds would have thinned and faded; there would be the rattle of cicadas and perhaps from far back in the bush a morepork uttering a single, plaintive cry. My gumboots swished quickly over dewy grass and made small rubbery clumps up the steps to the back porch. Always I remembered first to strip them off and wipe my bared feet on the doormat, as Mother had taught me. Then, opening the door, I moved swiftly inside, clicking it shut against the cold and dark and damp of evening. The house was always filled with the fragrance of cooking food, stew bubbling or sausages frying. Padding through to the warmth and brightness of the kitchen I came upon my father stooped over our huge old iron stove, feeding wood into its mouth; or turning and stirring food with a fork folded into his large, worn hand. And while he worried and muttered I made haste to prepare the table before he put out steaming meat and vegetables on two warmed plates.

But of all those autumn evenings there was one to remember clearly, a different end to a different day. Since morning there had been the promise of rain; grey clouds built on the hills, growing darker and finally smothering the weak sun. We hurried through our evening jobs. But it wasn't until we were about to sit down to the meal that we heard the falling patter of rain on the iron roof. Shortly afterwards there was a faint rapping on the door. Looking surprised, Father rose to answer it.

—I didn't hear any car, he said.

We were out in a lonely part of country and didn't often have visitors. At that time it was an even more pleasant surprise to have them, because Father didn't always know quite what to do with himself in the evenings the first year after Mother died. Most nights, if he couldn't find something to keep him busy, he'd fall back in his favourite easy chair, put up his stockinged feet on another chair and balance his steel-rimmed reading glasses on the tip of his nose. There would always be a big pile of newspapers for him to read; always too many, for all the time new ones arrived at the farm. Now and then, with sudden resolution, he threw out all those unread and began again with the very latest issue. But the pile grew again. Because some nights, too tired to work or read, he just rested in his chair and looked up at the ceiling through half-closed eyes. If I asked him anything, while I read or puzzled over homework, he answered only with effort.

And, after he'd sent me to bed, the living-room light would burn till late: from the warmth of my blankets I saw its reflection under the bedroom door. Sometimes, when I was awake longer than usual, I slipped from my bed, opened the door quietly, and tip-toed over the cold floor down the passage to the living-room. Often I found him still in his chair, sprawled asleep, the glasses balanced precariously on the tip of his nose while he made loud snoring noises in his mouth. Timidly, I moved closer and touched him lightly on the shoulder: he always woke with a jerk, and stared at me with wide-open tired red eyes as if I were a stranger, as if he had expected to waken somewhere other than under the cold glare of light in the living-room, with me standing before him small and frightened in my outgrown pyjamas. Presently he seemed to recognize me. Then, slowly and deliberately, he removed his glasses and said:

—You ought to be in bed. Asleep.

It was a stern voice, one that made me scurry back to bed. In a little while I heard the jangling of easing chairsprings as he lifted himself up. He went through to the kitchen, and presently the kettle hissed for his suppertime cup of tea. And suddenly my door swung open and the light behind showed him tall and upright. Bending, he gave me my glass of milk and a thick slice of fruitcake.

—And after this you better go to sleep.

And before he left he reminded me:

—Early to bed and early to rise makes a man healthy, wealthy and wise. Goodnight, boy.

—Goodnight, I murmured through my mouthful of cake.

And after a while I'd hear the rattle of his cup and saucer as he finished his tea, the splashing of water as he washed himself, the lights clicking out one by one, his feet whispering up the passage to his bedroom; and, finally, the slow grating as he wound his shrill-voiced alarm clock, and the wirewove of the big double bed straining as he eased his weight on to it. But I rarely heard him begin to snore, for I was tired too.

—I'm damn sure I didn't hear any car, Father repeated.

I followed him from the table. He opened the back door, and light played faintly on the damp face of a young Maori with a swag on his back. He smiled cautiously, as though uncertain of his welcome. The rain whipped under the porch roof and stung our faces. Father quickly invited the young man inside and closed the door. Still surprised, he asked:

—How'd you come?

—Walked from town.

The stranger spoke as though there was nothing interesting in the fact that he'd walked fourteen miles. He hastened to explain:

—Heard you might have a job going.

—Well, Father said. Well, yes, I might have.

He paused thoughtfully a moment.

—Well, dump that swag of yours. Tim boy—run and get the young man a towel to dry himself.

The stranger eased the load from his shoulders.

—It don't matter. Don't fuss me. I don't want to be no bother.

As I fetched the towel, Father said:

—Don't suppose you've eaten.

—No. I was walking to beat the rain.

—Well, you can eat with us then. You're pretty lucky. We was only just starting on the tucker.

Father spooned out stew and potato on a new plate while the stranger dried himself. I set another place at the table, and we all sat down.

—My name's Tui, he said. Tui Waritene.

—I expect you know mine already, Father said. Anyhow I'm Ned Livingstone and this is my boy Tim. We run this place between us, Tim and me.

—Yes, Tui said. They told me your last man left quite a while back.

Father frowned. Just as if nothing had been said. he asked:

—What part of the country you from?

Once that question was asked he could talk for hours, contrasting different places. Tui explained that he'd come up from the south lately, and liked the look of our district. When Father began to talk my eyes stayed on Tui. Even to me he didn't seem very old. His skin was the rich brown full-blooded colour, clear and smooth; different to Father's wrinkled, weathered face with its greyish stubble of beard which he never seemed able to shave. He smiled with brilliant teeth and a friendly twinkle in his eyes; his voice was soft and pleasant and made me think of restful places with cool shadows, deep grass, and running water. He was careful with his table manners and listened attentively to all Father said. It didn't seem Father would stop talking. And the more he talked, the more carelessly he ate. Stew splashed off the plate and soiled the table-cloth; little bits of food clung to the corners of his mouth. When he tried to eat and talk at the same time he never had good table manners: when Mother was alive she often reproved him for them after visitors left the house. Now, seeing his bad manners, I felt embarrassed and uncomfortable and responsible. I shifted in my chair, trying to catch Father's eye while I rubbed industriously away at the corners of my own entirely clean mouth. I desperately hoped he would see my meaning. When he at last took notice he regarded me sternly, the food still clinging to his mouth, and demanded:

—What's the matter, boy? Eh? You got St. Vitus' dance?

He glared as though ashamed for an idiot son. Tui was smiling at me in a friendly way, but I wasn't prepared for that yet, and lowered my eyes.

After dinner Father went out and Tui helped me with the dishes, drying while I washed. He wanted to know how I liked living on the farm. I told him I wouldn't ever want to live anywhere else. Did I like school? Not much, I said, because I'd sooner be with Father than sitting in class. And Tui said it was a great change to hear a boy talk that way. After a while Father came inside the house again, his clothes spotted with rain, and took Tui through to the living-room and said for him to make himself comfortable while they had another yarn.

I was sent to bed early. They talked till late. Or at least Father talked. I could hear his voice rising and falling, like the sound of sea, as he told Tui about the farm. One of the last things I heard was Tui asking about the job again. Father said, well, they could sleep on the subject and see about it in the morning. I was sure then, by the tone of his voice, that he already intended Tui should have the job. But it was Father's belief that you should never make things too easy for anyone. They never appreciated it, he said. And before I fell asleep I thought about the last man.

He was a Mr Smith. He arrived in winter, not long after Mother died, and left just before Christmas, staying nearly six months altogether. He was a young man too; but pale and thin and awkward in movement, much different from Tui. He was very quiet; he spent most of his spare time reading in his small bedroom and smoking cigarette after cigarette, so that for a long time after he left the stale nicotine smell haunted the room; and the smell, together with the tattered jumble of detective novels in the corner, infected it with the memory of his presence. Mr Smith rarely spoke to me; often he didn't acknowledge my existence. Father liked him, though, and slapped him on the back and called him Bill; I wasn't sure whether to like him or not. And it wasn't just because he passed me by without a flicker in his bleak eyes; or because of the times when he threw stones at friendly birds or kicked and growled at the cows when Father wasn't looking. I was always noticing things about him, like the way his lips trembled and his eyes shifted when someone spoke suddenly; or the way he sat out on the porch looking at nothing, his eyes growing big and watery while he smoked a damp-ended cigarette. They were things Father didn't notice. Though Mr Smith never said much, his clumsiness let Father make up his mind that he was a city man seeking a clean and decent way of life by working in the country. He was pleased to have such a sensible chap; he was very pleased with Mr Smith. Until one day, when we went to town, we returned to find that Mr Smith had left suddenly, stealing thirty pounds. Father stood in the kitchen, bewildered.

—No. It can't be. It can't.

A ripple of looseness went through him, and he slumped to the kitchen table, his head in his hands. And he said the words I could remember him saying, over and over, from the time I began to remember.

—There's no one you can ever rely on. Only yourself.

And, in a voice a whisper:

—Don't you ever forget that, boy. Don't ever forget it.

A little while afterwards the police called at the farm; they had been seeking Mr Smith for some time, under his real name, and for reasons of their own.

I knew how difficult the stolen money made things. Though we'd been working hard, the cream-cheques were poor, and there had been all the expenses for Mother's funeral. Not to speak of the thing called a mortgage which worried Father so much. And it was nearly Christmas.

—It's a day for those with money, boy. Not for us.

But it seemed to make no difference, for when I woke in the grey early light of Christmas morning I found at the foot of my bed, brightly wrapped, the model railway set I'd wanted. I began to play with it. Then I saw his bare bony feet splayed on the floor. He was still in his sleeping shirt, his legs pale and hairy, the sleep clinging to his eyes, the rumpled hair falling over his face, and the faintest of smiles playing about his lips. Presently he squatted on his haunches, farmer fashion, and while he rolled and lit his first cigarette of the day advised how to lay the rails properly and wind the toy engine.

Later in the morning he went to a cupboard and removed a single bottle of beer. It had gathered dust with time, and he polished it against his shirt and uncapped it with ceremony. He poured a few drops into an egg cup for me, and filled a large glass for himself. The beer frothed a cheerful smell.

—And go easy, boy, he said, raising his glass. Learn to be moderate. Cheers, now.

He drank while he prepared dinner, and presently he even began to whistle tunelessly. I couldn't remember having heard him whistle for a long time, not since Mother died.

When we were about to sit down to the meal, he suddenly remembered something. He went from the room and returned with three coloured-paper party hats. They were hats we'd used for Christmas dinner for years; Mother had always carefully folded them each year and put them away for the next Christmas celebration.

Standing before the laden table, he peeled off one of the hats and gave it to me; he watched with a smile as I put it on my head. Then he lowered his eyes and the smile slowly went from his face as he separated the two others in his hands. He took one for himself, then seemed to become rigid as he looked at the other. With a queer expression, he crumpled it in one hand, and threw it away. He sat down heavily, and I could see the big vein at the side of his temple beginning to throb.

—Eat, boy. Eat. Go on. Don't sit there like a ninny.

He forced the hat on his head: it ripped. Obediently, I began to eat. There was a fowl which he had killed, cooked, and dressed; it had somehow burnt in the oven, but there was still enough of the novel poultry taste to be enjoyed. And Mrs Fletcher on the next farm made a Christmas pudding as a present for us, filling it with surprise threepences. Father ate in silence. Astonished at my own boldness, I said:

—I bet I can find the most.

—Most what? he growled.

—Threepences, I said timidly.

He looked at me, startled.

—You do, eh?

—Yes, I said.

He seemed almost to smile. In no time at all he discovered four threepences. I found only one.

—What happened to you, eh? he grinned in triumph. You swallow all yours?

He stood up and looked at himself in the mirror. The torn hat was askew on his head.

—Don't I look stupid?

He grinned, and we laughed. For the rest of the day everything was all right. We spent the afternoon chopping out a rebellious patch of scrub and gorse. Father said people like us couldn't afford to be idle, not even on Christmas day. Besides, he added, idleness led to the habit of slackness, and if there was any such thing as sin, then slackness was the worst sin of all. He explained I should be glad to learn this so early in life. Some people went all through life without ever learning it. So many in fact, he hated thinking of them all. It wasn't, though, that he was afraid for their souls; he said he wasn't worried about nonsense like after-life. It was just that he didn't like the thought of them going into the darkness without ever knowing.

The sun baked the sky, and stung the sweat from our faces. We worked all afternoon, till our backs ached and hands chafed, and then it was time for the evening jobs. After tea he took me to the living-room, where he spread the railway set on the floor. But soon I wilted and fell asleep when I should have been watching him explain something. He must have taken me up gently and carried me to bed, for I remembered nothing more until I woke with the morning sun shining through my window.

One night not long after Christmas he jumped from his chair, waving a newspaper.

—My God, he said. They got him.

—Who? I said.

—Him. That Smith joker. They got him.

He pointed to a news item.

—Two years they give him. There, he said with satisfaction, they got him all right.

He fell back in his chair, reading the item again.

—Yes, he said. No doubt about it, eh?

He was silent a while. The newspaper rustled to the floor. Then his voice was changed.

—The poor young devil. Two years.

Presently he added:

—He probably didn't have a chance. It's just the way it is in them cities. It's the way people get.

He rose and paced about the room.

—I liked that young joker. I had faith in him.

He paced about for some time. Then he halted, stiffened.

—But there's no one you can ever rely on, he said. Only yourself.

He turned to me, and his face was hard.
—Remember that, boy.

2

Now the cold wet night of the young Maori stranger had come and gone,
receding beyond the days of deepening autumn and approaching winter.
Tui slipped so quickly into our life that it was hard for me to remember
back to the time when he was not on the farm. One day Father took me
aside and told me how pleased he was that Tui fitted in so well. But that
day too had come and gone, merging into the grey twilight of the season.
And there was only the present, the cold morning awakening, the beginning
of each day. When Father and I stepped out on the back porch, Tui would
emerge from his little room, washed and dressed and ready for work. There
were brief morning greetings and Father and he talked as they walked down
to the cowbails with me trailing behind. Sometimes the farm was under a
slow-dissolving fog, which might in time lift to reveal a sullen, weeping sky.
Other times, those which fastened on my memory, a heavy white dust of
frost covered hillside and flat, icy grass crunched under gumboots, and
warm breaths bloomed steam in the clear air as sharp voices crackled
through the brittle silence. Above, beyond the eastern hills, there was the
first glow of sunrise. Threads of mist hung in hollows and folds, soon to
be warmed away by the risen sun. But always, rain or fine, there was that
brisk morning mingling of awakened voices; and, later, while Father brought
our antiquated milking machine racketing and chugging to desperate life,
Tui's voice bursting into song above the noise. He had a good voice, and
I loved to hear it. He said he reckoned the cows gave up their milk easier
when you gave them a little song. Though Father never said anything, he
liked the changed atmosphere too, in his own way. Afterwards Tui was left
singing by himself while he cleaned the separator. Father cooked breakfast
and I got ready for school. Every morning after breakfast I had to excuse
myself, pick up my schoolbag, and hurry to the door while the two of them
still relaxed at the table, lingering over steaming cups of tea, rolling cigarettes
and talking. I felt badly about leaving them, but there was nothing I could
do about it, and so I'd be walking quickly down the driveway, turning now
and then to look back at our old unpainted house, tiny behind the trees,
with its chimney and faint blue wisp of smoke. Father and Tui usually came
to the window to wave goodbye. Satisfied now, I'd run the rest of the way
to the gate, where presently the school bus would call to take me the long
miles to the classroom.

I liked being with Tui. Towards evening, while the shadows merged and deepened through our valley, we winterfed the cows with hay from the barn while Father cooked a meal inside the house. Sometimes we chatted as we forked.

—Your Dad's a great man, eh? Tui said.

—Yes, I said, pleased.

—Yes, Tui said, he's a great man on the work. He never stops. All day and half the night. He's a great man on the work all right.

—He works pretty hard, I said proudly.

—Too much work's no good. What d'you think, eh?

Surprised, I only said:

—It makes you pretty tired.

—Too right, Tui said. Too right it makes you pretty tired. All work, no play, eh?

—Yes, I answered; though I still couldn't see whatever it was he meant.

—You got to have fun sometime, eh? You're a long time the corpse.

Paused in his work, leaning on his fork, he looked down at me as if he expected an answer. But I didn't know what to say.

Through autumn and winter, as the cows dried off and things became easier, Tui and I shared our spare time. On fine days we went for walks. Climbing the hills which rose steeply from the back of the farm, we came upon the sight of bushland tumbled out in a carpet, blurred and crumpled, of brilliant browns and greens. In the distance, greys and blues washed the purple line of the horizon. It would be strange then to look back and see the valley so naked where Father had burned and axed to sow pasture. As if flung back by storm, the bush hung ragged on the hills around. Burnt stumps jutted from the grassed earth; second-growth manuka strung itself weakly on erosion-veined slopes; bracken, fern and toi-toi clung weakly to weatherworn limestone cliffs. Thickening, the bush fell back over the hill-crests to flourish, lush and tall-treed, circling the valley. When an inflamed winter sunset lit the valley, it seemed an island in a wild sea.

While I skipped and scrambled along beside him Tui told me the names of trees and birds, and old Maori legends and tales about them. Guiding me by the hand, pointing things out, he explained how easy it was to live off the bush if you wanted, eating eels and birds, fernroots and berries and the juicy white insides of nikau palms. He told me his own adventures in the bush. And one day he let slip that his great-grandfather was one of the old chiefs who fought the pakeha in New Zealand's wars. After that I made him tell new stories, stories he had heard from old men. The thing that caught my imagination was not so much the actual resistance to the pakeha, but the picture of the brown men after defeat, fleeing through the bush before the clumsy advance of Britain's troops. And his slow voice made the picture come alive, so that sometimes I could almost imagine that these things were still really happening, so that I could see the long-dead tattooed men fleeting softly and shadowy through high fern, never to be glimpsed warring again.

He would tell the stories reluctantly. At times like these we would have halted our walk. I would sit on something, perhaps a fallen treetrunk, while he stood and talked before leafy curtains of evergreen. Sometimes startled wood-pigeons flapped heavily away at the sound of his voice. The sun, shafting thinly through the trees, streaked the fern and moss and maidenhair of the bush floor; and touched him, here and there, with its dusty pale lemon-colour as he moved talking, somehow sad and solitary, in and out of shadow.

Father didn't mind Tui spending time with me. He seemed pleased with everything Tui did. He said he was a pretty good sort of Maori. He worked hard, never complained; he was a big help around the farm. Pretty educated too, and sensible. Not like some of the Maoris who went gallivanting round spending all their money and having a good time. No, Tui worked hard and saved his money. He expected Tui was doing it with the idea of getting married, or something. Anyhow, whatever it was, he hoped Tui wouldn't leave us too soon; even a couple of years would be too soon.

The idea of Tui getting married interested me; I remembered it one mid-winter day when we were out fishing. The frost had melted from the grass, the sun was warm, and long white clouds feathered the sky. Below us the cold-running creek sparkled as we waited for eels to swim into the trap Tui had shown me how to make.

—When you going to get married, Tui?

He laughed.

—Married?

—Yes.

He laughed again.

—You get some funny ideas, he said.

I thought of when Tui and I went down to the town together. Maori girls, shy and hopeful, or haughty and proud, would often look at him as he walked the street. And I remembered that Tui never seemed to notice them at all.

—Aren't you going to? Not ever? I said hopefully.

—Sometime I might. No big hurry, eh?

—I just thought you might be going to.

—No fear. Not me. Not yet for a long time.

—Dad thought you was going to.

I spoke as though that somehow proved he really should be getting married.

—Hah, Tui said; his smile was big. Why, eh?

—Because you save up your money.

With his hands behind his head, he lay back and closed his eyes.

—Well, he said, you both thought wrong, eh?

There was a silence.

—Then why do you save up?

—To get money.

—What for?

—So I can do things.

—What kinds of things?

He rolled on his side, took out a tobacco tin, and began to make a cigarette. After a while, reluctantly, he said:

—Things I want to do.

—What kinds? I persisted.

—Well, he began. Then he fell silent, licking the tissue paper around the tobacco, and lighting the finished cigarette.

—Well, there's lots of things I want to do. Around the country. Like a bit of shooting. I need a good new rifle.

—That'll be good fun, I said.

I began to get excited at the prospect of all the good times we'd have together. But he didn't seem to hear what I said; he was still talking about the other things he wanted, for hunting and fishing.

—Gosh, I said. You want a lot.

—I want things like that. And money to keep me going. For clothes and food and smokes and stuff. I'm spoilt now, eh? I can't go living off the bush for everything.

I was slow to see his meaning. Bewildered, I asked:

—Then won't you be stopping at our place?

—No, he said. Think I'll have to be moving on for that. For what I'll be going to do. Don't think your Dad would like me spending all my time having fun, eh?

There was a long silence. The creek rippled, and a bellbird sang. I looked at Tui.

—You never ever told me you'd be going away.

—Not right now, he said.

—Don't you like it here?

—I like it all right. I like you and your Dad all right.

—Then what d'you want to go away for?

He sat up and folded his arms around his legs.

—I just think I'll have to be moving on one day.

Then he rose to his feet.

—We better have a look at that trap.

We raised it. There were five eels; three big, and two little. Tui let the little ones wriggle back into the creek.

—They'll be big next year, he said.

—Will you be here next year?

He shrugged.

—It depends, he said.

Things I'd been about to say fell back into my mind, like drops of water into a brimming pool; I was sad. Tui, singing, dropped the threshing eels into a sugar bag and slung it over his shoulder; as we walked home, I wondered if he might stay long enough for me to leave school and go away with him. But then I thought of Father lonely by himself on the farm: and I didn't know.

Presently we mounted a ridge and saw the trees and buildings clustered tiny on the green valley floor. We could only just distinguish Father's distant, solitary figure as he moved about the backyard, close to his workshop. He began to hammer at something; the hard, rhythmic sound rose up to us.

—He's a great man all right, Tui said. A great man on the work.

He paused, and added:

—You better not tell him what I been telling you. He mightn't think it's a good idea, eh?

3

Spring slipped behind us: the stirring and change, the swampy paddocks drying, the cows coming into milk, the calves tottering spindle-legged, the awakening green of the bush, the flash of rata blossom, the pink of puriri, the sharp new clamour of birds. And there was Tui, restless and alive, moving abruptly away from his work to stare at the bush along the horizon: staring, and then walking away, quickly, with me following until he tired and sat in silence. If we talked, the conversation circled slowly to alight on the things he would do when he left the farm, while his eyes lit and I wondered.

Then summer was upon us. Ahead were rainless months while the sun browned and killed the grass and dwindled the creeks to trickles; while fire crackled through the hills to bloom blue-grey smoke and send cinders falling like rain. Father would afterwards recall that we only came through that summer by the thinnest skin of our teeth.

—If that much, he'd say.

But the future was still pushing through the present into the past; and at night Father, settled comfortably in his chair, talked to Tui about this summer, next autumn, next winter, and about bigger cream-cheques and a smaller mortgage.

—It'll be a great thing, he said, when a man can go out there and plant his two feet down and look around and tell himself it's all his, eh?

—Yes, Tui said. It'll be a great thing, all right.

But he would seem uncomfortable in his chair; he shifted, and rolled another cigarette.

One evening after milking, while the farm was alight with a cool orange sunset, Tui came into the kitchen and told Father he wanted to leave.

Father was bent over the hot stove. He turned stiffly at the sound of Tui's voice. In a slow, bewildered way, he drew the back of his hand over his sweaty brow. Tui's eyes were dark and apologetic.

—Well, Father said at last. I'm sorry to hear that, Tui. I am sorry.

Tui was silent.

—I thought you'd be with us a bit longer.

—I think I'll have to be moving on, Tui said quietly.

—Well, I don't expect there's anything can be done about it. If you want to go, you'll go, and that's flat. I couldn't make you change your mind, eh?

Tui shook his head.

Father turned awkwardly to the stove again.

—I knew you'd be pulling out one day. The only thing is I didn't pick it'd be this soon.

Tui went to bed unusually early that night, leaving Father with his newspapers. Sitting near him with a book, I looked up suddenly at the sound of his voice. Then I realized he wasn't talking to me, but to himself.

—He must be going to get married. It's the only thing. That's why he's been saving so careful. Been putting away every penny. Probably counts on getting himself a bit of land one day too.

He was silent, and I began reading my book again. Presently there was a small rustle of paper and, looking up, I saw a newspaper slide from a limp, dangling hand. He slept with his mouth fallen open, and the deep lines on his brow relaxed. Moving quiet towards him, I saw his face as older than I had ever seen it before, and I noticed the new grey hair patching the side of his head. Gently I removed the glasses from his nose and set them on a table. Then I switched out the light and went to the kitchen. With the least possible sound, I set the kettle to boil for his suppertime cup of tea. While I waited I opened the window and, resting my arms on the sill, looked out into the mild summer evening. Stars peppered the sky above the dark hills, and from somewhere deep in shadow a morepork called, its cry long and lonely.

It was another clear day, that Saturday, and I was home from school. The sun, climbing clear of the hills, had still to smother the clean smell of morning. I sat on the porch. Tui was singing as he packed in his room; Father was out in the backyard, tinkering with the engine of our battered old Ford. He had promised to run Tui down to town, but the car had broken down earlier in the week and he wasn't able to get it running again. He made a lot of apologies to Tui, but Tui just said not to worry, he was used to hiking, and anyhow he really liked it better that way. It made no difference, though, because Father kept apologizing and making Tui more embarrassed.

Father was still swearing and muttering at the engine when Tui came out of his room, his swag dangling from his hand. He set it down, took out his tobacco tin, and began to make a cigarette.

—Well, he said, looking around and breathing the morning. She's a great sort of day to be starting off, eh?

—Yes, I agreed miserably.

Father came over and spread himself, large and loose-jointed, at the foot of the porch steps.

—Well, it's no go with the car, Tui. I'm sorry.

—She's right, Tui said. Don't worry.

There was a silence.

—She a nice girl? Father asked suddenly, twisting his head to look up at Tui.

—Girl? Tui said.

—Don't you think we can guess? Father said, smiling.

—There's no girl, Tui said quietly.

—We can guess.

—No, Tui repeated. There's no girl.

—Then why you going?

—It's just time to be pulling out, Tui said. Time to be moving on.

Father rose stiffly. He looked at Tui.

—But the money you been saving up. Aren't you going to get married? I thought you might of been thinking about settling down on your own bit of land or something.

—No fear, Tui said.

—But what about the money?

—That's for me. To keep me going through the summer. And for things I want, like a rifle and stuff.

—And that's all you worked for?

—Sure thing, Tui said.

He tucked the cigarette in the corner of his mouth and deftly swung the swag up on his shoulder.

—Well, I guess I better be starting off.

But he didn't move. He and Father stood quite still, looking at each other. And I saw it wasn't just Father who didn't understand; Tui couldn't understand Father either. There were the two of them there, neither understanding the other, and I stood between, only knowing that of all the hurtful things in life the most hurtful was two people not understanding each other. I knew that it was important that they should come to understanding, though I didn't know why and would never have been able to explain. I wanted to jump up and down between them, shouting words that would make them understand. But I knew no words, and was silent.

—Gee, Tui said. I almost forgot.

He went back into his room and returned carrying two parcels. He handed one to Father, the other to me.

—Presents, he said.

Father's face looked queer as his thick fingers fumbled with the string and paper; his parcel was small, but mine was long and thin.

—A fishing rod, I guessed, grinning at Tui.

But he just smiled, not saying anything.

And it was. Then wrapping fell from Father's hands to reveal a combination spanner. The bright, new steel glinted in the sunlight as he turned it over.

—You shouldn't of done this, he said, and his voice was as queer as his face. You shouldn't of—

—Forget it, Tui said.

—Thanks, Father said. But there wasn't no need—

—Well I better be starting off, Tui said, patting me on the head. You be able to have fun now, eh?

I nodded. My tongue was stuck dumb in a dry mouth.

—Oh yes, Tui said, taking an envelope from his pocket. I almost forgot this too. That's my sister's address. She usually knows where I am. If you have any troubles getting a new man you better tell her and maybe I can come and give you a hand for a while next year. O.K., eh?

—Thanks, Father said. That's real good of you.

He was not looking at Tui now. We followed him down to the gate. He shook hands and gave me another pat on the head. Then Father swung the gate shut while Tui walked away down the long white road. Dust puffed out under his shoes, leaving tiny clouds behind him.

Father leaned on the gate and I sat, my legs dangling, on the top rail.

Tui's figure grew smaller with distance. Now and then he would turn to wave. Presently we heard his voice rising into the morning, the faint song receding. Then he was gone; his voice too. Father thumbed his hat back on his head and began to roll a cigarette.

—Well, he said.

The sun was hot now, and the cool shadows of the trees splashed over us as we walked back up the driveway to the house, our feet brushing over the parched grass. A friendly fantail twittered round us, then wheeled away.

I expected Father to go directly to his car and begin tinkering again. Instead he came to sit beside me on the steps of the porch. While I fingered my fishing rod, he sucked at his cigarette, puzzling and frowning.

Presently he rose jerkily to his feet. He picked up the spanner and envelope together, turning them over in his hand. Then he lifted his eyes.

—There's no one you can ever rely on, he said. Only yourself.

He spoke in the same way as I might repeat some school lesson; mechanically, without conviction. Bewilderment had settled on him now, and he was saying the only thing he could find to say.

He looked down at the spanner and envelope again. Then, as though they contradicted him, he flung them away. The spanner fell with a dull sound; the envelope fluttered down limply.

—Only yourself, Father said.

Standing tall and straight above me, his brow puckered, his hands curled into tight fists, he considered what he had said. Then, breathing deeply and uncoiling, he moved loosely, almost shamefaced, to retrieve the spanner and envelope before he crossed the yard to where the rebellious engine waited for him.

LOVE STORY

1

THE sun burned in a bright sky; the town under the hazy hills soaked up the summer heat. Mr Jackson lay belly-up on an unshaded part of the baked back lawn. The Saturday sports edition covered his face; his many-patched working trousers were rolled at the knees above milky flesh, and tight and swollen at the crutch; his undone shirt buttons revealed a thin tangle of hair on the sweaty chest which rose and fell with erratic grunts. of sleep. He had been there since dinner; he had gone out of the house explaining he would do some gardening. He had done no more than survey the weedy ruin of the garden, sigh heavily, and settle himself comfortably on the lawn, taking the sports edition from his back pocket to make a cursory examination of the race results. But even that was half-hearted, and it was pleasant to let himself fall full-length on the lawn so that his heavy head rested on the parched grass. He also found it pleasant to cover his face with the sports edition and swallow cool mouthfuls of shade. Just as he had probably not intended to touch the garden in the first place, he had probably not meant to doze, let alone sleep; for it was far too hot to sleep in the open sun. On the other hand, though, a walk back to the shade of the house demanded energy; and possibly too a return to work which he had in the first place sought to avoid.

The girl Gloria had no intention of waking him. She sat slim and relaxed in the deep sag of the yellow-and-blue deck chair. Her body was almost entirely bared to the sun; she wore only a brief red two-piece sunsuit which fitted trimly to the firm young shape of her body. Her skin, pink and tender, was now beginning to sting; so she rose from the deck chair to walk back to the house. As she did, she glanced down at her father; and her small nose wrinkled.

The cool gloom of the house was edged with the crackling voice of the request-session announcer. Gloria stopped in the kitchen: flies sang above the unwashed dinner dishes, suicided against the speckled window. She turned on a tap, letting the first tepid flow of water splash over the ooze of gravy-fat on the sink-bottom and gargle down the plughole. When the water began to run cold, she filled a glass and drank quickly.

'Bring me a glass too, dear,' called her mother from the living-room.

Mrs Jackson had been listening to the radio since the meal, her body propped by cushions, her slippered feet folded comfortably on the end of the couch; she had smoked cigarette after cigarette, each lit from the butt of the last, and spilt ash dribbled down that part of her black dress which stretched tight over her bulky bosom. She was a large untidy woman with straggling black hair. Features which had once been not unattractive were effectively disguised with fat and age. There was a warm glass of sherry on the table beside her and, next to it, several dogeared women's magazines. These she thumbed through when the music did not appeal to her. She accepted the glass of water from her daughter, and sipped thinly.

'You're burning,' she observed, studying her daughter's firm flesh.

'I know,' the girl said sullenly.

'Hadn't you better put some cream on?'

'I was just going to. You don't have to tell me.'

'All right, dear. I was just saying—' What was she just saying? Mrs Jackson wondered. She couldn't remember. She was aware only of the cool disconcerting presence of her daughter; the sulky pretty face, high-cheekboned, tender-lipped; the dark hair and supple body. Mrs Jackson felt sad; she had been young and pretty herself once. What for? 'What's your father doing?' she sighed. 'Or needn't I ask?'

'He's out there,' the girl said. Her gesture could have meant any one of a number of things; she turned away as if to leave the room.

'Gloria,' her mother said softly, reluctant to see the cause of her pleasant sadness depart.

'What?'

Mrs Jackson began uncertainly. 'I was just thinking—'

'Yes?' the girl said querulously.

Mrs Jackson found it difficult to explain; she abandoned the effort. 'It doesn't matter,' she said. But she still thought: a pretty girl like me, all gone to waste. 'You're looking lovely today, dear. The red suits you.'

Impatient, the girl made to move away again.

'Why don't you take a magazine and have a lie down, dear? There's a lovely story in this one.' But the girl would not accept the offered magazine. 'Is something the matter?'

'No,' the girl said shortly. 'Nothing.'

'You shouldn't have too much sun,' advised Mrs Jackson. 'Too much is bad for you. You don't want that lovely figure of yours to shrivel, do you now? Now, if I was a boy—'

'You're not a boy.'

'I was just saying if I was—'

But the girl went quickly out of the room, out of earshot. Mrs Jackson sighed, shook her head, adjusted the volume of the radio, which, she now suspected, was giving her a headache (or perhaps it was just the heat, or the wine). She flicked idly through the magazine which she had offered her daughter. The story had been a beautiful one, a love story, about a boy and girl who decided to spend a weekend in a lonely cottage together before they were actually married; but, at the last moment, as they set a fire in the grate to warm the cold cottage, they looked at each other guiltily and knew that it was, after all, a mistake, and that afterwards they would only remember it with a shame which would destroy the true happiness of marriage. So they kissed each other and, linking hands, went home again to their separate, celibate lives; an ending happy and wistful. Mrs Jackson saw herself in the story, young and fresh (like Gloria) and ready for the bridal bed; she saw also, in the light of the story, where her own mistake had been. Not once before marriage; but many times. She should never have let it happen. That was why, she was sure, she had never commanded proper respect from Mr Jackson; he knew quite well he was the last in the long line. Not even the last, for that matter; though there had, after all, only been one failure since marriage, and that with a fly-by-night traveller Mr Jackson knew nothing about. One of these days she would have to have a talk with Gloria; to make sure she made no mistakes. But she didn't seem able to talk to Gloria any more: such a self-willed, restless girl.

I must make myself a cup of tea soon, thought Mrs Jackson. Then I will feel better. Mrs Jackson had great faith in cups of tea; she had been making them all her life in an effort to feel better.

Gloria, meanwhile, was in her bedroom. It was a tiny room with one window, lace-curtained, which gave a partial view of the backyard where Mr Jackson still lay asleep in the sun. There was a faded grey carpet on the varnished floor, placed so she could lower her tender feet luxuriously on to it when she slid from the warm blankets on a cold morning. The remaining furnishings were functional; a narrow single bed, a light-blue chest of drawers, a kitchen chair, and a wardrobe with full-length mirror. On the chest of drawers, between the boxed collection of trinkets and the cosmetic set given her last birthday, stood a framed photograph of her sister. She had run away to the city with an engine-driver on the railways; and eventually married him. But the engine-driver worked late shifts and his wife still liked dances and parties, and there was a divorce, the reasons for which confused Gloria at the time. Gloria's sister still lived in the city; sometimes she wrote letters. The photograph was an old one, taken before she went to the city:

plain, freckle-faced, with too-prominent teeth and a straight fringe of hair, smiling faintly with, perhaps, foreknowledge of the engine-driver, she looked down at Gloria every morning; and looked at her now, as the zip crackled under her hand and the sunsuit fell in two limp pieces to the floor. She admired herself naked in the full-length mirror, studying the white lines across breast and thighs which sharpened the new sun-colour of the rest of her body. Then she dressed in blue-flowered skirt and crisp white blouse. She touched lipstick lightly on her mouth, and she was ready. She pirouetted swiftly, the skirt snapping about her, slipped bobbysox and sandals on her feet, and then went back through the living-room. Her mother was still on the couch.

'Going somewhere, dear?'

'Out for a while.'

'You look so nice,' her mother whispered. 'Is it a boy?'

'Don't be silly,' the girl cried. 'Can't I dress decent if I want to? I'm just going out for a bike-ride, if you want to know.'

'Where to?'

'I don't know. To Sheila's place, I expect.'

'Then you better watch out for Sheila's brothers,' Mrs Jackson said, trying to be friendly.

Gloria did not stay to answer. She had no intention of going to see Sheila. She had no intention of going anywhere. She only wanted to get out of the house. She wheeled her bicycle down to the front gate, hesitated, and then chose to ride in the direction of the shops. Houses slept in the hot Sunday. Here a lawnmower chattered, there a man clipped his hedge, there a woman read a book on a shady verandah. Everyone else seemed to be passing the time in satisfactory fashion.

They met on the corner after dinner every Sunday. It was a casual arrangement, made simply because they found it easier doing nothing together, rather than singly. Sunday was always a difficult day. Saturdays were never so bad: they played rugby for the Lions second-grade team on winter Saturdays; and recently a new club had organized cycle-racing on the recreation ground on summer Saturday afternoons. They all competed in the cycle-racing. At the beginning of summer, when the season was new, they had been enthusiastic about Sunday afternoon practices. Use of the recreation ground was, of course, forbidden Sundays; so they conducted races for themselves over country roads. But the roads were rough and stony, and the summer had turned dusty and hot; and the novelty had gone. Lately, on Sunday afternoons, they remained more and more within the town. Sometimes still they made sporadic attacks on country roads, following parties of cycling girls who usually remained aloof. Mostly they stayed together in the town, arguing about what to do. That was how they were now, an untidy collection of bicycles and boys in the shade of a shop verandah. The long flat main street, shimmering with heat, was white and empty.

'Well,' Harry said. 'What d'you reckon?' Harry was the eldest, and the leader. Tall and lanky, with thin blotchy face, he was very pale in complexion and had stiff black hair shiny with brilliantine and slicked straight with a comb. He took a damp-ended cigarette from his mouth and jetted smoke; he examined the cigarette with mild interest, then looked from face to face.

'Who, then?' Mick said. Small and wiry, aggressive-faced, Mick was the only one ever to ridicule Harry's ideas.

'Hell,' Harry said. 'Anyone.'

'Who?' Mick persisted.

'There you are,' Harry said, pointing. 'There's a nice piece for you.'

They looked. The approaching girl was white and distant at the end of the street.

'Christ,' Mick said. 'Gloria Jackson? She's only a kid.'

'Old enough,' Harry said.

'Who are you trying to kid?' Mick snorted.

'Would she be game, though?' someone asked.

'They're all game,' Harry announced confidently.

'And so who's going to ask her?' Mick said with sarcasm. 'You?'

'All of us,' Harry smirked. 'That's fair enough, isn't it?'

'You'd have no show,' Mick said, dissociating himself from the idea.

The girl halted a little way down the street to look in a shop window. They watched her.

'Well, then,' Harry said. 'One of us can ask her.'

'Who?' Mick said.

'You seem to know her pretty well,' Harry said.

'You're doing all the talk.'

'Someone's got to think of things,' Harry said, unruffled.

'The one who thinks of them ought to do them.'

'What's all the argument about?' Harry demanded. 'Hell, it's only a matter of asking if she'd like to come along with us for rides Sunday afternoons.'

'I know what you mean,' Mick said.

Terry snickered. Terry, thinner, paler, shorter, was almost a three-quarter size version of Harry. But they were not brothers.

'Don't tell me,' Harry said to Mick, 'that we're going to get all fancy about it? You want us all to write her pretty little notes on blue paper asking her what about it?'

Terry snickered again, nudging a silent member of the group.

It was almost time for afternoon tea: his mother was working in the kitchen. Ralph went outside, wheeled his bicycle from the back shed, and began to pump the tyres firm.

'You going somewhere, sonny?' his mother called.

'I thought I might just have a practice run,' he said.

'Practice run?'

'For the Saturday afternoon racing. And the Easter sports too. I need to practise.'

Mrs White came to the back door, wiping floury hands on her apron. 'You know best,' she said. 'I still can't say I'm very keen on all this business. But now you've joined this club, you might as well do the best you can, I expect. As long—' Mrs White found it necessary to take a deep breath here '—as long as you don't start hanging round with some of those others, that Harry Williams boy and his crowd.'

'No,' he said, pumping till the muscles of his arms began to hurt. 'I'm just going for a run by myself.'

'I certainly hope so. Mrs McIntyre was telling me only the other day that it's only a matter of time before those boys land themselves in trouble. It isn't healthy the way they go hanging round the place all the time, whistling at girls and goodness knows what else. I'd hate to think of you getting like that. You won't, will you?'

'No.'

'I'd hate people to think I was letting you get mixed up with that crowd. It's bad enough what they think now, with you joining that club. I've raised you decently, and I like people to see that. I know I've brought you up in the way your father would have liked.'

Ralph said nothing. He was shining the chipped blue paintwork of his bicycle with a kerosene-soaked cloth. It was a heavy-frame sports model, not a real racer, not like the flash feather-weight bicycles from the city the others in the club owned, with thin wheels and delicate frames. But he had stripped brakes and mudguards, turned the handlebars down, and bought a cheap second-hand racing seat; these things, together with the shiny new toeclips on the pedals, almost gave the impression that it was a real racing model.

'I hope you remember your father in whatever you do,' Mrs White said. 'He may have had his faults but he was a good man. You do remember him, don't you?'

'I always do,' he said.

'And what else must you remember?' she asked.

'That my mother loves me,' he said.

'Good boy. You're a good boy to your mother.'

Stooping, Ralph clipped the ends of his trousers.

'You won't stay for afternoon tea, sonny?' she appealed. 'I was going to make you some scones.'

He hesitated. 'I won't be long,' he promised. 'I'll just ride a little way and then come back again.'

Mrs White smiled, smoothing back a wisp of hair; she looked very tired. 'I'll be waiting for you, sonny,' she said.

'I won't be long,' he repeated.

She watched, the smile growing faint on her face, as he wheeled the bicycle down to the gate, swung up into the saddle with an inexpert flourish, and then rode out of sight. Frowning now, she turned inside slowly, wondering, with a small twinge of fear, if she had done right in allowing him the bike-racing.

A pity she hadn't suggested he play cricket instead; if he had to mix with other young people, cricket was nice and quiet, and more respectable. But the year before, when he asked, she told him she thought cricket, like the rugby she also denied him, too dangerous; that hard little ball flying through the air all the time, bruising people and breaking their teeth. And then this summer, when he came pleading for the bike-racing, his face eager and shining, she did not have the time to think the thing out properly. Otherwise she might have remembered the cricket, and suggested it. She had been confused: she had seen danger in another denial.

I could have mentioned the cricket, she told herself. I wish I had mentioned the cricket.

Ralph's crouched shadow rode alongside him over the white road; then swung out and away as he turned into the main street. The tyres hummed and, as he completed the turn, the shadow returned small under him again. Already his leg-muscles ached, his heart hammered in his chest, his breath rasped his throat. He fought to keep the handlebars steady, strove not to jerk the smooth running of the chain; he seemed to be going faster than ever before. Perhaps if he reached this speed on a Saturday afternoon he could win a race. He needed more practice. It was only practice that made you fast; made you a champion. One day he might even be as fast as Mick Parker; Mick won all the junior races. The road ahead was a fuzzy white, becoming distinct only under his front wheel.

There was a flash of blue and white at the edge of his vision; his name was called. Still travelling at speed, he looked up, looked around behind him, and saw Gloria Jackson dismounted from her bicycle in front of a shop window. She waved, smiling. He waved back, an awkward movement that almost lost him his balance, and made the bicycle lurch. As he regained control he wondered if she meant him to stop and talk with her; he wondered if he should turn back. But he was only playing with the thought; he knew he would not. He hardly knew her really, though he had seen her often at school and around the town afterwards: her eyes were too troubling. Still, he wished he could stop.

He was well down the main street now. His name was called again, this time by several voices. He saw the group on the corner: Harry Williams and Mick Parker and others from the club. Even while he checked his pedals, his mother's face insinuated itself. But there was no harm in being friendly. After all, he raced with them Saturdays; he couldn't very well ride past them Sundays. They were not like Gloria Jackson whom he could ignore because she was a girl. He liked the casual way they called his name: as though he belonged.

He turned back to the group on the corner. He stopped before them and swung off the saddle, his body beginning to tremble and drip sweat from the effort of the ride.

'You was going pretty good,' Harry said. 'We was watching you all the way down the street.'

'Going to clean up them Easter sports aren't you, Ralph?' Terry said, winking hugely at the others. 'Eh?'

There were one or two laughs: Terry decided the joke was good for some more. 'Ralph's the coming champeen,' he declared. He was right; there were one or two more laughs, though from the same people. Mick did not smile.

Ralph grinned uncertainly. Mick slapped his shoulder in friendly fashion. 'You was going well,' Mick assured him. 'So don't you take no notice.' Ralph smiled gratefully, confusedly, at Mick. He liked Mick; he was always nice. He looked sour, but he wasn't so bad when you knew him.

'Look,' Harry said. 'Here she comes now.'

Gloria was riding towards them, on the other side of the street. Her long legs wheedled the slack chain slowly; her dark hair fell loose over her shoulders; her gaze was fixed somewhere ahead.

They called her name. She gave them a remote, mild smile and continued along the street.

'Playing hard to get,' Harry sniffed. 'That's all.' He paused. 'Wait a sec— what's she doing now?'

They watched. She turned across the road, dismounted, and leaned her bicycle against the verandah-post outside the milkbar. Then she went into the milk-bar.

'Now's our chance,' Harry announced.

'You go right ahead and do your stuff,' Mick said. He was tired of Harry; he often wondered why he hung round with them Sunday afternoons. But there was always the hope something might happen. 'Go on. Go right ahead,' Mick urged.

'Hell no,' Harry said. 'We'll all go.'

'I thought so,' said Mick. 'You're all talk. You're scared.'

Harry disregarded Mick; he turned to Ralph. 'You want to be in this too?' he asked.

'In what?'

'We're going to ask Gloria if she'll come for rides with us Sunday afternoons,' Harry said, certain lewd emphasis.

Terry sniggered: it was like a danger signal.

'I don't think I'd better,' Ralph said quickly.

'Frightened?' Harry said.

Ralph didn't reply.

'Mummy's little baby,' Terry needled.

'Leave him alone,' Mick said. 'He doesn't have to if he doesn't want to.' Ralph looked weak and pathetic; Mick felt sorry for him. 'You do whatever you like. And if Terry doesn't shut up then I'll crack his nose in.'

Ralph didn't look at Mick. He stood blinking bleakly in the bright sunlight. He didn't belong any more.

'Well,' Harry said. 'We're not going to stand here talking about the price of fish all day, are we?'

'I didn't know you called it fish,' Terry giggled.

'You got a one-track mind,' Mick told Terry. 'A dirt track.'

'Who said we was worried about a price anyhow?' Harry said.

'All free,' Terry said, grinning as he inserted a cigarette between pale lips. 'Eh?'

They rode off towards the milk-bar and Gloria Jackson. Mick went with them. He felt ashamed of himself: not so much for leaving Ralph by himself, as for letting Ralph see him go with the others.

Ralph watched them roll down the street, park their bicycles, and file into the milk-bar. Then he pedalled home slowly.

2

There was applause from the thin assembly of spectators as the leaders in the junior race flashed across the finish-line: Mick first, then Harry and a bunch, Terry and another bunch, and Ralph trailing. The impetus of the final sprint carried them well around the track. Uncrouching, straightening, backpedalling, they cycled slowly across the green field to the pavilion.

Ralph rode apart from the others. Head down, breath still sobbing, he watched his front wheel husking over dry grass. Some distance from the pavilion, away from the spectators and other riders, he propped his cycle against a wire fence. He lay flat on the ground, trying to contain the fluttering of his body. Presently calmer, he sat up, unbuckled his headgear, and hung it on the handlebars. New riders began to circle the track before the last race of the afternoon.

Then he saw Gloria. Detaching herself from the spectators, she moved into a group of junior riders. Mick, Harry and Terry were there; and some of the others who met on the corner on Sunday afternoons. They were still arguing about their race. Mick, after congratulations, was proud-faced.

A whistle shrilled, a pistol banged, and the senior race began. Headgeared, taut-faced, the riders leapt from their saddles, jerking pedals, making speed, whining past.

But he did not see the senior race. He watched Gloria.

Her dark head was only just visible above a wall of masculine shoulders; a wall reinforced by a tangle of cycles flat on the ground. She bounced with excitement as the senior race ended; then the boys circled about her.

As he rode home, along the main street, he saw their cycles, with Gloria's at the centre, parked outside the milk-bar. He rode home.

Next day, Sunday, he excused himself soon after dinner.

'Where are you going now?' Mrs White said.

'To practise. I told you last Sunday I need to practise a lot.'

'Sounds a lot of fuss and bother over nothing.'

'It's not,' he defended. 'I've got to practise.'

He saw her temper. He already knew the next question.

'You sure you're keeping away from that Williams boy and his crowd?' she asked.

'Of course I am.'

'I wish you'd chosen something else,' she said. 'Cricket or something.'

'You wouldn't let me play cricket,' he reminded her.

'You were younger then,' she said. 'It'd be different if you asked me now.'

'Anyhow,' he said, 'I'm not keen on cricket.'

Mrs White relented. 'You won't be away long, will you? Promise?'

'I promise.'

'And what must you remember?'

'That my mother loves me,' he said.

Ralph did not practise. He rode first past Gloria's house, but glimpsed only the deck chair empty in the backyard. Tar oozed and bubbled along the hot streets. He rode along the main street. The boys were not in their usual place on the corner. He idled his cycle past the milk-bar; there was only one customer inside.

They had gone.

Yet still he hoped he might come upon them, as if by accident. He spent the afternoon riding roads which spoked out from the town, but did not see them. Towards evening he turned, at last, for home.

At about the same time they came riding into the town. The boys were crouched over their racer handlebars: only the girl rode upright, shoulders squared, long-legged and proud, hair damp and twisted.

At the end of her street they said polite goodnights to her. They left her riding home; and then travelled bunched into the main street. A string of blue sodium lamps illuminated the long bare street and its closed shops; a patch of yellow showed outside the open milk-bar. But they did not go there; they dismounted, by general consent, on the strip of lawn opposite the post office. They lay on the grass. Above them, moths and mosquitoes whirred and battered uselessly against the pale face of the town clock. Its minute hand jerked soundlessly from numeral to numeral. They did not speak for a time; they lit cigarettes and thought.

'Well,' Mick said.

'A bit of a dead loss,' Harry muttered.

No one denied it. They had taken the road which spiralled thin and white above the town. After the long climb in the heat of afternoon, they descended, with whining wheels and a rush of cooling air, into a lonely part of country. Tar-seal gave way to a road of clay and pumice which wound through poor farmland and strips of bush; this road in turn dwindled to a stony track beside a sunlit river and through a gorge walled by tall limestone. Gorse and blackberry fingered at them, catching in their clothes and chopping in the spokes. Then, with the track almost lost in fern and paspalum, they found a pool, a sparkling backwater curving out from the flow of the river and almost hidden by a tall stand of manuka; it was calm and clear, sandy-bottomed, and fringed with rocks and fern. They lingered at the edge of it, excited by the discovery; and more mysteriously by the mood of the day.

She left them without awkwardness, explaining she would find somewhere to change. After she had gone, stepping erect and serene into the grey and green concealment of the bush, her sandals crackering away over dry sticks, they were left looking at each other with embarrassed smiles. They were not quite sure what they should have expected her to do, even now. Their smiles became foolish; lowering their eyes, they undressed quickly, scuffing out of shirts and shorts and underclothes. She called a warning; and then she stepped out of the bush, only a little self-conscious in her trim bathing suit. Again their eyes darted here and there.

Mick explored the pool for snags. There were none; so the other boys followed. They floundered clumsily, ducking, laughing, splashing, water glistening their pale bodies in the sunlight. She was poised at the edge of the pool; they clamoured for her to follow. Even when she lowered herself into the pool, they still boasted and squabbled and fought, seeing who could remain underwater longest, who could win a race the short length of the pool. Always just at the edge of horseplay, she trod water with a remote smile. Once or twice she allowed herself to be drawn into the frolic. Playfully someone would grab for the rippling shape of her body; but she would anticipate it and slip swiftly beyond reach.

Suddenly cold and shivering, they climbed from the pool, towelled themselves, and fell in a close circle about her; yet she, with her pink hairless body surrounded by scrawny limbs, seemed unconscious of holding court, seemed to consider herself merely one of them. Cicadas crackled and birds flitted through trees and the river made gentle sounds.

Yet the silence seemed immense.

Harry told jokes. They were only mildly funny, and soon it was quiet again. Each was stirred by the same impulse to reach out and touch her; each waited for another to make that move. Nothing happened, and the magic ebbed from the day.

The sun sank behind a wall of the gorge, and shadow travelled across them: clearly the day was at an end. She excused herself and returned into the bush. Admitting that the moment had gone, and feeling better for the admission, they dressed and rode home with her; she was still in good spirits. They would meet again next Sunday.

Insects ticked against the clock. Sunday idlers clattered along the other side of the street. Mick flicked away a cigarette: it fell in a brilliant shower of sparks. 'I think I'll be getting home,' he said. And at last they dispersed.

3

Mrs White handed him his lunch-parcel. 'Oh yes,' she said. 'And in your lunch-hour could you go round to Hannah's and buy me some cottons. It'll save me making a special trip.' She described the kind she wanted. 'Anyhow,' she added, 'ask Gloria —what's her name?—of course, Jackson. Ask Gloria Jackson. You know her, don't you? Of course. What am I thinking about? You must have known her at school. Nice girl. Pretty. Rather bold, though. Probably the kind to get into trouble sooner or later. She always serves me.

She'll know exactly the kind I want. Just ask her. That's a good boy. Goodbye now, sonny.' She kissed him. 'And what must you remember?'

That my mother loves me.

Miss Jones, the typist, racketed at her desk. Now and then, as she shifted in her seat, he glimpsed, with the lift of her red pleated skirt, the nylon curve of her leg.

Miss Jones was blonde and pretty; her fingers were long and clever, and an engagement ring flashed on her left hand.

That my mother loves me.

Miss Jones would marry Fred Saunders soon. Fred was a farmer's son, and first five-eighths in the Lions senior rugby team; he was good-looking, popular with the girls. A lot of girls wanted to be Mrs Fred Saunders in place of Miss Jones.

Miss Jones was a fine girl, a decent girl; she wasn't the kind of girl who suddenly hurried out of town to have a baby. Miss Jones was the kind of girl his mother liked.

She paused in her work, looked up, and caught his eye. 'You look all hot and bothered this morning,' she said. 'Something the matter?'

'Nothing,' he said weakly.

'It's the heat, I expect,' she said. 'It worries everyone this summer.' She smiled sweetly and chattered the keys again.

That my mother loves me.

His mother had chosen him the job in the bank. It offered security, she said; and if there was one thing you needed in this life it was security. He began at the bank after he passed his school certificate. Boys like Harry and Terry and Mick didn't wait till they passed school certificate: Harry delivered groceries, Mick worked in a garage, and Terry in the auction mart.

Gloria didn't wait either. She had left school six months before, as soon as she turned fifteen.

He felt the heat again.

Perhaps she would be out at lunch, leaving only withered old Miss Hannah to serve him. But what if she wasn't?

'You sure you feel all right?' Miss Jones said suddenly. 'You don't look very well to me.'

He felt guilty: she had caught him watching her again. A fan whirred stale air in the silence. His body was burning.

'I'm all right,' he said. He bent over the papers on his desk, and felt released sweat trickle down his body.

After the white glare of the main street, the shop was dim and musty. Floating outlines became solid; and the dry wool-and-cotton smell prickled his nose. Gloria was smiling behind the counter. 'Hullo,' she said. 'How are you today?' She spoke in a light, cheerful voice. He found himself looking down at the undergarment which she was folding into a small parcel: then he was embarrassed. He raised his eyes and explained what he wanted.

'I saw you racing last Saturday,' she said, walking across to the cottons counter. He followed slowly.

'I didn't do well,' he said.

'But you've only just started to race, haven't you? You can't expect to win straight off, can you? You haven't had as much experience as the other boys.'

'I'm not very good, though,' he said.

'That's just being silly,' she declared. She began to wrap the cottons he wanted. 'You could be as good as anyone if you wanted to.' She looked at him: her eyes were friendly. 'Do you go for rides Sunday afternoons?'

'Sometimes.' He nodded. 'By myself,' he added quickly.

'Why by yourself? Why don't you go with Harry and the others?'

'I like to go by myself,' he said.

She did not seem to disbelieve him; she handed him the small packet of cottons. 'That'll be two and six. I went out with them last Sunday. We had fun.'

He was quivering, as if with fright; and his hands were sweating. He dropped his half-crown and picked it up: he couldn't look at her.

'We went up the Ohemai gorge,' she continued. 'Have you been up there?'

He shook his head; his mouth was quite dry.

'It's lovely there. Really lovely.'

'What did you do there?' he heard his own strange voice say.

'Oh,' she said, seeming unconcerned and entirely truthful. 'We had a swim in a beautiful little pool there, and sunbathed. You know.' The cash-register jangled: she handed him a receipt. 'You ought to come one Sunday. You'd enjoy it.'

'Yes,' he said, backing away from the counter and clutching his packet and receipt.

'You come,' she said softly, experimentally.

4

He wheeled his cycle off the road, through a patch of long grass, and hid it behind a ragged cluster of pongas. He lay beside it, in the ferny speckled shade, close to the dry heavy smell of the earth. He waited for perhaps a half hour.

Then he heard their voices as they pushed their cycles up the steep hill. Gloria's voice, light and circling; Harry's laugh, loud and braying; Terry's shrill echo, Mick's hard chuckle, and a medley of other male voices. They drifted past, up the road, leaving him with the oddly lonely sounds of cicadas and birds. He counted to a hundred. Then, hesitantly, another hundred; and he wheeled his cycle back to the road. Below, the white town shimmered in a tawny bowl of hills. He set his wheel in the opposite direction. Crisp chips spat from under his tyres as he pedalled with effort up the rest of the hill; then the road plunged down into open hilly country.

He was not long in catching them. They were riding slowly, spread wide across the road, with Gloria at the centre. He made it seem an accidental meeting.

'Fancy seeing you,' Gloria said.

'What d'you know?' Mick said. 'Getting in some practice?'

Mick and Gloria parted to let him slide into the slow-riding group. 'Just having a ride around,' he explained.

'Coming with us?' she said. 'We're going up the gorge.'

'Come on,' Mick said.

It was noticeable that Harry, Terry and the others did not make the invitation; they pedalled in silence.

'All right,' Ralph said, as if persuaded.

'You could have a swim too,' Mick said. 'You got your togs?'

'Yes,' Ralph said. 'I thought I might go for a swim myself.'

'Hell,' Harry said with sarcasm. 'Isn't that a coincidence?'

His pretence had, after all, been useless. Gloria smiled warmly at him. She knew.

The day was windless; heat gathered thick in the gorge. They stood at the edge of the pool.

'It'll be good in there today,' Mick said. 'You bet it will.'

'I think I'll change now,' Gloria said. She went off into the bush with her bathing suit parcelled in a towel.

Harry had taken Terry to one side. They lit cigarettes and whispered. Harry laughed.

'What's all the talk about?' Mick demanded.

'Aha,' Harry said with mystery. 'We're just talking about who's going to be first.' He winked meaningfully at Mick, and made a sly nod in the direction of Ralph, who had his back turned.

'First?' Mick said. 'What are you talking about?'

Harry made another sly nod towards Ralph. 'First turn with her, silly,' he said. He jerked his thumb in the direction Gloria had taken.

'What?' Mick said. 'What are you—'

'We think Ralph should have first turn, eh?' Harry said, attempting another wink before Ralph turned round to face them with bewilderment. 'He's the guest.'

'Lay off,' Mick said sharply.

'What's wrong?' Harry said with pretended hurt, and innocence. 'That's right, isn't it? The guest gets first turn.'

'Shut up,' Mick said.

'Look,' Harry said, ignoring Mick and turning to Ralph. 'We take turns, see. We can't all go at once, can we, eh?'

Ralph stood quite still. Mick's face was angry. Terry was giggling nervously. Someone laughed. Harry was still explaining. 'And you got to go first, see?' he finished.

'No,' Ralph said. 'Not me.'

'Leave him alone,' Mick said. 'Don't you take no notice, Ralph. He's trying to fool you.'

'Come on,' Harry said, beginning to bluster. 'We can't waste time. Don't you like being offered favours? Eh? You're a rotten sort. Go on. Go after her. All you need to do is go after her. You don't need to be told the rest, do you?'

'Perhaps mummy didn't tell him,' someone said.

'Go on,' Harry said, pushing Ralph. 'After her. Quick.'

'Stop it,' Mick shouted. 'Don't you take no notice, Ralph.' Mick jumped between Harry and Ralph: he seemed about to hit Harry. Terry and one of the other boys fell on him, dragging him away. 'Don't you take no notice,' he cried, fighting to free his pinioned arms.

But it was too late. Harry sent Ralph stumbling off into the bush, after Gloria.

Mick fought off the two boys. 'You sod,' he said to Harry, striking at him. The punch went wild and Harry hit him and he was pushed from behind. He fell heavily on rocks: the hot gorge sang around him. Harry laughed, and kicked him as he lay there.

'Why don't you go home? You want to spoil everything.'

'You sod,' Mick said. He rose painfully.

'Didn't you see?' Harry said with glee. 'Didn't you see? He really wanted to go after her.' He laughed. 'Yeah. He did.'

'Liar,' Mick said.

Harry was unconcerned. 'This'll be fun,' he announced confidently to the other boys. Mick was finished; Harry was leader again.

'Your kind of fun,' Mick said. 'Not mine.'

'Yeah,' Harry said, still delighted. 'He really wanted to go.'

Mick ran from them. Holding his hurting ribs, he crashed through bush to the track. He retrieved his cycle and rode down the gorge: slowly, wondering if what Harry said was true.

Dry fern crackled under his feet. 'Gloria,' he called.

'I'm over here,' she answered, soft and surprised.

She had gone to change further from the pool than he thought. He found her in a small clearing. Though she had not altogether fastened her bathing suit, this did not trouble her. Her clothes were tumbled in a bright heap on a log. She was smiling.

'Ralph?' she said. 'What do you want?'

He didn't say.

'Is something wrong? I heard shouting.'

He was still silent.

'You sure nothing's wrong?'

'Yes,' he said at last.

'Did you just come to pay me a visit then?' she asked, still smiling. 'That was nice of you.' She was twisting her towel in her hands, as if it was wet and needed to be wrung: but the towel was quite dry. She was uncertain, perplexed. 'I like visitors,' she added in a voice without conviction.

'They said—' he began. 'I mean, Harry said—'

'What did they say?'

He told her. At first she seemed amused. Then she bit her lip and frowned. He looked at the ground.

'It's all lies,' she said. 'What they told you is all lies. You didn't believe them, did you?'

He had to look up now; but he looked beyond her face. 'No,' he said guiltily. 'I didn't believe them.'

'You sure?'

'Yes.'

She bundled her clothes quickly. Then she took his arm. 'Come on,' she said. 'We'll show them.'

'Where you going?' he said.

'We'll go somewhere else,' she said impatiently, tugging at him.

'What about the others?'

'We won't worry about them any more. Come on.'

'What about our bikes?'

'We'll get them later on. Come on. Stop arguing.'

He followed her up the gorge. There was no track, and they picked their way through bush tangled with supplejack. Eventually they came to another pool. It was smaller than the other, and shallower. It was calm; a limb of rock separated it from the river. At the centre, where it was sandy, the water was clear and trickles of sunlight played.

'Isn't it lovely?' she said. 'It's far enough away. They won't find us here.' She paused, and looked into his face. 'What's wrong?'

'I forgot my togs. I left them at the other place.'

'Never mind. You can swim in your shorts, can't you? Afterwards you can take them off and let them dry. You can cover yourself up with a towel. Don't worry—I won't look. Come on. I bet it's beautiful.'

She dropped her clothes and towel and shed her sandals. Her body flew lightly, arching and straightening in a neat dive: there was a quick explosion of water, and spray hit his face. She rose spluttering, hair swimming. 'Come on,' she urged. 'It's wonderful.' He stripped shirt and sandals and followed.

They emerged quickly, shivering, at the sound of the calling voices. First the voices would call her name, and then almost as an afterthought, they would call his; mostly it was Gloria's name.

Placing her finger over her lips, she took his hand and drew him down into a small cave of fern. They lay there quietly, grass and sticks under their bodies.

The voices, angry now, grew louder, then fainter.

The tension left them. She rolled on her side and looked at him gravely. The voices had gone.

'Funny Ralph,' she laughed suddenly, jumping out of the fern. 'Quick. Let's have another swim.'

They were close on the grass, their bodies browning. The sun coppered the top of the gorge and shadow crept across the river.

They made their way downstream to the second pool. On the abandoned bank silver-foil glinted among crumpled chocolate papers and cigarette-packets. His towel and swimsuit had been flung into the water: they still floated, though almost sinking, some distance out from the bank. He pulled them in with a long stick.

'Aren't they terrible?' she said. 'I never knew people could be so nasty.'

They walked out to the track. Their cycles were gone. They found wheel-tracks and finally located them hidden behind flax-bushes. The air had been let out of the tyres.

'Why are people ever born to do nasty things like that?' Gloria said, almost tearfully. 'I don't know.'

He carried the cycles out to the track and pumped the tyres hard again. Then they began the ride home. Shadow covered the gorge now: the bush had turned a gloomy green colour, and only the tops of the tallest trees were lemon with sunlight.

They had not ridden far, not more than three hundred yards, when they heard voices sharp in the silence, and feet smacking through undergrowth.

Five boys ran out to block their way and drag them from their cycles. They held him and forced Gloria to the edge of the track. He fought at their hands, and kicked and bit. Gloria screamed. A fist clubbed each side of his head, then crashed into his face and chopped down on the back of his neck; he fell to the track, and rocks bit into his back. Two of them sat on him, one on his stomach, one on the side of his head. There were three of them with Gloria. He couldn't see what they were doing to her. But she was still screaming.

And then they went suddenly, the five, moving quickly, their legs jerking their cycles away.

Ralph crawled to Gloria. She was crying more quietly now; mostly the sobs merged in a moaning sound. He cradled her head and untangled the hair from her face.

'Gloria,' he said through swollen lips.

Mick, after he left the boys, did not ride back to town. He swam in a stretch of river further down the gorge. He found exhilaration in fighting swift current. His arms and legs flailed the fast water as he tried to swim upstream. He made, however, little progress; and finally he dragged himself from the water to fall on the bank limp and tired, and at peace.

Birds sang around as he rested in the sunlight. He thought of his single visit to the city: of the crowded stadium and the silky colours of the riders flashing around a floodlit oval of concrete. That talked bright things to his tired mind. One day soon he would go to the city and find a job; and ride the floodlit track. He would do well: everyone seemed agreed on that. They said it was remarkable how a boy with so little competition on a rough grass track in a country town could develop so quickly and record such good times. He would, they predicted, be a champion. There was his triumph over Harry and the others. They would never ride the floodlit track.

The thought pleased him. Suddenly it was late afternoon, and a lone bird sang up river. His mind was hot and confused, though his body was cool; he splashed water over his face and dressed. He looked with disbelief at the perilous part of the river in which he had swum; and was bewildered at his lunacy. He could have been ripped by a snag or knocked unconscious and drowned. His challenge of the river seemed stupid.

He found his way back to the track and his cycle. Then he heard the panicky voices and saw Harry and Terry and the others whirring down on him. They seemed to be running away from something; he did not know, then, that they were fleeing themselves. And he leapt out across the track to stop them.

'What's wrong?' he shouted.

'Get out of the way.'

He jumped quickly to avoid being run down. And they shot past, leaving him alone.

He pedalled back up the gorge. He was not long in coming to them. The two walked together slowly, Ralph's arm supporting Gloria; with their free hands on either side, they pushed their cycles. Gloria's clothes were dirtied; she was crying, and tripping. Ralph's face was bloody, and his shirt torn.

Mick dismounted and approached. He relieved them of their awkward cycles: he pushed them along behind the pair. Manoeuvring three was difficult; he managed in the end.

5

The mayor was a little gnome-like man. With short-sighted squint, he peered across his desk at the senior-sergeant.

'And the girl?' he said softly.

'Four months under the age of consent. Three months gone.'

'The family?'

'Ordinary enough. Mother's a bit scatty. Used to be quite a girl in her day, so they tell me. The old man's supposed to be henpecked, but I wouldn't know about that. Works at the limeworks, on the furnaces. Decent enough chap. Plays the horses in a quiet way and drinks a bit on the side. But not enough to cause any trouble.'

'Ah yes,' the mayor said. 'Yes. It shows you, doesn't it? The most ordinary of families. Yes.'

The senior-sergeant remained silent, vainly waiting for the mayor to elaborate. He was old too; a silver-haired old man with tired face. Younger, he won a reputation with a vigorous attempt to enforce the liquor laws in a disrespectful part of the country; his career there was brief and perilous, terminated by his transfer to a quieter rural district.

'No option but to lay the charges, I suppose?'

'No option. Not when the girl's pregnant, you see. And the mother's complaint.'

'It'll mean unpleasantness, of course,' the mayor said, frowning wisely, tapping his pencil slowly on the desk.

'Unpleasantness? Yes, I expect you could call it that. Particularly in view of the White boy.'

'White boy?'

'Ralph White. Mother's a widow. Done her best to bring him up well, by all accounts. Father was killed in the war. El Alamein. Jack White. Carpenter for Evans' Construction, if I remember right.'

'Yes, yes. Of course.' The mayor was still frowning.

'Surprising, really. Of course we haven't got anything like the full story yet. The girl didn't name anyone. When the mother complained she told us the girl had been connected with some of the bike-racing boys.'

'That was it, was it?' The mayor leaned attentively across the desk. 'The bike-racing crowd, eh? I've seen them around, all right. Hanging round street corners. An unhealthy element.' The mayor fell silent, considering unhealthy, hairy-legged boys.

'Of course it was easy to work from there,' the senior-sergeant continued professionally. 'What we do know now, for certain, is that a gang of them started taking her out with them Sunday afternoons. Practice rides for the Saturday races. Practices, all right.'

The mayor smiled faintly at the quip.

'But just how many are mixed up in the affair it's hard to say. They all started taking her up the Ohemai gorge at the beginning. Then, from what I can make out, there must have been some kind of row between the boys. Anyhow, after the first couple of Sundays, there was just this boy Ralph White and another boy, Mick Parker, tagging along with her. Parker's an interesting case. Never had any trouble with him before. Works in Butterfield's garage. Quite a promising young rider too. You might remember you presented him with a big silver cup at the Easter sports. Won it against outside competition. Doesn't care much about anything except bike-racing, from what I hear. Seems—or seemed—a good enough boy. His father—you might know him, old Bluey Parker, always turns up for the Anzac day parades—was mustard-gassed in the first war. Bit of an alcoholic. The boy more or less supports both his parents.'

'So you think it's just the two of them?' the mayor said. 'Just this boy Parker and this boy White. That right?'

'I'm pretty sure that's right.'

'Well,' said the mayor, sighing. 'That doesn't sound so bad, after all. The way I first heard the story was that there might be up to a dozen or more boys involved. I don't mind telling you, I was worried. It's bad for the town. You know what I mean?'

'I said I'm pretty sure. Not absolutely sure. You see, on one hand there's the Williams boy. Harry Williams—you know, Sam Williams' kid. A real tall streak, covered in pimples. Always been a larrikin, though we've never been able to blame him for any actual trouble. Mind you, we've had our suspicions. But suspicions never proved anything. Never had much of a chance after his mother cleared out. Sam never worries about any of his kids. Always let them roam the streets till all hours. Well anyway this boy said they never had anything to do with the girl, he and his cobbers.'

'You think that's true?'

'More or less. Because it's Parker and White who've been seeing most of her. No doubt about that. But on the other hand Parker says Williams is telling lies. Parker says he and White have got nothing to do with the girl being pregnant. He rambled on with a long involved story about how the Williams boy and his crowd knocked the girl and the boy White about one day out at the gorge. And about how they—he and White, that is— were supposed to have invented a story of an accident to protect the girl, and so on. I couldn't make head or tail of what he said, myself. It didn't make sense. It seemed to me he was just trying to push all the blame on the Williams boy for what he and White had done.'

'And what about the White boy? What does he say?'

'He didn't say anything. That's what makes me pretty sure. He just kept his mouth shut. Very nervous boy. Listened to all I had to say and wouldn't answer anything. Almost as if he expected it. Queer, really. Couldn't get anything out of him, not even yes or no. And then, just as I was going, he opened his mouth and asked me what would happen to the girl.'

'What will happen to her, by the way?'

'That's for the Child Welfare to decide. She'll probably be taken away somewhere for a while. Best thing, in her condition.'

'Unpleasant,' said the mayor.

'Complicated,' said the senior-sergeant. 'But I expect we'll have it all sorted out by the time we go to court. When the girl knows who we've collared, she might come out with the truth. Or enough truth to help us, if you know what I mean. No one ever really tells the truth. I learnt that a long time ago.'

'Yes,' said the mayor. 'Complicated.' He paused, flicking fastidiously at some dust on his desk. 'It'll be, well, unpleasant for the parents, Senior.'

The senior-sergeant shrugged. 'I saw Mrs White this afternoon. Soon as I tried to discuss the thing with her, she blocked her ears and ordered me out of the house. Then she broke down and asked me to tell her everything. Almost as if she was expecting it too. It was all very painful.'

'Yes,' said the mayor, catching eagerly at the new word. 'Painful.' He made a small whistling sound as he coughed. 'I don't envy you your job, Senior.'

There was silence in the dim office. A fly spiralled down from the ceiling, walked with unconcern across the mayoral blotter, and rose to the ceiling again. The senior-sergeant climbed from his chair. 'Better be getting along,' he said.

The mayor also rose. 'Yes, well, yes I really do appreciate your coming here this afternoon to acquaint me with the facts, Senior. You're a busy man. All this really isn't in my sphere, of course. I just felt it would be a help for me to know the facts; not morbid curiosity, you understand. You know how quickly wild rumours get around this town, and in my position—'

'I understand.'

'There's just one thing, though. This club—'

'Club?'

'The club that organizes the bike-racing.'

'Yes. Rather unfortunate for them.'

But the mayor didn't seem to be listening; he looked through some papers in the wire basket on his desk. 'Yes. The whole thing's bad for the town. That's my concern, of course. Now, let me see. Ah, yes, the agenda for the next borough council meeting. Here we are. Now I suppose you know that this club leases the recreation ground from us for the bike-racing. It's an annual thing, on the agenda for the next meeting. I think that possibly, after this, we may have to, well, reconsider—'

'I'm sorry. I don't understand,' murmured the senior-sergeant.

'It seems perfectly clear to me, Senior, after all you've told me. They represent an unhealthy element.'

The senior-sergeant shook his head. 'Well, of course I wouldn't know about that. You've got your job and I've got mine.'

The mayor looked up from his agenda, frowning. 'That's true, Senior. And you needn't worry. I'll be giving this a great deal of thought. A great deal. It's a bad business for the town.'

'No doubt about that,' replied the senior-sergeant, moving for the door.

'A painful business,' said the mayor.

6

That night Mick worked late at the garage, finishing an urgent job. He was impatient to leave; he needed to see Ralph, and talk to him. He was more concerned with Ralph than Gloria. After all, Gloria could more easily look after herself. They should, he thought, after that day at the gorge, have told the truth; and not invented the story of a cycling accident. Now no one would believe it. At the time it seemed simple enough; and necessary, to protect not only Gloria but Ralph too. Mick had never touched Gloria; and that was the truth. And Ralph?

He could not, he knew suddenly, answer for Ralph.

In the thickening autumn night, a sickle of moon faint in a black cloudy sky, he worked frantically to finish the job in his square box of light at the back of the garage. Tools spilled over the oily concrete around him; his face and hands and hair were smeared with grease. He was a small baggy figure in his soiled khaki overalls; his fingers were nimble, and his face was sharp and bad-tempered.

Then, still working in haste, the job unfinished, he heard the news. The news spread quickly that night.

He left the job unfinished, the tools spilled over the concrete. He shed his overalls. He fetched his cycle and began to ride.

He did not know where to ride. He circled about in the main street. Then, as if to pick up the trail, he rode to Gloria's house. A black police car gleamed outside. The old house was patched with lighted windows, and voices came faintly. He did not listen. He rode past the house, the lighted windows, the gleaming police car.

He still did not know where to ride. Of all the roads he might choose, of all the roads the three of them had ridden in the fading summer; of all the roads just two were riding now.

But he rode. He did not find them.

Towards morning, considering, for no reason, that they might not have headed for the city and that they might be hidden somewhere near, he found himself alone in the silent gorge with the sound of a morepork and the sound of the wind. He dismounted, and let the cycle crash to the side of the track. He cupped his hands around his mouth, against the wind, and began to call their names.

But the wind snapped at his voice, tricked the names into separate, then mingling echoes.

When he stopped calling, he fell forward, into long grass. The sky was starless, the sickle-moon hidden; and the gorge dark.

Mrs Jackson lit herself another cigarette. The people had gone now. Mr Jackson had fallen asleep on the kitchen couch. All the lights in the house were still burning. It was as if there had been a party; and the party was over.

What a performance, Mrs Jackson thought tiredly. She slumped into a chair, blowing smoke.

I will make myself a cup of tea soon, she thought. Then I will feel better.

No lights burned in the White house. When the senior-sergeant called to see Mrs White he found the place black in the night. After he had knocked several times on the door, a light snapped on above his head and Mrs White looked out. Her face was crumpled and her eyes were bloodshot.

'What do you want?' she demanded. 'Him? He's not here. He's gone.'

She slammed the door and the light went out. The senior-sergeant made his way down a dark path to the front gate. He had all the information he wanted; he had only come to check that the boy had gone too.

The senior-sergeant went to organize the search parties. They would not get very far. That kind never got very far.

7

When Ralph returned from work that evening, Mrs White met him in the kitchen. Her lips were thin and tight and very pale. A harsh sound burst from her throat; and, choking and wordless, she began to strike him. She struck downwards, on the top of his head, on his shoulders; so that presently he was beaten to the floor. It was over then; and Mrs White collapsed across him, still hitting weakly, and sobbing.

He picked himself up and left the kitchen. Outside, a breeze blew bright leaves about his feet as he wheeled his cycle down to the front gate and swung up into the saddle, not looking back.

Near the Jackson house he left his cycle, crawled through a hedge, and crouched behind a small shrub. In the blue dusk he waited until her window yellowed with light. Then he moved softly and swiftly across the lawn and tapped almost soundlessly on the window. Curtains rustled apart and Gloria looked out, bewildered and frightened, and then smiling. She seemed to understand perfectly, for she slipped on a coat, slid out the window, and fell into his arms. He led her across the lawn, under the hedge, to where he had rested the cycle.

She sat on the bar, her legs dangling. The pedals turned, the chain rasped, and they wobbled out into the road.

They avoided the main street and its bright sodium lamps, evening-walkers and picture-goers. They took dim back-streets, past timber yards and railway sidings, and rode clear of the town. Behind them, under the massing clouds and sickle-moon, the lights of the town grew faint. The cycle pumped forward steadily, the chain whirring, the wheels bumping, the spokes hissing, the lamp jiggling, the feeble light dancing over the white road and dusty drooping fern and gorse; over the white road moving slowly beneath them, and not the road ahead, long and dark and climbing.

Cloud Riders

THE PAUA GATHERERS

1

After dinner, after the third and worst argument of the day, he vanished behind a slamming door.

The crisp pretty black-haired girl found small things to do. She passed dishes through soapy water and whisked a broom over the floor. When the condition of the flat satisfied her, she felt calmer, more in control. She went to a couch, relaxed on cushions and raised her eyes slowly to the closed door.

She could wait now, smoking, reading and listening to the clock on the mantelpiece. Or she could walk. After all, it was Sunday, the day lonely people idled through city streets. Eyes would watch from shabby doorways as her heels ticked through the streets; ticked her past lifeless window displays and aimless people. But when she returned the door would still be closed against her, and the silence heavy.

A small hysteria rose: she felt trapped in this room, this flat, this city. She jerked to her feet and snapped on the radio. A solo saxophone jazzed into the grey afternoon.

There was a sound of protest from his room. Her fingers strangled the saxophone. She lit another cigarette, looked in the mirror, removed a fleck of tobacco from her lip, took up a book, riffled pages and placed it down again. She stubbed out her cigarette in the iridescent bowl of a paua-shell ashtray and walked to the window.

The city lay below, the houses strewn around the harbour and heaped up the hills; the scene was cheerless in the flat winter light. Her first view from here had been different, on a warm summer day with cool breeze along the narrow wooden streets. They stood at the window together, seeing the dappled buildings under blue heat-haze, the dark harbour shimmering beneath straw-coloured hills, white yacht-blades cutting calm water. In a rare mood of enthusiasm for the discovered flat, the new city, Tim took her arm.

The girl stood at the window alone. She imagined how he would be now: tense while the point of his brush discovered line, fidgeted with colour. And she, in this room, waited confused, uncertain, unable to settle, only knowing that summer had gone; that it was winter, and she was alone. And she couldn't have complained, or even begun to explain. 'There are books,' he would say with a vaguely irritated gesture, indicating the titles cramped along the shelves. 'You can read, can't you? Other people find something to do with themselves, don't they?'

Other people found something to do with themselves.

There were two escapes.

Auckland, with its neon nights and rain fresh on the streets, was an escape from that lazy small town where white streets curled among green willows. She had gone there, to university, on a scholarship.

The coffee-shop, with its urgent young people in unfashionably fashionable dress, was an escape from that suddenly-dismal university world of clatter-tongued undergraduates.

Sandy had analysed her; Sandy the radical, who sometimes took her off to his proletarian parties in slummy Freeman's Bay, where kegs flowed and fights flared. 'You see, Ann,' he said. 'You don't belong to that, any more than I do. You come from working-class people, like most of us; and that's your trouble, you see, you're far too serious. You want ideas; they don't. You want ideas, to make something of yourself. They want an education, to make money.'

Ian, desperately earnest, trying to atone for his past on a small-town newspaper by writing obscure and erotic verse, told her more bluntly, 'You're sincere. If you want to get on in this world, forget it.'

There were the candlelit parties, with flung mattresses and blasting radiograms, in poky Grafton rooms; and the people from the shadows. Joe, who wrote morbid sketches about rapes and suicides until the day he took a job in an advertising agency and then slashed his wrists seriously enough to be taken to a mental hospital; Alex the actor, disillusioned and homosexual, who wept after the only time he tried to make love to her, and told her about his mother.

They came to the room she took in the city after she left the student hostel. Came hungry for food, thirsty for coffee; depressed, for sympathy. If they came alone, she allowed loveplay, smiled and turned them out; if they came together, she entertained them, laughed with them, and after the last coffee saw them down the stairs and locked her door before retiring. Sometimes, as she edged between the sheets, she heard returning feet come hesitant up the stairs, a knock on the door, the rattling chain; and then the feet slowly down the stairs again.

Tim arrived so suddenly that she only recalled in flashes, like fragments of an old film, his enthusiasms, silences, hates and tenderness. Finally there was the morning awakening in his room, his body beside her, the raw light seeping beneath the ragged blind, the puddled saucers and streaked brushes, the scatter of paintings with harsh shouts of colour, the deserted easel, their clothes limply mingled on the chair beside the bed.

It was an awakening, after the hurt, the cry in the night, to the questions. To Tim the questions could only be a joke. 'Like all the rest,' he said. 'You all like to look free and easy. But deep down you're inhibited as hell. Full of phony middleclass ideals. But it wouldn't really be much fun going to bed with the Bible, would it now?' He couldn't understand. It wasn't what she meant at all; it was a thing she couldn't explain. She couldn't explain a father's knobbled hands, a mother's expectation.

And when Tim announced that he was leaving Auckland, shedding the old skin and the old way, the old life and the old people, the questions gathered like the unanswered letters from home. She couldn't explain the move south, deserting university, abandoning the scholarship; the plunge down country to the new city.

And to defeat. Soon it would be over; in one week or another, on one day or another, the express, gathering speed, would racket north. No doubt he would adapt with time, freeze into solo shape.

She didn't mean to argue, didn't mean to hurt. But the questions, dictated she did.

There was a knock on the door. She woke to the present, to the wind in the curtains.

Ted stood on the step; she was glad it was Ted. He was Tim's only real friend, a rolling stone who moved about the country from season to season, beachcombing with Maoris in Northland, sheelite-mining in the Alps, cutting tourist tracks at Milford Sound. Lately he had been living in the city; he was their only regular visitor.

He grinned from his black-bearded face and, duffle-coated, a small canvas bag swinging from a shoulder, he slouched in the door. 'And how are the kids today?' he said cheerfully, in his soft Irish voice.

She tried to smile in the particular way she always smiled at Ted. But quite suddenly she was blinking back tears.

He slipped his arm about her and helped her into a chair. 'There,' he said. 'What's all the trouble now?'

'Nothing, really,' she said. 'Nothing, Ted. You just caught me at the wrong moment. That's all.'

'There now,' Ted said. He dabbed lightly at her eyes with a red handkerchief. His face gentle, he stooped over her, one arm still about her comfortingly. 'Better?'

'Yes, Ted. Better.'

'The old man locked away again?' he said. He sat down, crossed his legs, and began to fill his pipe. Ted never worried for long; she liked him for it. He was a comfortable person; he always put her at ease. She liked Ted to keep her company.

'Yes,' she said. 'He's busy.'

'What's the masterpiece now?'

She shrugged, wondering if Tim had been listening behind his closed door, and felt a dead weight of tiredness.

Ted looked at her curiously; and changed the subject. 'Well,' he said, slapping his knee. 'What do you say to a meal of paua tonight?'

'Wonderful.'

He looked at his watch. 'Low tide's at four. I better get weaving. It's an hour out to the beach from here.'

She hesitated. 'Would I be a nuisance if I came?' she said quietly. 'I'd love to get out—'

'Fine,' he said. 'I hoped you'd come.'

'Then why didn't you ask me in the first place?'

'Because I like people to please themselves.'

She heard the slap of Tim's sandalled feet; his door sprang open. He emerged smiling, cool and tall in his paint-smeared black sweater; the front patchy with tobacco-ash.

'How's the boy?' he asked Ted.

'Just fine.'

'Going somewhere?'

'After paua. And Ann has just decided she'd like to come along with me.' Ted seemed oddly apologetic.

Leaning in his door, Tim lit a cigarette. 'Good idea,' he said casually. 'But it's a hell of an afternoon to go after them, isn't it?'

Ted shrugged. 'Maybe they'll taste better today.'

Tim laughed shortly: she sensed tension between them. She hurried into the bedroom and returned zipping a windbreaker.

'You have to go right away?' Tim said.

'Why?' Ted said. 'You want to come too?'

Tim shook his head. 'I'd like to,' he said.

'Then why not?'

'Too much to keep me busy.'

'Give it a rest. It's time you got out of that room.'

Tim looked doubtful. 'I'll see how I go,' he said. 'I might just follow you out to the beach.'

'Right,' Ted said.

The tram jolted towards the beach. Ted, remembering the tears, wondered whether today was after all the best time to speak to Ann. Perhaps not; it would be taking unfair advantage. And anyway he was not sure yet that he would be able to say what he wanted. She might not understand; she might turn away.

Yet today he had her alone, clear of the flat, even if only for a short while. It might be his chance.

The tears had surprised him. They could mean that everything was ending after all; that all he had to do was wait. But first he would have to be sure of the words, sure of the time.

There was no sign now of the tears. Her face, nipped by the wind, glowed; twists of dark hair tangled from under her yellow head-scarf. She darted glimpses of the passing suburbs through the dusty tram window; and, talking to him, her quick hands gestured.

Curious, she and Tim. Yet what kind of girl should he have expected for Tim? And which Tim?

The first he remembered clearly. They met in Auckland—Auckland, that impassive city sprawled casually over a green South Pacific isthmus— not long after he arrived in the country; in the dust and dag-stink of a woolstore. New to the city, a refugee from an austere and lonely childhood on a depressed backblocks farm, that first one had been shy and timid. It was an achievement, after the small beginnings of friendship, to persuade Tim to show the work which obsessed him.

Tim took him home: by rattling tram and then by foot through side streets, lit by sunset, where lilac shadow played on old wooden houses: down a narrow path, tangled with weed, around a ruin that had once been a sly-grog shop and brothel and now supported a dozen Maori families: and then through a rusted corrugated fence and into a small shed where a weak bulb hung from the slanting tin roof showed Tim fumbling beneath an old iron bed. He displayed his drawings carefully, explaining that he had no training. And beneath the crudeness, the childish crayon, was a talent and a passion to understand which informed the features of his people—the crab-faced landlady, the fat boozy watersider, the black-bonneted salvationist, the passionless old coal-heaver—with a wry compassion.

He helped Tim, encouraged him, found him a better place to live and work, loaned him money for paint and brushes, sketchbooks and canvas; and introduced him to others who might help. And when he was satisfied he could do no more, that Tim had all he needed, he went deer-culling for a year.

And then he found the second one. More assured, Tim moved with confidence in a fresh circle of friends. They met more as equals now.

On Saturdays, under dark walls hung with yellowed pictures of forgotten racehorses and boxers, they drank together in a small waterfront pub where they joked with their friends—Josef, the Dalmatian fisherman; Harry, the retired burglar; Andrew, the disillusioned evangelist turned alcoholic. For Tim they were friends only now; no longer subjects. His subjects were after the fashion of his other friends.

Then there was the third. The seemingly taller Tim, almost a stranger, who had shaken off all friends, not only the simpering hangers-on, the corduroy theoreticians, but even too the friends of the waterfront pub (because there was his work, his paintings built with blocks of violent colour knifed with heavy lines). Yet they found their way back to friendship.

Finally, after a long spell out of cities, Ted discovered him gone from Auckland; there was the story of the girl who had left with him.

'A skinny little bitch,' Hans, an effete continental poseur, had told him. 'Absolutely characterless and uncreative. Out to suck him dry. You see.'

'She might do him good,' Bridget said hopefully, examining her long cigarette holder with interest, when Ted went to her flat.

'You think so?' he said, while wondering if Bridget was remembering her own affair with Tim; she had been Tim's first woman.

'She's only a child, really. But you never know, do you?' Bridget's plucked, pencilled eyebrows arched with question. 'She might be just what he needs. There's something gone wrong with him somewhere, hasn't there, Ted? Inside him, I mean. When I remember that time you first brought him up to see me—' She made a small gesture of despair. 'I don't know. Do you?'

Ted spent the night with Bridget; slept with her because it was expected of him. He found no more than he knew he would find: despair.

Once, younger, he knew everything with certainty; now he knew nothing. Once he had run barefoot over cobbles through Dublin mist; once scrambled brilliantly up the ladder of learning away from the priested religion of his father. And then discovering no retreat, no ladder to descend, no path back through the mist.

But he had found something in his friendship with Tim.

In the morning, dressing-gowned and showing her age, Bridget demanded, 'Well? Why don't you stop talking about him? Go down to Wellington and see him—or them, rather. See what it's all about.'

'All right,' he said. 'I'll go.'

'Don't think it's because I want you to go, Ted,' she said. 'Because I don't. I like to have you here. But you know what I mean, don't you? It'd be interesting to know what he—'

'I know,' Ted said.

'And remember,' she added, 'if you want to come back, you're welcome here. Any time. And, whenever you want it, I can always arrange a job on the magazine for you. Any time.'

'I know that too,' he said.

So he travelled to Wellington and found the flat high above the city; found Tim more aloof than ever; and found the girl Ann. She was vivid and birdlike among the brightly covered old furniture, the yellow cushions, the checkered sisal floor-matting, the walls hung with French prints. (Tim wouldn't allow Ann to hang his own work. He had—so she told Ted—offered contradictory excuses, saying first that it would be vanity, and then that he was working on new things not ready to be seen yet. But whatever the reason the unhung paintings accumulated in his room, always shut from sight.)

After the greetings, the drinks, the restrained reunion with Tim, he said, 'Maybe I'll stick around one or two weeks. Find a place to live and pick up a job on the wharf.'

One or two weeks—he had been in the city three months now. Why? Tim had said, far too simply, 'This is Ann.'

Seeing her loneliness and Tim's neglect, he felt at once sorry and angry. He soon saw she needed his company; he took her to concerts and films, and helped her through the long winter evenings, reading to her, listening to music with her.

When he understood himself, and remembered his loyalty to Tim as a friend, he tried to keep away from the flat.

But it was no use. Tim, surprisingly hurt, wanted to know why he stayed away; and Ann missed him through friendless weekends and evenings. It was no use: if he really wanted to remain loyal to Tim, he could have left the city then; instead he used the excuse that Ann needed him to cover his need for her. And there was the second excuse, that if he waited, waited long enough, there might be no disloyalty.

If he waited. But the waiting had grown too long now, the Wellington winter too cold, the north too attractive. He could escape from this dilemma as he had escaped all others; find peace with rugged men who asked no questions and posed no problems. Who worked hard and drank hard; and accepted him.

The tram banged to a stop. 'Here we are,' Ted said. They swung down from the footboard.

The suburb was sunk in peninsula hills at the end of the harbour. They climbed clear of the houses and a road led them down through a cutting to the open sea. Then the beach, bleak and deserted, spread in a grey sweep below them. The ebbing tide left reefs of black rock.

They took a thin path down to the beach. The coarse sand rasped underfoot as they picked their way across.

With the wind flushing her face, she turned to Ted, laughing. 'Know something?'

'What?'

'Who cares if we don't find paua?'

'Me. I like them.'

'And I just like getting out, getting away—' She stopped, suddenly aware she had said too much. 'I like that smell of the sea,' she added lamely.

'Who doesn't?' he asked, grinning easily.

She was surprised at her own calm.

He helped her over the rocks, his hand brown around her pale wrist. Then, seeking the grey-shelled paua, they peered into shallow green rock-pools and into crevices where the sea still swirled.

2

They had been gone an hour. He still couldn't call stop. He should get out, look around, let everything fall into place again.

It would be too easy to lose his grip. There were enough irritants already.

Yet he was sorry now for what had happened. He couldn't blame her for anything. She followed her logic; he followed his. It seemed impossible to express himself clearly anywhere but here, and then only by way of bitter geometry.

For too long he had lost himself among other people. That was why he had come to this new city, to find himself again. But people still confused him; left him unable to see things calm and clear as he had once.

He needed to be alone, free of her. For her good and his. That was what the geometry said.

Without thinking, he had slipped into a coat.

Then why lie to himself? If he really wanted to be free, why follow them? He knew Ted too well not to know what was happening, not to know why Ted had stayed in the city so long. On Saturday afternoons, when they drank together, their desultory conversation and bleak pauses only reminded him of conversations when they laughed at themselves, at each other, and felt no hurt.

Then Ted could have her, he told himself.

So why follow them? The dead faces and wooden seats in the jerking tram gave no answer.

At the terminus he met the bite of sea air. He began to walk briskly through the suburb. Then he slowed, seeing suddenly the neat homes in the Sunday quiet, the gaunt trees against the sky, two boys riding a trolley, a squall of small girls with tumbling curls and dangling dolls, an old woman forking a grey flower plot to chocolate. How long since he took notice?

He climbed above the houses and into the cutting, frowning, bewildered at himself. Walls of yellow clay parted to reveal the beach, the surf along the long margin of sand. He saw two distant figures moving about on a stubble of rock.

He paused, thoughtful; then he stepped down from the road, where they might have seen him. Screening himself behind patchy scrub, he slid down the bank by degrees, nearer to the beach. A little way above it, he sat on a rock, his feet resting comfortably on a curve of clay.

Their voices were faint: from where he sat he saw them framed by fern and broom.

Gulls circled noisily above them as they searched.

'His trouble,' Ted was saying, 'is that what he's doing is hypothesizing himself out of life. He's got the fool idea into his head that he has to get clear of it to look at it properly. Ideas about ideas. No rough edges, no mystery. It's all cold and hard.'

'Yes,' she said, and then was silent.

'I'm boring you.'

'No, Ted. Not at all.' She raised her eyes above the sea to the wheeling gulls. 'Ted,' she said quietly. 'Do you think he loves me?'

The sea sucked at the rocks.

Ted, head down, avoided her eyes. Like a woman, he thought. Always it had to come down to the personal.

'Do you think he can?' she said.

Ted shrugged, watching the confused weed tangle up in the swell. 'Don't ask me,' he said.

'Be honest. Forget you're his best friend.'

'He's too reductive to be seductive.'

'But it doesn't have to be like that—not always, does it?' Because, she thought, Tim was not like that, not always.

'We're not doing much good here,' Ted said. 'Best to move on a bit. The tide'll beat us if we don't find something soon.'

Light was seeping from the afternoon; and the pleasant feeling had left her.

'I wish I could do something to help,' Ted said, reaching out to lift her over a broken shoulder of rock.

'Thanks, Ted. But there's nothing.' Of course there was nothing; why persist? But it was one thing to be logical; another thing to leave Tim.

Ted rolled his trousers and waded into new crevices. She stayed above him, pointing to where she thought she saw the colour of the shells among the surging weed. Then he would feel underwater, knife in hand, for the paua. He found some small ones. 'They'll do,' he said. 'If we don't find more.'

Presently he straightened, hands on hips, the sea washing about his knees. 'The tide's coming in pretty fast,' he observed in a flat voice.

'Is something worrying you?' she said.

'Me?' He laughed, without conviction.

'Something is worrying you, isn't it?'

He didn't answer; she watched him climb slowly from the sea.

3

He was building it carefully now. Their two figures in the foreground; and behind them the sky, the thin light on the sea, a spray dancing over black rock, a flight of gulls and a far off fishing launch. The emphasis strong, their colour rich against the leaden day.

Ted, stooped, would be gathering the shells into his canvas bag, his back curved, the blue tartan shirt falling loosely about his waist, his brown corduroys lifting above his pale bare ankles, the black of his hair flowing to the stub of his beard; the pipe jutting, the face absorbed and serious.

And Ann? Standing, looking down at Ted, arched slightly, the head-scarf fallen loose and yellow about her neck, the open green windbreaker snapped by the wind, revealing the red sweater beneath, the gentle line of the small breasts. The hair cascading about the face. The face half-hidden.

Why not? He had no paper, no sketchbook; he began to draw on the back of a cardboard tobacco-packet, working through the idea with a pencil stub before it left him. He looked up to see that they had moved further along the beach. Their voices were lost altogether now. In a moment he would join them.

He thought he might speak to Ann then. Instead, scrambling from the sea, he dried himself and pushed the shellfish into his bag. She said nothing; she merely watched him curiously. Too conscious of her, his thick fingers fumbled clumsily with the bag. He closed it, slung it on his shoulder, and suggested they walk a little way along the beach to see if more paua could be rescued from the rising tide. He did not look at her.

'Tim didn't turn up, after all,' he said. Why should he feel guilty? He had said nothing, betrayed no friendship.

'Has that been worrying you?'

'Why should it worry me?' He discovered an irritation in his voice.

'It has been worrying you, though. Hasn't it?'

'It would've done him good to get out,' he said irrelevantly. 'He never gets out. Cooped up in that room all the time.'

She was silent. The sea hissed under the darkening sky. She felt spray on her face.

Suddenly he swung about to look at her; his face was agitated. 'All right,' he said. 'So you know. You needn't be so damn smug about it.'

She looked bewildered, hurt. 'What?'

And then he saw, and was sorry; she had not seen.

'What is it? What have I done?' Her words lifted away in the wind. But she knew.

She felt chilled and tired. Ted's voice was quiet; she could scarcely hear it above the sound of the sea.

'I'm sorry,' he said. 'I just wanted to have a talk with you this afternoon. It doesn't matter about what. It doesn't matter now.'

'What doesn't?' she asked.

He looked at her.

'Getting dark,' he said. 'Shall we get moving?'

He jumped lightly across a gap in the rocks, then waited to catch her. 'All right?' he said, observing her curiously.

'All right,' she said.

She jumped. Her feet slipped on greasy rock; a sob leapt unexpected from her throat and tears stung her eyes. But Ted's arms caught her before she fell. He swung her up to him, and planted her down firmly. She clung to him; he did not push her away.

'It's all right,' she said, recovering.

He did not release her. His hand slid gently down her loose hair and then, with sudden urgency, lifted her face. He was warm against her, and gentle; his lips tasted faintly of tobacco.

Then he let her go.

'I'm sorry,' he said brokenly. 'I forgot myself. It's just that—' He raised his arms in appeal, then let them fall helplessly. 'I'm sorry.' He turned away and she caught at his arm, despairingly.

He saw them come together, the two figures in the fading light, to become motionless, silhouetted singly on black rock above the white lines of surf. Presently they moved along the beach, becoming indistinct against the darkened sand. Then they were lost to sight behind a finger of land. He scrambled down to the beach, trying to catch sight of them again. Sand slid under his feet; he stumbled and pitched forward. He rose and ran along the beach, the sea in his ears. But he saw only a grove of pine and a derelict boat-shed. He stopped running. Breathing heavily, he looked towards the shed. Then he looked down to see that one hand had fastened tight around sand. He opened the hand and let the grains dribble between his fingers. Then he turned stiffly and walked away.

4

The wind, creaking through the pines, slapped the broken boards of the shed. He could hear the waves beating over rocks, up the sand.

Her white face was lost, her body withdrawn into the darkness.

'I expect we'd better go now,' he said. His voice sounded faint to himself.

'I'm sorry,' she said presently.

'For what?'

'You've got to understand,' she said.

'What?'

'That—' She hesitated.

'That it doesn't mean anything?' he said. 'Because I know that already.'

He slumped back to the floor, turned his face to a chill draught of air.

Escape was one thing; sanctuary another. He was familiar with the first. He might learn to live with the latter.

'I'm sorry,' she said. 'It's my fault.'

'We can go now,' he said presently, but he made no move.

'Yes,' she agreed. She was calm. She reached for Ted's hand and found it. 'Yes,' she said. 'We can go now.'

From his room he listened to them enter the flat. The tap of Ann's heels, the scuff of Ted's heavy shoes. He heard them talking in the kitchen as they prepared the meal, hammering soft the paua-steaks.

He concentrated again. Glancing at the crude notes on the tobacco-packet, he worked quickly, building with thick strokes of black pencil. Then he was lost. The figures were angular, the rocks inflexible too.

From the kitchen he heard the hiss of gas, the pop of flame. Presently the smell of the frying steaks seeped into the room. He heard percolating coffee, the low voices.

He began again. It was better; the stiffness was going. Important that he understand.

She called his name.

He held the drawing to the light. It was rough still. The incoherence mattered less by the minute.

She called his name again.

He seemed to have mislaid anger.

Ted had built a crackling fire of resinous pine. They sat before it, eating the paua.

He congratulated them on the meal, tried to joke with them. Ted smiled weakly. Ann was aloof. So he fell silent too.

Ann rustled through the silence as she cleared the dishes and poured coffee. When she finished she sat cross-legged on the floor between them. She was wearing slacks now, and black sweater, and looked trim and neat and boyish.

'Working on something new?' Ted said finally.

'You might say that.'

There was no large interest apparent in Ted's face.

Tim began to feel desperate. Running a hand abstractedly through his hair, he tried to summon up conversation.

Then he saw they were both looking at him.

At least not at him. At the sand which showered from his hair.

He affected not to notice.

5

Ted stood at the door. His pipe fixed between his teeth, he gave his full attention to fastening his duffle-coat. 'I meant to tell you earlier,' he said. 'I think I'll be pushing off this week.'

'Pushing off?' Tim said. 'What's the hurry?'

'No hurry. I've just been thinking lately it's time to push off north again. It'll be warmer.'

There was a pause. Tim looked at Ted.

'You don't really have to go, you know,' he said.

Ted lowered his eyes and fidgeted with the top fastening of the coat. 'I've been here long enough. Time to be moving on again.'

'I wish you didn't have to. I'll certainly—I mean, we'll both certainly miss you.' Tim was aware of Ann standing beside them. 'You'll see us again before you go, won't you?'

'I'll try,' Ted said. 'But I'll probably be busy. I might just push off tomorrow, or the day after.' Ted thrust out his hand suddenly. 'So here's just in case.'

The handshake was austere. Ted's eyes looked dead. Tim wished there was some way to reassure him. There was no way.

'We'll be seeing you down here again, won't we?'

'Sure thing,' Ted said, without conviction.

He opened the door. Thunder slammed beyond the hills and lightning made the horizon vivid. New rain began to spit through the darkness.

'Anyway I'll be able to get in touch with you?' Tim thought at last to say.

'Through Bridget, probably.'

'Bridget?'

'She seems rather on her own now.' Ted shrugged. 'Besides, she promised me a job on her magazine. Any time I wanted it.'

'And you want it now?'

'I didn't say I wanted it.'

'But you used to say that was one kind of thing you'd never—'

'I used to say I'd never do a lot of things.'

Through the open door they looked out upon the wind and rain, the growing storm.

'I'd better go,' Ted said.

Ann spoke at last. 'Goodbye, Ted,' she said quietly.

'Goodbye.' Ted raised a hand in salute. 'Be seeing you.'

They watched his back disappear into the rain and dark, heard the dwindling sound of his footsteps. The front gate clicked shut.

Tim closed the door. Ann switched off the radio and turned to face him. They were alone now. The fire crackled and rain hissed on the windows.

'I'll sleep on the couch tonight,' she said simply.

He turned away, without hope.

'Whatever you like.'

'And I'm sorry,' she said.

'For what?' he said, swinging sharply.

'For everything. For you.'

'I don't want sympathy,' he snapped. And more quietly added, 'I expect you'll be going too.'

'Surprised?'

'Not really. With Ted?'

'No. I'm not going after Ted. You heard what he said.'

'Then where?' he said, perplexed.

'Home.'

'Home? Back to your people?'

'Back to my people.'

There was a silence. He looked at her bleakly.

'I'll marry you. If that's what you want.' He might have meant it.

'But don't you see?' she cried.

'Not enough, apparently.' he confessed.

Outside, the first of the storm was spent.

'You have the bed,' he told her finally. 'I'll take the couch. I'll be working late.'

'Shouldn't you get some sleep?'

He shook his head. 'I've got something to finish.'

'At this time of night?'

'To start, then.'

He turned into his door.

'Tim,' she called.

'What?'

'Nothing,' she said.

'Nothing?'

'Coffee?'

'That'd be fine. Thanks.'

'Much to do?'

'Too much.'

He swung his door shut and she raised her eyes slowly, with dull dread, to see it close against her for the second time that day. Remembering Ted, she gave a small cry, too low to be heard, and darted to the window. But there was only the rain; the rain on glass, and bright lights bleeding.

PLAY THE FIFE LOWLY

1

SHE ran, her legs jerking steadily forward, her feet striking echoes from the moonlit streets. Quick swallows of air rasped her throat and stung her lungs; her coat slapped back and forward, as though trying to impede her progress. She still called his name. Once she thought she heard an answer; once a voice in faint, mocking song.

But there were only deserted corners where the wind sidled through rustling papers, and streets leading to more empty streets: and these with the same decayed shops and secretive houses.

She paused and, in the moment the echo of her own footsteps died, she heard the other feet ringing behind her.

2

They were not the first city feet Helen had fled. Earlier there was the night when other girls in the flat rustled away with their sleek boy friends; when she forsook her fireside chair.

It had been pleasant at first: her heels clipping over pavement, the rain-cooled darkness, the harbour lights. And there was the shabby wharfside milk-bar where, from a rainbow juke-box, a thin masculine voice wheedled for the return of lost love. Sipping her milk-skinned coffee, she watched the Saturday-night drifters: sad, shuffling old men; middle-aged women with dusty furs and shapeless hats; sallow young men with pin-stripe suits, nicotine-yellow fingers and tragic faces. She felt an affinity with them: she was like them, she told herself, one of the harmless strays of the city. When she walked home, that proposition fell apart. A figure lurched out of shadow, a bottle smashed and a slurred voice called. She began to run: unsteady feet hammered behind her. Once she fell, shredding her stockings and skinning her knees. But she was running again, not stopping until she slammed the door of the flat and leaned limp against it, listening, for the footsteps that never quite came.

Sometimes, waking from a dream of smothering, she thought she heard the feet again: it was almost as if the quick, ringing footfalls were always there, always ready to burst into earshot. She remembered them more calmly at other times. Then she would put down her book, silence the radio, approach the mirror, remove her glasses, and tell herself: I am twenty-five, not pretty, and will never be married.

Such nights were before Gerald. Not that she could regard Gerald as more than a casual friend, a Saturday friend. He was mild, pleasant, courteous, but hard to take seriously. And when she realized she had aroused his deeper interest she was not sure what she should feel. Pleasure, she supposed, firstly: that was only natural. Then regret. She was already wording her rebuff.

Yet she was no longer sure she could once again face the nights in the flat alone; the nights when not even books or music could camouflage the truth.

Tonight, in the restaurant, as Gerald leaned intimately across the table, fingering his engraved cigarette case and exhaling smoke smoothly, she decided there was no reason why she should not, after all, marry him. As she half-listened to his murmured confidences, she avoided his eyes and, turning her head slightly, studied his reflection in a wall-mirror: he was even handsome, she supposed, in his boyish way. In his neat suit, starched shirt and college tie, he always seemed so much younger than herself. She glanced at her own reflection only briefly. He could be likeable enough: she would have to be content with that.

And then, leaving the restaurant, he ended her compliant mood. He spoke curtly to the girl behind the cash-register about a noisy drunk the girl had allowed to enter the place. He was needlessly unpleasant, and it brought back all she tried to forget: his pompous mannerisms, his opinionated monologues.

As they drove to the party, he sat stiff behind the wheel, his face impassive; and she knew he was examining a new approach, calculating her response. She was almost certainly in for another uncomfortable talk.

The street into which the car turned was broad and prosperous, with large white homes set back among well-ordered greenery.

Gerald silenced the engine.

'Well,' he said, speaking for the first time in minutes. 'Here we are.' He paused, fumbling through his pockets for cigarettes. She waited, tightening her coat about her neck, stiffening slowly.

'You know . . .' he began, inserting a cigarette in his mouth.

'Yes?'

'It ought to be quite fun tonight,' he added lamely. His fingers fidgeted with his lighter: the flare lit his face forcing a smile.

'Any particular reason?' She felt calmer: he surely wouldn't attempt to say anything now; his moment had escaped him.

'A bit of a joke, really,' he said, tilting back his head to exhale smoke. 'But Tom Anderson's been invited.'

'Tom Anderson?'

'You must have heard us talk about him.'

'Was he the one—'

'—the one that went all arty after college. Really went off the deep end. Everyone knew he'd come a flop. He did, all right. Hit the booze and got T.B. and God knows what else. Trailing round with all types. I hadn't heard anything about him for years. Mike met him in the street. Thought it might be fun to invite him along tonight.'

'Wasn't he your friend?' Helen said, remembering conversations where her interest had been lit.

'Just a friend,' he corrected quickly. Dismissing the subject, he slid his arm around her. He seemed about to make another attempt at serious talk.

'Tell me more,' she said evasively.

'About what?'

'About this Tom Anderson—and what he's like.'

'He's not all that interesting.' He drew her towards him. His hand felt clumsily at her face. 'Helen,' he began.

'But you still haven't told me—' she protested.

'I wish I hadn't mentioned him,' he said petulantly, jerking back into his part of the seat. He shot open his door. 'Come on. Let's go inside.'

Beaming, a glass wedged in a huge fist, Mike met them at the door and led them inside. Guests grouped and regrouped rowdily. Almost all the boys, like Mike, were friends of Gerald from college days; to Helen they all seemed to possess the same clean features and tricks of speech. She often had difficulty remembering names, telling them apart. Only Mike was distinctive: heavy and shapeless, lumbering and loud-voiced, but always the leader, the one who had held them together since college.

At the bar, as Mike poured drinks, she looked about foreseeing the nature of the evening ahead. First, tipsy but not yet drunken, they would conjure names and events from the past to hide lapses in conversation: 'I say, did you hear about Hamish?' 'They tell me Robin . . .' 'You remember that time?' 'I always laugh when I think back . . .' Later, as alcohol took effect, they would return from rumour and reverie to the present; to back-slapping, name-calling, boasting and high-pitched frolic pursued with vast seriousness, as though they desperately wanted, now the novelty of adult life had worn thin, to escape from themselves and win back their schooldays. The girls present—the limpid girl friends and affectionate fiancées—would appear shocked at first: it was almost necessary they show some measure of disapproval. But later, they would join with the boys in feverish dancing, stamping conga-lines and suggestive games. And at the end there would be illness and upsets, tears and flushing toilets, and frantic petting on the verandah, in the bedrooms, and in car back-seats.

In another room a radiogram played: through a doorway Helen could see couples scraping listlessly around the floor.

'Well,' Mike said, handing out their drinks. 'Anderson hasn't arrived yet.'

Gerald frowned. 'I'm rather hoping he doesn't.'

'Why?' Mike demanded, regarding Gerald shrewdly. 'Don't you want to see your old cobber?'

Helen, perplexed, saw colour show in Gerald's face. 'Anderson's—well, all right,' he continued to stammer. 'But, I mean—inviting him here . . .' He faltered, and began to sip his beer.

Mike laughed hoarsely. 'Gerry,' he said, 'you know something? You're getting stuffy in your old age.' He slapped Gerald roughly on the back. 'And you want to know something else? I should've thought you'd only be too glad to see your old friend Tom. You're the reason I asked him along tonight. That's a fact.'

Helen felt irritated: they were leaving her outside. Mike seemed determined only to hint, and Gerald to remain reticent.

'What's so terrible about this chap anyway?' she said.

'Ask Gerry,' Mike said with a malicious grin.

'For God's sake,' Gerald said sharply.

The situation was uncomfortable. Mike's head was cocked slyly and Gerald's eyes were downcast. Helen was relieved to see Sylvia, Mike's fiancée, swaying towards them. Sylvia always had some serenity, even when drinking heavily. Tall and blonde in blue, she was smiling warmly at Helen.

'One guess to know what you're talking about,' she declared tipsily; her large glass of iced gin slopped and chinked in her hand. 'My God, Helen did you ever see anything like it? You know something? I think this chap's only a rumour.'

'You're only a rumour,' Mike said. 'And a vague one at that.'

Sylvia frowned dully, slow to discern insult. 'Don't you talk to me like that,' she snapped finally.

Mike, mildly amused, turned his back on her. 'By the way, Gerry,' he said, 'did you hear about Tony?'

Sylvia touched Helen's arm. 'Let's get out of here,' she said.

She followed Sylvia from the room. Near the door they passed a group conversing loudly.

'I always said Anderson—'

'—but, really, the way all these so-called talented people think they own the world.'

'My God,' Sylvia said as they moved down a quiet passage to the rear of the house. 'You wouldn't read about it. Talk about fowls pecking one with a broken leg.'

'Are you and Mike having trouble?' Helen asked quietly, as Sylvia led her into a bedroom.

'Trouble?' Sylvia crowed. Standing before a mirror Sylvia began to brush her hair. Her voice was sibilant. 'When Mike finally got me to bed it hurt his hothouse feelings when he found out I already knew the routine. Thought he was going to be the conquering hero. Instead he turns out the lamest runner in the race. Now he's finding excuses not to get married. Funny, isn't it?'

Sylvia brushed her hair even more vigorously. 'I think it's absolutely hilarious,' she went on. 'Because the funniest thing is I don't even want to marry the randy clot anyhow. Stupid, isn't it?"

Helen didn't answer.

'Well—isn't it?' Sylvia demanded.

'I'm sorry it's gone wrong,' Helen said softly.

'Gone wrong?' Sylvia laughed without mirth. 'If I had any sense left I'd get out while the going was good. But, there comes a time when it's now or never. For me it's now—or else.' Sylvia turned from the mirror. 'Well, pet, and what about your trouble? How's dear Gerry? Still serious?'

'Still serious.'

'A stayer, isn't he? When d'you think he'll get sick of it?'

'I haven't the faintest idea.'

'Don't tell me you're weakening?'

Helen shrugged. 'Hadn't we better go back?'

'In a moment, petal,' Sylvia said, clicking open her purse. 'Just a wee daub of warpaint for a weary old warhorse.' She inclined towards the mirror, half-stooping and peering intently at her reflected face as she worked the lipstick. 'Funny,' she murmured. 'But I had an idea he'd get you sooner or later.'

'What do you mean?' Helen said.

'What I say,' Sylvia said primly. Satisfied now, she replaced the lipstick and clipped shut the purse. 'Anyway, just how ridiculous can we get? I ask you.'

'What's ridiculous?' Helen said.

Sylvia threw her arms wide. 'Every damn thing. Here's me fighting like hell to get married when I don't want to get married. And there you are fighting like hell not to get married when you really want to get married. If that's not ridiculous, what is?'

Sylvia glanced finally into the mirror; she pinched and smoothed her frock. 'Do I look all right now? My God—my knees still feel weak. You know what time I started tippling today? Eleven this morning. Had to— to face up to him tonight. Ought to feel weak, poor things, shouldn't they?'

Helen didn't answer; she was listening to loud voices at the front of the house.

'What's that?' said Sylvia. 'Don't tell me. This character must have actually arrived. We'd better have a look. Before they pick the meat off him.'

As they moved to the door together, she caught at Helen. 'Look, darling, before I forget. Perhaps I was shooting off my mouth too much just now. But you won't say anything to anyone, will you?'

'Of course not.'

Sylvia squeezed Helen's hand. 'I didn't really imagine you would. It's just that I'm in a big enough mess now without—' She stopped, frowning. 'Do you ever feel cramped up and suffocated?'

She jerked Helen through the door. 'Come on. It's all free.'

The commotion had shifted from the front door to one of the rooms. When they pushed into the room they found attention centred on a varied group. There were four Maoris, two boys and their girl friends, young and bewildered in the alien atmosphere. The boys wore gaudy shirts and had guitars strung round their necks; the girls were flounced and floral. With them was a delicate youth with thin feminine features; he wore a yellow turtle sweater, and curls of fair hair tufted from beneath a black beret. He was surveying the room with apparent unconcern. If he had been the only one with the Maoris, Helen would have mistaken him for Tom Anderson: he seemed more the fragile male she pictured. She hadn't expected the tall dishevelled figure which dominated the odd group: red hair flared above a squarishly attractive face set on broad shoulders. His unbuttoned wool tartan shirt peeled from the chest to reveal red hairs on pale flesh; his soiled corduroys were hitched askew, and a flap of the shirt hung out; bare feet were sandalled loosely.

'Give drink,' he commanded. 'And we give music.'

Mike stared foolishly, seeming to hesitate between hostility and obedience: he paused indecisively, then went to the bar. 'What do you all want?' he said from the silence. 'There's gin and vodka and scotch and—'

'Forget it. Beer.'

Helen was aware of Gerald standing beside her. 'Serves Mike right,' he said. 'He should have known there'd be trouble.'

'What trouble?' Helen said. 'There's no trouble.'

'No trouble?' Gerald laughed shortly. 'You're a bit innocent, aren't you?'

Sylvia, who had been listening, turned on Gerald. 'What did you expect him to do? Come creeping in on hands and knees? Or did you just want him to stand up against a wall so you could throw darts at him?'

'I was talking to Helen—if you don't mind,' Gerald said stiffly.

'All right,' Sylvia said. 'Don't get shirty.'

Helen moved away.

'What d'you think you're doing now?' Gerald demanded, lunging after her. He was flushed and panicky.

'I thought I might help Mike with their drinks. Someone could be polite after all.'

Their exchange had become an incident. People stared; and from the other side of the room Tom Anderson regarded them with amusement. She broke free of Gerald and went to the bar.

'Can I help?' she asked Mike.

He raised blank eyes; sweat beaded his upper lip. 'Oh—yes, thanks,' he said. 'Thanks. Thanks a lot. What a mess this is. What a mess. What would you do?'

Gathering up the filled glasses on a tray, she moved slowly across the room. Tom Anderson stood protectively before his friends; he intercepted her.

'And who do you belong to?' he said. 'Gerry?'

'To no one,' she said and sped away.

Gerald was with Mike at the bar. He ignored her, but she overheard him say, 'After all, Mike, it's only a question of squeezing them out, isn't it?' Near them a large group talked in animated staccato. 'What a hide, though—' 'Those tar-babies and that fellow in the sweater—if you ask me...'

'Well,' said Sylvia, coming to stand beside Helen. 'There's only one thing for it. Get tight and watch the fun. Like a gin?'

They sat singing in an alcove, a recessed window seat; the Maoris occupied the seat, the fair delicate young man was arranged languidly on the floor, and Tom Anderson squatted on his haunches. Around them the party continued weakly: voices were unnaturally high. Only the newcomers appeared to be enjoying it. Elsewhere there was determination not to acknowledge the disaster; and the guitars and Maori voices made the scene absurd.

'What's with your boy friend?' Sylvia said. 'He's a cat on hot bricks.' Helen looked towards the bar and saw Gerald still talking earnestly to Mike.

Someone carried the radiogram in from another room in an effort to drown the singing. Then, the fair young man, who had apparently developed a dislike for a rather elegant girl sitting near him, said something insulting. As if they had been waiting for that moment, Gerald and Mike sprang across the room to where the fiancé of the elegant girl now menaced the fair young man. Trying to pacify everyone, Tom Anderson moved into the argument. The radiogram roared unchecked, smothering voices: the six of them, the five boys and the girl, postured and grimaced like dumb characters in a tableau.

Tom Anderson managed to end the altercation. The gathering dispersed, with warnings and meaningful gestures.

'Pity,' Sylvia murmured with a click of tongue. 'I was just beginning to enjoy it.'

With a new rush of music, several couples began to spin about the floor. The group in the alcove did not attempt to sing again. After persuading the Maoris to join in the dancing, Tom Anderson spoke softly to the fair young man, who had sulkily taken a place in a shadowed corner of the window seat. The only response was a violent headshake. Then, ignoring the young man, he took up a guitar and began to idle his fingers over the strings while looking out over the room. He saw Helen: he winked broadly, grinning, and raised his glass to her: she moved her eyes away.

'Well,' Sylvia said drily. 'Don't tell me you've made a hit.'

Gerald came towards Helen. 'Dance?' he said, almost apologetically. She slipped into the crook of his arm and let him slide her away.

Over his shoulder, as they danced, she watched Mike approach Sylvia and say something. Sylvia hesitated, bracing herself, and then she hissed a reply. Mike backed away as though stung.

'I'm sorry things have gone wrong,' Gerald was saying.

Sylvia's blue frock flashed towards the alcove. Helen's view was obscured for a moment, and then she saw Sylvia dancing with Tom Anderson.

Gerald stiffened. 'Do you see that?' he said.

'What?'

'Sylvia.'

'I know,' she said calmly.

'The sooner Mike wakes up to her the better. I've been trying to make him see.'

'What's wrong with Sylvia?'

'Ask yourself.'

'I wish you'd remember that Sylvia's my friend,' Helen said in a small, even voice.

'Please yourself.'

There was a pause.

'And there's just one thing I'd like you to tell me,' she said.

'What's that?'

'Why are you so twitchy about Tom Anderson?'

'Look,' he said with irritation. 'Can't we just quietly forget about him? He'll be gone soon, anyhow.'

'Why?'

'Because we just got him to promise to clear himself and his menagerie out of here soon—that's why.'

Helen was silent. She knew what she had to do. There was only the one question to ask.

'Dear old Gerry's girl friend, eh?' Tom said. They were dancing. His voice was low in her ear. 'Friend, is it—or fiancée?'

'Friend.'

'Well, well. And when shall it be fiancée?'

'I don't know—that it will.'

'He's asked, I suppose.'

'He's asked.'

'Well,' he said with his friendly smile. 'Dear old Gerry.'

Close, his face lost its crude strength. In the eyes were webs of red. He regarded her quizzically.

'Why is he so afraid of you?'

'Who?—Gerry?' he asked, with affected surprise.

'You've seen him tonight.'

'Have I?' he asked.

'You were good friends at college, weren't you?'

'Excellent friends.'

'Then why does he hate you now?'

'Perhaps,' he suggested, 'he's just forgotten—that we were friends.'

'He hasn't forgotten—you know that.'

'Well, then—I can't understand it. Can you?' He smiled winningly again.

'Tell me what you and he were like at college.'

'Well,' he said, pausing briefly. 'He used to keep me company when I wandered the countryside with my sketchbook. He was never much of an artist himself, as I remember; not that I was either, come to think of it. Also he used to produce poetry of a rather badly written variety; a pastime in which I encouraged him, since there might have been something there. That satisfy you?'

He paused for breath: there was a wheeze in his throat.

'And Mike?'

'Ah, yes. There was Mike. The big bad philistine.' He wheezed again, and added, 'I was expelled. Mike informed on me. Liquor on college premises. Girls over the college wall.'

'And why did Mike inform?'

'Let's say that perhaps he wasn't a patron of the arts and would have preferred me to give my full attention to rugby, a game at which I sometimes excelled. Not a puritan, mind. Not Mike—I never did find out where he got his own liquor from.'

'And what about Gerald?'

'Yes—alas, poor innocent Gerald. Betwixt and between.'

He appeared, suddenly, to have dismissed the subject.

The dance was faster now. Faces twitched in and out of focus, points of light blinked. She was out of breath suddenly, leaning against him, his stubbled chin prickling her cheek.

'Enough?' he asked.

'Yes.'

'Then let's have a drink.' He steered her towards the alcove. 'You will drink with us, won't you?'

'Of course. Why not?'

'I'd hate to get you into trouble with Gerry.' Strangely, he seemed to mean it.

'You haven't met Derek yet,' Tom said as he led her into the alcove. 'Helen, Derek. Derek, Helen.'

The fair young man didn't rise from his seat; he raised cool eyes briefly, his face still pouting.

'Derek plays the violin,' Tom said. 'He's enchanting when he plays the violin.'

Derek didn't look up again.

'Excuse him, won't you?' Tom said, as though apologizing for a child.

The cough came without preliminary: one moment he was smiling at her; the next he was doubled up with the violence of it. And then, as quickly recovered, he smiled again. 'Let's drink,' he said.

She looked at him quickly. If there was distress she was too late to see it.

She realized, for the first time, that he was drunk, though his manner and speech did not show it. He tilted back his head and drank with a flourish, his neck-muscles rippling.

'Tell me something,' he said as he wiped his mouth with the back of his hand. 'Think you'll marry Gerry? Or shouldn't I ask?'

'You shouldn't ask,' she said lamely.

She remembered that Sylvia too had vanished from the room. Perhaps to be ill.

'Who are you looking for?' Tom said. 'Gerry?'

'Sylvia.'

'Sylvia? Ah, yes, Mike's fiancée. She danced very nicely.'

'I think I should find her,' Helen apologized.

'It's all right—if you want to go,' he said, touching her arm lightly.

'How do you mean?'

'I mean it's all right if you want to go. Everyone else seems to be leaving us.'

The room was beginning to empty: the radiogram had been disconnected and carried through to another room. Apparently Mike had decided to isolate the unwanted guests altogether.

The Maoris returned to the alcove; their brown skins were shiny with sweat from the dancing.

'I think we better go now,' one of the boys said, showing white teeth.

'Nonsense,' Tom said. 'Let's make more music.'

'I think we better go,' the boy persisted.

'More music,' Tom insisted. *'Kapai te* music.' He began to talk persuasively.

'Really, Tom,' Derek appealed in his thin, affected voice. 'Don't you think all this has gone far enough?'

'Everyone sit down,' Tom commanded. 'We're just getting started.' He turned to Helen. 'Aren't we, Helen? You will stay, won't you?'

And his eyes, hinting again, seemed to add: after all, there is no real need to say anything; we understand each other, don't we, you and I?

'I'll stay,' she said faintly.

'Really, I think—' Derek began to protest.

'Shut up,' Tom said mildly.

He drew up a chair for Helen and sat himself on the arm. The Maoris crowded back into the window seat, and Derek slipped unwillingly to the floor.

Everyone else had left the room, but at that moment Gerald returned to stand at the door.

'Helen,' he said quietly.

There was a silence. Sylvia wobbled into the doorway to stand behind Gerald.

'Helen,' he repeated more sharply.

He stood only a few yards away, at the other end of the misty room. It seemed a greater distance.

She shook her head. He stared with disbelief, then turned away.

There was the sound of Sylvia's high laugh; Mike came and Sylvia allowed herself to be led away, still laughing. The door slammed and there was silence.

Tom touched her arm lightly, gratefully; she did not look at him. The guitars were strummed.

It was after midnight: out in the passage goodbyes were said as another group of guests departed.

From other rooms came the subdued sounds of the diminishing party: its dying fall infected even those in the quarantined room. Tom Anderson plucked a borrowed guitar and sang alone.

Lights had long been turned out. Moonlight found chinks in the curtains.

> *When I walked out in the streets of Laredo*
> *When I walked out in Laredo one day*
> *I spied a young cowboy all wrapped in white linen*
> *Wrapped in white linen as cold as the clay*

For one moment it seemed the song would break off altogether; she felt the body beside her arch and quiver. But this time he smothered the cough quickly. His finger found the tune again.

> *'I see by your outfit that you are a cowboy'*
> *These words he did say as I boldly stepped by*
> *'Come sit down beside me and hear my sad story*
> *I'm shot in the breast and know I must—*

Moving her eyes slightly she met Derek's steady stare; moonlight and shadow met on his face. His eyes continued to regard her with contempt and distaste: she looked away quickly, trying to check her trembling. For one moment she was afraid she might cry out.

> *It was once in the saddle I used to go dashing*

The door sprang open: light leapt across the floor. Mike entered the room and, peering uncertainly into the dark, sought Helen out.

First down to Rosie's and then to the cardhouse

Mike spoke quickly, slurring his words. 'Sylvia—she needs you. Says she won't talk to anyone else. I can't do anything with her. She's squiffy as hell. I can't—' He caught at her arm in dumb appeal. 'She won't talk to anyone but you.'

Get six tall cowboys to carry my coffin

'Please,' Mike said. Please.'

Six purty maidens to sing me a song

She needed to escape the room, the eyes, the song, the singer. Insistent and mocking, the voice followed her as she moved off with Mike.

O beat the drum slowly and play the fife lowly

'You leave me,' she said to Mike over-loudly. 'I'll look after her.' The voice pursued her still. It had taken on another and dangerous dimension.

When I walked out in the streets of Laredo

She slammed the door. She leaned against it, her hot cheek pressed to the cold panel. Then she turned to face the bedroom.

Faint smoke lingered towards the ceiling, and on the table beside the bed stood a depleted bottle of gin and two large glasses, one overturned in its own puddle. The bed was crumpled. Sylvia lay face down, one brown arm crooked out from her body, the hand clenching and unclenching a corner of the bedcover. Hair tented her face.

'Get out,' she said, jerking convulsively. 'Get out you bastard.'

'It's only me,' Helen said quietly. She went to the bed.

Fingering back her hair, Sylvia raised her face. The skin was puffy, the make-up smudged by tears; her eyes were bleak. 'I'm sorry,' she murmured. Her breath caught in her throat; she smiled, crookedly. 'I'm sorry,' she said again.

'Are you all right?' Helen said.

'I'm all right.' Sylvia tried to smile again. 'There's only one thing wrong with me. Too much thinking.'

'Thinking?'

'About how it's only a dirty cheat, the things they put in music and poetry.'

She gave Helen no pause for reply.

'No? You'll find out what a cheat it is. There's no beautiful things. Just

116

randy bastards and chemists' shops.' A shudder rippled through her body. 'Where's your Gerry, anyhow? What've you done with him?'

'He's somewhere. I don't know.'

'Poor old Gerry. He doesn't know what to make of you. He thinks he might be in on a win if he had an intelligent wife. But you only get him all balled up. What he really needs is a decorative blonde like me. So you've been with them—with the others, all night?'

'Of course.'

Sylvia laughed. 'I knew you didn't understand.'

'What don't I understand?'

Sylvia's laugh rang again. 'Tom Anderson's not interested in you. He's playing a game with Gerry. Can't you see? He—' Her voice broke. Helen tried to force her back to the pillow. The hysteria subsiding, they fought wordlessly. Presently Sylvia lay silent. Helen drew back from the bed.

'I'm sorry,' Sylvia murmured. 'It's not true what I said. I didn't mean to say it—I don't know—' She sat up and pointed to the door. 'Go on. Before it's too late to try. Go back and find him.' She seemed to choke. 'And God help you.'

Outside, there were voices: a door banged; someone laughed. Helen ran from the bedroom. Along the passage Gerald and Mike blocked her way.

'It's all right,' Gerald said. 'They've gone. We got rid of them.'

'Where did they go?' she said.

'They've gone,' Gerald repeated. 'Gone.'

'Sylvia,' Mike said, as Sylvia came stumbling along the passage. 'You should've stayed—'

'What do you think you're doing?' Gerald said to Helen.

'Can't you see?' she said. 'I'm putting on my coat.'

He caught at her shoulders. She tried to burst free, but he held tight, beginning to shake her. 'Can't you see—can't you . . .' The words bubbled in his throat; his face quivered. She couldn't be angry. She could only be sorry.

There was not even choice now. Even if flight was futile, pursuit pointless, she might at least know her own face in the mirror.

Confused, struggling, the four were bunched in the narrow hallway. Sylvia's hand smacked twice across Mike's face. Mike, recoiling, lurched against Gerald, and Helen broke free of him at last: she escaped through the front door into a silent world laced with moonlight: trees, gardens, and then streets, pale, empty and echoing.

3

Somewhere she had taken a wrong turn. She was lost. The familiar city was behind her; ahead it was new and strange. Sagging and weed-tangled, rickety buildings lined the way; and unlit windows.

She ran still: she ran until the feet ringing behind her slowed and a voice called her name. She leaned against a wooden wall and waited until Sylvia, limping, came to stand beside her.

They looked at each other without words; their breathing sobbed. A loose shop-awning flapped in the wind. Sylvia moved nearer.

'I should have made you understand,' she said. 'It was no good. That boy and—'

'But I knew,' Helen said.

'You knew? Then why—'

There was a pause. They were clinging together as though in fright. The wind grieved through overhead wires: it slapped and rustled, nipping them with cold. Sylvia lifted her head and tried to speak.

'No,' Helen whispered. 'Don't say anything at all.'

KNOCK ON YESTERDAY'S DOOR

1

Turning without hesitation into the remembered door, he escaped from the hot world where trams banged between old wooden buildings, where the dying sun left cooling veins of colour in the sky. Inside the house worn carpet tracked up the stairway and then his feet struck creaks from the warped wood; at the top of the stairs he took breath, and moved down the dim passage to the door of the flat.

He heard a woman singing.

His knuckles hit three times on the varnished wood: inside the flat the song was silenced. Sandalled feet slapped towards the door; the door swung open a little way.

'Who is it?' Val said, peering into the gloom; her voice was tremulous, slight. 'Who—'

The open door let an angle of light fall into the passage: he moved into it. 'Only me,' he said. 'Roger. Remember?'

'Roger? But—' Her arms jerked in a small theatrical gesture. 'Roger,' she repeated softly, pleased now.

There was an awkward moment. Then she opened the door wide.

'Come in, Roger,' she said.

He moved past her, into the flat, gathering the faintest smell of perfume. And then he stood in the small living-room, embarrassed, out of place. Val always made him feel large and clumsy. She closed the door and turned her back on it; the snapping lock sounded final. He was trapped with her; there was no escape. She leaned back against the door, looking at him in astonishment still. His confidence was gone already. He wished he had not come.

'So,' she said. 'After all this time.' The crisp voice conveyed nothing.

'It's a long time,' he agreed inadequately. He had a giddy feeling; liquor lay warm in his empty stomach.

'Fancy,' she said. 'Roger. Back from the dead. Nobody's heard anything about you in a long time. Not since—'

'No,' he said quickly. 'I've never written letters.'

'I imagined you might be settled somewhere by now. Married, probably. In a little, well-weeded garden of content.' She paused. 'You're not, though, are you?'

'No.'

'Not settled, not married, not in a little garden of content.' She sighed, smoke circling from her ovalled mouth. 'You disappoint me.'

'I'm sorry about that,' he said sullenly.

'Sensitive Roger,' she laughed. 'Poor old sensitive Roger. That's what Peter used to say.' She smiled, and added decisively, 'You haven't changed.'

'You aren't giving me much chance to prove anything else, are you?' he said with irritation. Awkward in the centre of the room, he was aware of growing discomfort. The heat of the day was suddenly more oppressive.

'For goodness sake, Roger,' she said with friendly sharpness. 'Loosen up. Relax. You look awful just standing there. Take off your coat and sit down.'

He obeyed.

'And stop looking like a startled rabbit. You'll stay to eat, won't you?'

'If you've plenty.'

'Of course I've plenty. Don't be so stuffy.'

A side of the room was partitioned with a curtain. Inside stood an electric stove, a half-size refrigerator, a sinkbench, and shelves of crockery and food. She began to click switches and bang pots down on the stove. 'It'll just be some poisonous hash,' she said. 'But you won't mind, will you?'

He tried to smile. 'I always did like your hash, remember?'

'Did you?' Smiling vaguely, she moved with method about the stove. 'Well, haven't you anything to tell me?' She began to peel onions.

'About what?'

'About what?' she repeated, mimicking his voice. 'Good God, man. About yourself. Where've you been? What've you done?'

'Who knows?'

'Don't you?'

Liquor was alive in his stomach again. 'What do you want to know about?' he demanded. 'The time I worked in a timber mill? The time I was a fisherman? Or the time I navvied on a road gang?' He was, he knew, boasting now; but he wanted to impress her, perhaps shock her.

'It all sounds interesting,' she said.

'I'll tell you about Jack,' he said. 'Jack was my cobber in the timber mill. Jack and I went on the bash every Saturday. In the first town out of the bush, twenty miles away. Drink all day and pay a visit to the local house at night. Nice girls. Every Saturday.'

'Sounds lively,' she murmured.

'The other stories are much the same,' he confessed.

Val was chopping the onions with a slow, meticulous motion. 'If alcohol's your problem,' she said, 'there's some sherry on the mantelpiece. Sorry about the other thing, though.'

He sat silent: her serene voice shamed him. He let his gaze wander. The room had not changed in two years: the old furniture Val had covered and painted, the rattan-shaded lamps, the record-player, the Dufy prints, the drawing of Peter, the candle in the empty chianti bottle on the mantelpiece, the decanter of sherry beside it. He appeared to be looking at an abandoned outpost of the republic of letters. Peter's desk remained prominent in a niche walled by bookshelves. The effect was of a shrine: the typewriter cased, papers and manuscripts in neat stacks, pens and pencils arranged in a rack, and an ashless ashtray. It was plain that Peter had long left the desk. Peter always worked in demented confusion, papers flooding the desk and falling to the floor.

'No,' Val said softly. 'You haven't changed, Roger. You're still full of yourself.'

'And I suppose Peter wasn't,' he said bitterly.

'He could forget himself sometimes.'

'You've got to live with yourself all the time.'

'And with other people,' Val added quietly.

'Remember that Sartre play you acted in?' he said. 'The one Peter thought so decadent? Hell is other people.'

'Heaven, too.'

'What do you mean?'

'Heaven is other people too, Roger.'

'Charming thought, anyway,' he said.

'One day,' Val said evenly, 'you might grow up. Meanwhile, do you want some sherry or not? Because I do.'

'I'm sorry,' he muttered. 'I forgot.' He fetched the decanter of sherry and poured two drinks. His hands were still unsteady. She left the stove and accepted her glass gracefully.

'Well,' she said, smiling. 'Here's to the return of the wanderer.' Their glasses touched lightly. 'Two years,' she said. 'And all that time you were running away.'

'If that's what you want to call it.'

'It's true, isn't it?' She paused. 'Didn't it work?'

He shrugged. Then he fell into a chair and looked at his sherry. 'No,' he said.

'And why have you come back?'

'Why does anyone?'

'That, if I may say so, is begging the question.'

'All right. I was curious. I wanted to see how different things were.'

'Things are different here, anyway,' she said, going back to the stove. 'That's obvious.'

A savoury smell drifted from the cooking food. He felt the sherry travelling down to his stomach. He had not eaten since he left the train. He brooded all day in pubs, hoping whisky might give him courage.

Why come back? The question had become tedious. He had begun to ask it when the express hissed along the platform in early morning sunlight. Why come back? Certainly not from curiosity. He needed to see if he had changed; he was sure he had. Yet here, in the familiar room where he thought he might discover the new self, he found himself slipping back into the skin of the old, truculent and cynical. He wanted to be honest. That intention seemed to be foundering. He felt lost, and helpless.

Perhaps they would talk of Peter presently.

If he could not see himself, he could at least see Val. Lately she had become lost behind Peter; now she was living and vivid, again the girl he knew.

She turned from the stove. 'Soon,' she promised. 'Nearly ready,' she said, moving towards him, slipping an unlighted cigarette into her mouth.

He had always watched with pleasure the economical movement of her limbs: the quick brown arms; the neat ankles and long legs; the firm thighs stirring behind a light skirt. He had known her before Peter. The two affairs could not have been more different: his own an end to agonized adolescence, the loss of innocence (though not the loss of hers: that body seemed never to have been a stranger to love) on the creaking springs of the old metal-posted bed where he spent the restless nights of his student life; the other a cautious courtship and marriage. Then she was no longer the girl, Val, who thrilled with whispering limbs and husky voice as no one since had done. She was a stranger; his best friend's girl, his best friend's wife.

She surveyed him gravely. 'You know something?' she said. 'It's comfortable, having you around again.'

He remained silent. Her expression grew cheeky. 'There's only one thing, though,' she added.

'What's that?'

'I can't argue as well as Peter.'

'You don't do badly.'

'Really? But you've no idea how much out of practice I am. I haven't heard a respectable argument since—well, since.'

2

Peter was never slow to make himself heard.

At college there were collisions with teachers; he always seemed to win before teachers took shelter. Peter, with the insolence of adolescence, accepted nothing; questioned everything.

The college was a modern one, with new paint and fresh concrete, and bright classrooms; the headmaster a mild grey and mostly tolerant man. But Peter bewildered him; after a classroom disturbance, he often escorted Peter to his study and begged him to be more moderate. Roger, on the other hand was nothing if not temperate.

Through college they were together in school debate; together in the backline of the school rugby team. In their last year they jointly edited the college magazine; and together resigned when publication of Peter's contributions was forbidden after a panicky staff conference. The headmaster saw, in an article on modern education and a piece of political satire on the atom bomb, anarchism flowering darkly in his airy new college. Roger's own contribution, a harmless piece of nature verse, remained in the re-edited magazine; Peter, kind though rarely condescending, saw promise in it and advised him to write more. But because he saw what Peter left unspoken he never wrote another.

Peter's university politics all but estranged them. That remained odd. It was Roger who had the working-class and radical credentials. Peter's father was a doctor of liberal opinion imprisoned and ill-treated as a conscientious objector in the first world war. Disillusioned with all political and moral remedy, he died while Peter was at university, a tubercular and prematurely frail old man who had long purged his self-respect to become an acceptable member of society. On the other hand, Roger's father was once a militant union organizer. He still smoked a pipe with his old leftist cronies and mourned the lost revolution in the corner pub, and once a month presided over bleak meetings of his Labour Party branch. Roger had seen him arrested as a picketing strike leader.

Roger accepted his father's defeat; Peter had only contempt for his father's surrender.

Peter had still to feel the pressure of the world. Roger had lived with it all his life. He remembered his handcuffed father, the schoolboy taunts. He had learned to keep his distance, keep his silence.

So now he kept a distance from Peter. They would differ; he found literary allies in Koestler and Gide. 'All right,' Peter said. 'So Stalin isn't a Christ who walks on water. So what? Do you deny a religion because of the immorality of a priest?' Even if he accepted Peter's Communism and new sharp-talking friends with reserve, they still saw each other often. After evening lectures at university they sometimes wandered talking through the city, through bright streets and dim lanes, and along the waterfront past fishing boats and glittering water.

At university he moved among a different set; a drifting common-room element, sporty and party-going. Sometimes there were questions: 'I say, aren't you a friend of that Peter what's-his-name, that Commo character? You are? I thought so. You're a Commo too, I suppose. What's that? You're not? Well, what do you know about that?' Peter was soon singled out for abuse by the right wing in the university; and for jest by indolent common-room intellectuals. Communism in the 1950s was an anachronism, a foolish survival from the 1930s; the 1950s knew better. Roger would argue this and other things with Peter. 'I take it, then,' Peter answered calmly, 'that you approve of the way things are now?'

'Don't be absurd. Of course not.'

'Then what alternative is there?'

'Doubt,' he argued. 'Of everything.'

Then he found Val. He met her after a play, a drearily produced Ibsen piece in which her acting was the only thing of interest. She was naive and impressionable; and he, for a time, must have impressed her.

Inevitably, Val met Peter. He had seen no significance in their meeting; not even when his undergraduate liaison with Val came to an end. He saw other reasons for the break.

So he felt no grievance when he learned Val was living with Peter. If he felt resentment at all, it was not for Peter taking Val, but for Val coming between himself and Peter. When they married Roger was best man. Other things were less happy, not least when Val's father, president of his city's Chamber of Commerce, discovered Peter's political affiliation.

Roger saw less of Peter. His degree uncompleted, Peter left university in despair of students and intellectuals after the collapse of the radical club he had organized there. It had flourished under Peter's erratic leadership; and then died when his efficient, cold-eyed party-lining friends began to take over behind scenes. Students in sympathy with Peter's initial rebellion soon drifted away. Peter chose to blame the drifting students, and not his friends.

He took a job as an unskilled labourer and became active in trade union politics. And now that Roger no longer saw Peter about the university, he had often to get news through Val, when he met her in a corridor. 'He's just the same,' she would say with a swift, deprecating gesture. 'Busy with his Party work nearly every night of the week. Did I tell you he's been elected president of his trade union? Oh, yes—and he's still trying to find time to write a novel.'

If he called around to the flat to see Peter, Val would of course be there, moving lightly about the room while they talked, singing softly as she dispensed coffee or cooked a meal. Marriage seemed to give Peter strength. He argued against Roger with confidence. The world might, in Roger's eyes, be falling to pieces; but Peter, deftly sorting the pieces, would show dialectical shape where Roger could see only confusion; see hope where Roger could see only despair.

But something was wrong now. Peter's fluency had always had a glib edge; with sincerity, it had not seemed so important. It now became irritating. He was no longer questioning, gently exploratory. He marshalled words for defence and attack along a fixed front. Peter had all the answers and no questions.

Roger felt betrayed. All this time he had been perversely wishing Peter right. Was it he who had changed, or Peter?

So their arguments mounted. Rancour too.

Caught between Peter's formulas and the complacency of his other friends, he cried finally, 'Only one hope for us all. The bomb. And let it come quickly.'

Peter turned away in disgust.

Val laid two bamboo mats on the dining-table; then arranged knives and forks for the meal. 'Remember the night when you and Peter had that big row?' she said. 'I didn't ever think we'd see you again.'

'You nearly didn't,' he said. 'It was almost a year, wasn't it?'

'Too long,' she said.

Finished with university, he found himself aimless in the world. After their final, seemingly irrevocable argument, he never saw nothing of Peter; and Val almost never. He did hear, through a remote connexion, that Peter's trade union had sent him to a peace congress at Vienna, and that he had travelled back through the Soviet Union and China. The person who told him was impressed by the fact that Peter had met Sartre, but knew little else.

He was tired of the people he knew, the parties. He toyed briefly with the idea of joining the army to go to Korea; then rejected it, for no reason other than the probability of his own discomfort, and the possibility of his own death. He told himself there was no moral issue. He took a job on a newspaper. He told himself there was no issue there, either; that his cynicism might serve him well.

'The bomb,' he would say, drunk and joking, in pubs, at parties. 'The redeemer of us all.'

So that, eventually, even his own shiftless set of companions sickened of him. They saw him as someone with a mental quirk; a tiresome oddity.

3

'Why did you come back?' Val asked.

'That's twice you've asked me that.'

'The other time, I mean. Not this time.'

'The reason's probably no different, then.'

'From curiosity? Surely not.'

He hesitated. 'Because I needed to,' he said.

'And you needed to this time as well?'

'Yes,' he agreed.

She smiled then: the smile discovered dimples in her cheeks. 'Like to wash before the meal?' she said.

'Love to.'

In the bathroom he stripped to the waist and splashed cooling water over his sticky flesh. As he towelled himself, he thought of Val; and found, in thinking of her, a mellow, warm sensation. He looked about him absently, seeing objects—limp nylons hanging to dry, face cream, hairpins, uncapped toothpaste, squares of white material tumbled in a container, a streaked tin of talcum, safety pins—that his mind made no attempt to sort and classify; so that he might as well not have seen them at all.

When he turned back, it was to Peter, not to the hope Peter might have offered.

In the flat again, after a year, it was as if there had been no year. Nothing seemed changed. Val's welcome was warm; and Peter, sliding his chair back from the untidy desk, rose gravely to his feet, hitched up his corduroys, and drew up another chair for Roger as though they were about to resume a conversation discontinued the day before. He ran a large freckled hand through his hair and grinned slyly at Roger. There were warm minutes as Val fetched coffee, and then all three began to talk quickly. He saw, with astonishment that Peter was as glad to see him as he was to see Peter. He didn't attempt to account for this.

For he didn't observe Peter as older or altered. There was still the surface swagger, the angry brilliance. He wanted to find the old Peter; he found what he wanted to find.

Certainly Peter's life was changed. He had abandoned his union position to return to university. And he was no longer out at meetings most nights of the week. The explanation seemed to be that Peter was giving a good deal of his time to writing. Peter must have made the decision—or the Party made the decision for him—that he would be more effective politically as an intellectual than as a worker.

He felt close to Peter again; Val too. When they argued, Peter was less dogmatic, if no less optimistic. They often found agreement. Peter presented his writing for approval. The polemic for left-wing magazines was skilfully argued. But Roger could feel no enthusiasm for the other literary work, a sheaf of stories. The approach was mechanical, the characters wooden. There was also the distinct beat of an ideological drum. Roger hid his disappointment.

Only once, in the months that followed, did he detect something irregular. It was a summer evening: they had been on a beach picnic. They returned tired and salty and flushed with sun, and, after taking turns with the shower and eating a light meal together, they were working about the flat. Val ironed the weekend wash while he and Peter cleaned and dried dishes. He liked slipping into their domestic routine.

Roger was talking of the virtues and failings of a once mutual friend. Peter, teatowel in hand, lazily ignored the damp dishes gathering on the sinkbench. Sitting legs astride a back-to-front chair, he listened to what Roger said; a fist propped his chin and his face was attentive. Beyond the curtain partition, Val sang as she ironed.

The friend was an ex-Catholic. Among Catholics he was anticlerical: yet with non-Catholics he took up a curiously defensive position for the church, and even argued in favour of much he attacked in different company.

Then he found himself talking of intolerance. The fish-eyes, the fanatics, were surely always the danger. He used as example Peter's radical club at university. It had been successful so long as it was loose. It died as soon as the fish-eyes, the dogmatists, arrived to squeeze it into austere shape. Rigid form always pressured out the original idea. It was, he added, the same in art as in politics.

When it occurred to him that the conversation had become one-sided, he glanced sidelong at Peter and saw his face surprisingly troubled.

Roger looked away quickly, guiltily. He seemed to be intruding on private territory. 'You see what I mean, don't you?' he resumed hastily, without much regard for what he said. 'The laughing boys might make the revolution, but it's the fish-eyes who determine it in the end.'

He turned to Peter. 'You're not saying anything,' he observed.

The pensive expression was gone: Peter smiled and blinked. 'Absolutely, old chap,' he said. 'Absolutely.' He levered himself up from his chair. 'Don't worry yourself about him. He'll snap out of it. Ex-Catholics are like that.' Peter paused. 'What's wrong, old chap? You look a bit startled. Did I lose the thread somewhere?'

Roger was perplexed rather than hurt by the discovery that Peter hadn't been listening. It was not like Peter. Nor the dark expression. On the other hand Peter and he were differing less. He was even tempted to tell Peter that he was ready to involve himself, to join Peter in the Communist Party.

The occasion never came.

He called at the flat one afternoon and found Val alone. She had been weeping; her eyes were bleak. Guessing a domestic quarrel, he pretended not to notice; and asked where Peter had gone.

'Christ knows,' she said bitterly. 'I thought he'd be with you somewhere.'

'Why me?'

'Why you?' she snapped. 'As if you didn't know.'

'Know what?'

'The performance he's been putting on for you. Since you're his only friend, the only one he can perform for now. And you're making it no better. Oh, yes—you kid him along, get him going. I wish to hell you had to live with him.'

He heard her out. Peter had been expelled from the Party months before. The ostensible reason given was breaches of Party discipline; the real reason that Peter refused to accommodate some solemn directive. Since his expulsion there had been a campaign of invective, to discourage other dissenters. That was why Peter's life had quietened; Old political friends avoided him; and Roger was one of the few visitors to the flat.

'I thought it might have done him good, having you here again,' Val said. 'I thought it might have got him outside himself. But all you've done is given him your own bloody sickness.'

'But look, Val,' he tried to explain. 'He almost recruited me—' But it was no use; Val was too distraught to grasp his meaning.

'You act so terribly innocent. Stringing him along. Making it worse.'

It was no use trying to make her understand when he couldn't understand himself. He left her then; he had never seen the flat or Val again until tonight.

4

In the darkening room, meal finished and coffee-cups drained, they sat silent on the cushioned window seat. Outside, the city was bright in the blue dusk. Traffic noises came faintly through the open window.

She stirred. She said quietly, 'You see, I blamed myself first. It hurt too much; so I blamed you. But it wasn't either of us. Not anyone, really. And even if there was someone to blame, it wouldn't matter. Not now.' She paused. 'So don't blame yourself. Or imagine I do. You weren't to blame.'

He wished he could believe that. For he had never questioned the lunacy of those last two weeks.

He found Peter drunk and maudlin in a waterfront pub which once Peter frequented with his leftist friends. Ignored by the same people, he drank alone in a corner. He reviled Roger and Val as well as old friends; no one could be excluded from his disillusion.

Peter assured him he had left Val for good. He laughed when Roger suggested he return to her. 'What?' he demanded. 'And have her swallow me down in some little suburban swamp? Get me bogged down with a house, a kid and a garden? Do you think she's different from any other woman? Do you?'

Roger saw unreason; he saw everything sharply. For months Peter had argued with Roger's scepticism, pretending everything the same. The masquerade was over. What price an iconoclast without a faith?

As for Val, Roger might have argued injustice. Hadn't she been loyal? Her kind of faith outlasted the most seductive ideology. He was too shaken to argue anything.

'I'm finished with this bar,' Peter announced. 'I know better ones. Coming?' And, of course, he followed. Even a disenchanted iconoclast needed an acolyte.

He pursued Peter from one bar to another, one city to another. The chase was never less than demented. There were bars smelling like urinals, parties with smashing windows, awakenings in hotel rooms with peeling wallpapers, cracked mirrors. Could fury go further? It could.

At the end there was the key waiting to be twisted in the ignition; the car ready to be stolen.

They had been at a party; he missed Peter suddenly. He went outside in time to see the headlights flare, the car lurch off into the night.

He ran after it, calling out, stumbling, falling, running again.

They were silent once more: he was conscious of her proximity. Her reflective face was lit by the lights beyond the window. She leaned forward, elbows on knees, hands linked loosely. Finally she moved. She clicked a switch and the room filled with warm light. The windows became dark mirrors which caught Val's bright reflection as she drew curtains.

'I must see how Peter is,' she announced.

His stomach lurched. 'Peter?' he said faintly.

'He's been a bit feverish all day. The heat. I fed him and put him to bed before you came.' She went to the bedroom door.

A sick mind, he thought; a sick mind feeding on fantasy. She must have seen his expression; she drew back from the door. 'What's the matter?' she said. 'Didn't you know?'

Of course: the flat was different, Val was different. But he had still been seeing another flat, another Val. Even in the bathroom: the tumbled white squares, the streaked talcum, the safety pins; his eyes had declined to interpret their meaning. Then just what had he expected at that moment? Peter to come walking in the door?

5

The skid-marks ran up a steep angle of road, over a grass verge, and stopped at the edge of a bank. The car, carried by its own momentum, must have hurtled some distance through space: they found it, bashed and tangled, at the foot of a slanting power pole.

In the dazzling headlamps they gathered about the flung figure with shredded clothes and torn face. A car sped away to fetch doctor and ambulance; but the haste, Roger saw, was pointless.

Peter opened his eyes, once, and saw him. Recognition came slowly. While engines hummed and brakes screeched and the crowd grew, the years dwindled to minutes, and the minutes to seconds, and they looked at each other.

'Here it comes,' someone shouted.

There was an ambulance siren and flashing lights.

Peter stirred, the pain shocking his body and twisting his face. He smiled weakly and his dry lips moved. The siren grew louder. No words came.

The eyes shadowed and closed: he withdrew from the body in a slow, sighing motion. The sudden void was filled with the strange voices, and the fading whimper of the siren.

Their movement into the room woke the child. It stirred, eyes blinking open, small hands clutching, pink lips parting. It had kicked in restless, fevered sleep, churning the miniature sheets and blankets in the cot.

'Hello,' Val said softly, taking up the child. 'Hello, Peter.'

Seeing Roger, the child buried his face in Val's neck.

'Doesn't like strangers,' Roger observed lamely.

'Fancy you not knowing,' Val said.

'It would never have occurred to me.'

'A year and four months,' she said.

'Then Peter—' he began, shocked.

'I knew,' Val said. 'But Peter—' She shook her head. 'He never knew. At least I don't think so. I didn't want to tell him. It would have been— well, just one more complication.' She paused; she was frowning now, and withdrawn. 'At least I think so. It would have been just one more thing to blame me for.' She paused again, uncertainly. 'I don't know. Perhaps he guessed I was pregnant. Perhaps that was the trouble. Then again, if I had told him, perhaps he wouldn't have gone. I've never been sure. I wish I knew. I've never been sure.'

She found a smile and held the kicking child high for inspection. 'Don't you think he's a fine boy?' she said.

'Yes,' he said thickly. 'A fine boy.'

The child glimpsed Roger again, and began to cry. Val stroked his back soothingly. 'Peter doesn't think you look friendly,' she said shrewdly. 'Why don't you say something nice to him?'

'Like what?'

'Like "Hello, Peter."'

Roger took the child's tiny bunched fist. 'Hello, Peter,' he said, feeling foolish. 'Hello, Peter.'

Then he saw likeness. As it puckered painfully, the soft child's face was suddenly the face in the headlights. He turned away quickly.

'What's wrong?' Val said.

'Nothing.'

He forced himself to look at the child again. The likeness was gone; he must have imagined it. Small grey eyes now regarded him curiously, without fear. 'Hello, Peter,' he whispered. The child smiled uncertainly.

'I shan't be long,' Val said. 'I'll settle him down for the night. Go and make more coffee if you like.'

He went gratefully from the bedroom, made fresh coffee, sat on the window seat. Val was some time with the child. He could hear her crooning softly. He pictured her bent over the cot; painful to picture. Presently she backed out of the bedroom and closed the door quietly. 'He's all right now,' she said.

'Sorry I frightened him.'

'You?' Her eyebrows lifted; she seemed a little amused as she poured coffee and relaxed in a low chair. 'I thought it was the other way about.'

Her insight irritated him. 'Why should I be frightened of a baby?' he said.

She shrugged. 'You would know.'

'What are you getting at?' he demanded. 'That I'm jealous?'

That was the point: he could see that.

'Partly,' Val said.

'I still don't see it, then.'

'I can't explain,' she said. 'Stupid to think I could. He was never a hero to me, I knew him as he was. That was enough.'

'Meaning I had illusions?'

'Didn't you?'

He thought on his answer. 'I'm not tending his shrine,' he pointed out.

'He's very dead, Val.'

'Of course,' she said calmly.

'Just another failure. Like his father. Like mine. Like me. He didn't amount to anything either. Nothing he said mattered; nothing he wrote. History had moved on. He missed the train by all of twenty years anyway. He found himself waiting on the same empty platform as me. He couldn't take it. Now tell me to get out.'

She declined to. 'Is that what you want?'

'Not especially.' Nevertheless, he had risen.

'Someone once said there is no such thing as success. There are only different kinds of failure.'

'Possibly.' He found himself looking at the drawing of Peter, then looking away. It wasn't the face of a conspicuous failure. Nor was it that of a success. On the other hand, Peter must have mattered. For why argue with the face now?

'Anyway it's not the point,' she said.

'No?'

'The thing is that he tried.'

'He what?'

'Tried,' she said.

He was beginning to sweat again. He resumed his seat limply. She was right: Val mostly had been. Now she had to spell it out for him.

'Some people never try,' she said.

6

He was not long leaving. Val accompanied him to the street. They stood together in the mild evening.

'What do you plan to do now?' she asked.

'Some thinking. Some reading. Perhaps even some writing.'

'Meaning what?'

'Someone has to try making sense of things. I might have twopence worth to put in.'

'Better than nothing,' she suggested.

'My thought too,' he said.

They were silent. Then he went on, 'It was all worse than he knew. Or perhaps he did know and didn't want to. Anyway he didn't live to see the horror of human engineering. The fake trials, the executions, the concentration camps.'

She didn't flinch.

'Now it's back to one thing at a time. Each day as it comes.'

'Perhaps,' she said.

'What about you?'

'There's Peter,' she said.

'Of course.'

'Otherwise I'm back teaching. Sometimes I manage a play. As you say, one thing at a time; each day as it comes. Like today, for example. You will come again?'

'If you'd like that.'

'I would,' she confessed. 'If you want books, quiet, perhaps a desk too, you know where to find them. I knew there was a reason for keeping things as they were. Who knows?'

He wasn't willing to speculate either. Most of her face was in shadow. 'I hope,' he began, but failed to finish.

'So do I,' she said.

Her lips darted against his cheek. She ran into the house. He heard her feet creaking up the stairs; and, more faintly, a child's cry.

He stood still for a time. He was less exhausted than he might have been. He would not take a tram into the city; he would walk back to his hotel through bright streets and dark. He wanted to hear his own footsteps, see his own shadow leaping ahead. Not that it was all he wanted. The rest could wait.

A young couple dawdled past him laughing mysteriously in the summer dark.

He began to walk.

In the Blind Canyon

MARIA

HE first saw Eleanor, after so many years, in Soho one summer afternoon. She was half-concealed in a doorway, a sketchbook held awkwardly before her; her face had that concentrated, almost tormented expression he had once known well. She had a pencil fixed between her teeth and was industriously rubbing away with a finger at something he could not see. When he cried her name, she started and her eyes widened with fright. Then, as if seeing him were the most predictable thing in the world, she took the pencil from her mouth, smiled quickly and held up a hand for silence. He slipped into the doorway beside her. 'What are you doing here?' he said. She held up the finger again. 'Please,' she whispered urgently, and ignored him. Looking over her shoulder and raising his eyes from the vivid black lines of the drawing, he saw from her viewpoint, through two dusty distorting sheets of plate-glass, the small scene a little way along the opposite side of the street. In front of a short stretch of brick wall spattered with torn posters, three girls smoked and ambled along sunlit pavement. Their figures were long-shadowed in the late afternoon; the cigarette smoke curled upwards in the sultry air. It was a lifeless day and passers-by were infrequent; a car snarled sluggishly around a nearby corner; a cash-register rang from an espresso bar. And the girls paraded hopefully. Their beat was confined at one end by an alley; at the other by a line of cascading garbage cans.

'Good old Eleanor,' he said. 'You haven't gone abstract yet, I see. Still the good social realist.'

'Shut up,' she said. 'Just for a moment.'

Idling lazily in the sunlight, the girls re-arranged themselves. One, a short plump creature in tight red frock, called amiably to someone across the street, whispered something behind her hand to her companions, and burst into shrill laughter. Eleanor turned the page of her sketchbook and began a fresh drawing. He could see she had done several.

'Wouldn't it be more convenient if you sat in a car, or something?' he said. 'It might be more comfortable.'

'Please be practical,' she hissed, 'and shut up.' Her pencil snapped back and forward over the new page. He observed that she noted a scene in an impressively neat fashion. Her style had always been precise.

One of the girls reclined against the wall, her knee jutting forward, as she looked in her handbag for cigarettes. She was tall, long-legged, and remarkably well figured; she had long black hair and a darkish complexion. She wore a blue suit with a split skirt that flashed white petticoat as she jiggled in her handbag.

'The tall one's new,' he said.

'You know a lot,' she said. She turned to a new page.

'Aren't you sick of it yet?' he said.

'You don't have to wait for me.'

'I don't think it's healthy for girls to stand alone in doorways here. Had any pick-ups yet?'

'Lots,' she said briskly, and went on drawing.

'What the hell is all this anyway?' he demanded. 'Is this all you can find in the old world? Garbage cans and tarts?'

'Oh God,' she said. She banged the sketchbook shut. 'What's the use?' She glared at him. 'Well, you might at least be decent enough to take me to coffee—now you've spoiled everything.'

They left the doorway. 'And you,' he said, 'might at least say how pleased you are to see me.'

'All right. How pleased I am to see you.'

'Fine. That's settled anyway. How are you keeping? How long have you been over here?'

'I'm keeping well, thank you. And I've been here just two months.'

'I wish at least you'd *act* pleased to see me.'

'Oh,' she said. 'But I am.'

'Act interested, I mean.'

'I'll try.'

'Now,' he said. 'Let's begin at the beginning. I expect you won a scholarship or something.'

'It's or something. Let's wait till coffee. I'm parched.'

Eleanor, he thought. Sweet, prim Eleanor. He hadn't seen her for three, four, nearly five years. She was unchanged, still the quaint old-fashioned Methodist girl from a lush Taranaki dairy farm who walked briskly into art school out of a bright Auckland summer morning.

'How's everyone at home?' he asked, over coffee. 'Tell me all the news.'

'The country's bankrupt,' she said, 'but apart from that things are fine.'

'For example,' he said. 'How's Ed?'

'Ed? Well, Ed went into advertising, you know. He was a great success.

He bought a big car and crashed it. Now he's in a wheelchair for the rest of his life.'

'Well, that's an encouraging start.'

'You want to go down the list? Well, there's Eric. Remember Eric? The pale little nervous boy with the tic who painted awful nudes? Well, he was in a mental hospital two years. Now he's fine; he's given up art and gone Polynesian, up in Northland among the mangroves somewhere. Then who else do you know? Well, there's Norm. You know, the quiet one, did ghastly abstracts. He found out he was colour-blind; and got married. And Peter? Yes, of course you must have known Peter. Well; Peter gave up painting and began writing a novel. He gave up the novel and began writing short stories. He gave up short stories for poetry. And he gave up poetry for the development of an entirely new literary form. He worked on that two years and then went into business. Now who else? Oh, yes—Robin. Robin announced there was no possibility of a native art being created in New Zealand, became homosexual, and got arrested last year for forging cheques.'

'Enough,' he said. 'You haven't mentioned the girls yet.'

'Well, there's Sheila. Sheila had two abortions and married a racehorse trainer. Marjorie went teaching among the Maoris; haven't heard of her in years. Beverley had a fling at documentary films in Wellington. Susie married a Catholic and has three babies now. Barbie became the mistress of that terrible little poet creature on the North Shore, pined for love when he dropped her, and got TB. Sarah's very successful as a dress designer and Evelyn's absolutely magnificent as a gossip columnist. Now who else?'

'There's yourself. You seem to have survived.'

'After a fashion.'

'You look as virginal as ever.'

'Thank you. You always say the sweetest things.' Once, long ago, she would have blushed. As she had in the days when, drab and timid and a butt for jokes, she came to their rowdy student parties.

'Now can I have my turn? What happened to you after you came over here on that scholarship?'

'Quite simple, really. I lost interest.'

'And stayed here?'

'And stayed here.'

'I think it's disgusting,' she said. 'Really disgusting. All that money gone to waste. And what do you do now?'

'As little as I can. Sometimes I work in a gallery.'

'And don't you want to go back?'

'To that dump? Never.'

'You know,' she said accusingly, 'I suspect you've become a rootless cosmopolitan.'

'Probably,' he said.

'I'd be ashamed to admit it.'

'But you are not the one admitting it, my dear.'

'After a while you all talk alike, look alike. You all want to be so, so individualistic, and you're the most regimented crowd I've ever seen in my life. Walk through Greenwich Village, along the Left Bank, through Soho— and what do you find?'

'Us,' he said. 'The rootless cosmopolitans.'

'You know,' she said. 'I don't think I like you.'

'I don't mind, so long as you pay for the coffee.'

'You make a religion of art, and when art turns empty, what have you got?'

'Rootless cosmopolitanism, as you say, my dear.'

'You've got no values. Nothing.'

'All right. So you don't like me.'

'I'm sure I don't. Now, shall we go?'

They walked back along the street. There was only one girl, the tall dark one, left in front of the wall. 'She's very pretty,' Eleanor said. 'I can't understand it. Why does she do it?'

'Shall I ask her? I'll say the lady wants to know.'

'Don't be ridiculous.'

'I'm serious.'

'You dare make a fool of me and I'll—'

But he crossed the street jauntily, hands in pockets, and began to talk to the girl. Eleanor paused uncertainly, hot and flushed, on the other side. He talked to the girl for a while. Then he walked back.

'Why don't you come and meet her?' he said. 'Her name's Maria and she comes from Spain. Came here to work for an uncle who runs a cafe. But he was not a nice man. Now, as you see, she is independent of him— more or less.' He took her arm. 'Come and meet her.'

'Really, I don't—'

He steered her across the street. 'You always want to observe the wicked world from a distance,' he said. 'Now be brave. Meet it face to face.'

'I hate you. I—'

'This is Maria,' he said.

The tall girl smiled down at Eleanor.

'Go on, you old puritan,' he said. 'Be polite. Say something.'

Eleanor stood blinking in the sunlight. And the tall girl still smiled. One idle day, some two weeks later, he took a bus out to Notting Hill Gate, to the address Eleanor had left with him. He was some time finding the place; it was an old house just off Portobello Road. She lived up two flights of creaking stairs.

'Hello,' he said, when she opened the door. 'Just wondering if you'd like to see a little more low life.'

Her room, facing the sunlit street, was large and bright. It was neat and tidy, everything in place. Eleanor was dressed, in businesslike fashion, in slacks and paint-smeared check shirt.

'You're low life enough for me,' she said. 'Thank you.'

'Well,' he said, 'if you're working, don't mind me. I'll just make myself at home anyway.' He fell into a chair.

'I can see that.' She went to the gas-ring in the corner. 'I expect you want some coffee.'

'The hospitality overwhelms me.'

'Why can't you talk like a normal person? Behave like a normal person?' She lit the gas and filled the percolator. 'The strange thing is I thought you were rather fun, once. I used to like you.'

'I must say you always showed it marvellously.' He rose and walked about the room. 'Mind if I look?' He nodded towards some drawings and water-colours in a dustless corner.

'I don't doubt you'll look anyway. But go ahead.'

'You're improving,' he said presently. 'I always thought you took yourself too seriously to get anywhere. You worked so hard. Had an exhibition yet?'

'In Wellington. Just before I left.'

'Sell anything?'

'Two pictures.'

'Quite. Another prophet without honour departs.'

'Not at all. You see, I don't happen to see the need for forever carrying a chip on one's shoulder about one's country. And using it as an excuse for doing nothing. Like some people.'

'Well hell,' he said. 'You dear old patriotic philistine.' He paused. 'Hey, what's this?' He held up a drawing of a woman's head: it was sharp, austere, high-featured, rather striking.

'Don't you remember? That's the girl we met. Maria. I ran into her again.'

'Just by chance?' he said.

'Of course,' she said.

'Really,' he said. 'Amazing.'

'We took coffee together.'

'And she sat for you?'

'Yes.'

'How wonderfully fortuitous. And did you try to save her soul?'

'Why do you have to give such an excellent impression of being an imbecile?'

'You surprise me.'

'As a matter of fact, I found her rather a pleasant girl. Isn't *simpatico* what you say?'

'Only rather unfortunate in the choice of profession.'

'It seems to me, for all your talk, that you are the one who wants to erect barriers.'

'So naturally you'll invite her here for coffee one day?'

'Naturally.'

'My God,' he said.

'As a matter of fact, she wanted to see the drawing when it was finished.'

'They'd love to hear about this at home, wouldn't they?' He dropped back into his chair and laughed. 'Dear me. It's too rich to be true.'

'I think you are deliberately misunderstanding me. Her life is her own business. I'm not trying to change it.'

'Oh no,' he said. 'Of course not. Nothing could be further from your mind.'

She poured the coffee. 'Do you take sugar?' she asked, coldly.

When he next called, on a Sunday afternoon three weeks or a month afterwards, he found Maria curled on a couch. 'Surprise, surprise,' he said. '*Buenas tardes.*'

She sat up uneasily, her large ear-rings swinging, and looked to Eleanor for reassurance.

'You're worse than a bad penny,' Eleanor said. She turned to Maria, smiling. 'You remember him, don't you?'

'Yes,' Maria said. 'I remember.'

'Well, seeing how you've come all the way up the stairs, you might as well stay for a bit,' Eleanor said.

He sat. There was a silence as Eleanor fetched coffee.

'You are of New Zealand, also?' Maria said at last, tentatively.

'Unfortunately,' he said.

'Please?' she said, puzzled.

'Yes,' he said loudly. 'I am.'

'Oh,' she said. 'Eleanor tells me much of New Zealand. It is interesting country, no?'

'No,' he said.

'Please?'

'Not very interesting.'

'But it is of much beauty. Eleanor tells me of its beauty.'

'Really?'

She sat in distinct discomfort now, her hands fidgeting in her lap. Eleanor slipped between them with the coffee. Maria rose suddenly. 'I think it is my doorbell I hear,' she said. 'I think I must go.' She went across the room, out the door and down the stairs.

'What the hell is this all about?' he demanded.

'Quite simple, really. Maria is living downstairs.'

'Off the streets?'

'And happier for it,' Eleanor said aggressively.

'All right, all right. I didn't say a thing.'

'If you only knew what that girl has been through. All the people who lived off her.'

'You surprise me. And what is she doing now?'

'Well, she found things a little difficult at first, you know. But then she had an idea. Thought of it all herself. It wouldn't have occurred to me.'

'Really?'

'Yes. She's become a model. Apparently there's quite an extraordinary demand for models in London, you know. All a girl does is put up little notices advertising herself on notice-boards around the city.'

He looked at her incredulously. Only Eleanor could be so naive. 'And is she doing well?' he said.

'Wonderfully. Her rooms are directly underneath here; she's fixed up a kind of studio. She has her own telephone on that floor, fortunately. It's ideal. People come to her—she doesn't have to go to them. Amazing, isn't it? It's just because there is such an extraordinary demand. In the last couple of weeks she's had all sorts of customers.'

'I bet,' he said.

'Nothing moves you,' she said. 'Does it? I think it's wonderful that a girl can make such a clean break.'

'I must confess it incredible.'

'There you are,' she said. 'Even you have to admit it.'

He found he had to stand up and walk about the room to stop himself laughing outright. 'You must feel proud of yourself,' he said.

'Of course I am,' Eleanor laughed, bouncing off the couch to pour more coffee. She looked pretty and absurdly young today. 'But just the same, you know, you've got to give her credit. After all, I hardly had to do anything, apart from giving her encouragement at the right time. Basically she's a nice girl.'

'I'm sure.'

'I'm glad you think so. Try to be a little more pleasant to her, won't you? Remember she's been through such a lot. Underneath she has really a sensitive nature.'

'You must see quite a lot of her now.'

'Of course. She's in and out of here all the time when she's not working. Insists on cooking me paella and all kinds of things. She's teaching me Spanish. We might even go to Spain together for a while towards the end of the year. She comes from a fishing village near Alicante.'

'You're certainly having a jolly time together.'

He circled the room again, noticing some new drawings of Maria on the workbench, and then finally sat beside Eleanor on the couch. She was suddenly self-conscious; she looked down into her coffee. He reached out and turned her face towards him; he held her chin tightly cupped between thumb and forefinger. 'And how is Eleanor?' he said. 'Do you still remember old friends?'

'Why should I?' she said, shaking his hand from her face. 'I've never had friends.'

'Come, now,' he said persuasively. 'Wasn't I a good friend?'

'You?' She laughed.

'I did my best to help you. Didn't I?'

'I was always under the impression it was some kind of competition,' she said. 'To see who could first deflower the silly virgin from the cow-country and boast about it. And all that happened, so far as I could see, was that you came nearest to winning.'

'I think you're unkind, Eleanor.'

'You don't think I came twelve thousand miles to have all this over again, do you?'

'Didn't you expect to see me?'

'Oh, I knew I'd run into you again,' she said. 'Sometime or other. Unfortunately.'

He lay back on the couch, sliding an arm around her. 'Why don't you relax?' he said.

She still sat stiffly.

'If you want to try again, after five years, the answer is still no,' she said. 'Understand?'

But when he drew her down beside him, she did not at first resist. Her head rested on his shoulder; stared at the ceiling.

'You've been lonely, haven't you?' he said. 'I've been lonely myself.'

Her eyes were still staring, as if in surprise. She said nothing.

'Why can't we be friends? Instead of pecking at each other?'

'That's for you to say.' She closed her eyes, almost in pain.

'Why me?' he said softly.

He was stroking her hair, turning her face. Her stiff body began to flutter. Then she jerked away and a slap jolted his teeth together. She stood erect, hands on hips. He looked up at her in dismay.

'Why you?' she said. 'Because you've got to learn to stop playing with people.'

'But—'

'But nothing. Behind that mask of yours there's nothing left. Nothing. The person who fashioned that mask died a long time ago. Talking to you is like knocking on the door of an empty house.'

He rose clumsily, angrily. 'If you don't want—'

'No. Stay by all means. But don't expect me to be fooled.'

'Fooled?' He laughed. He zipped his jacket and made for the door. 'Fooled? That's rich, coming from you. Fooled? Oh my God.' He stood, for a moment, in the open doorway. 'You really believe that crap about your precious trollop being a model, don't you?'

'You're a pig,' she cried. 'A dirty-minded pig. God damn you.' She rushed at him, trying to thrust him through the door. Then she swung the door shut on him, bruising his shoulder. 'Get out. Go on. Get out.'

'You know something?' he smiled. 'I think I will.' He went heavily down the stairs, two at a time. The door slammed behind him.

It was on the third notice-board he found, below Patsy (36-22-36) and above Dixie (34-20-34): Maria, new Spanish model, now available. The neatly typewritten card had only one spelling mistake. There was a telephone number.

My God, he thought. How easy.

His face still burned. He went into a pub and sat over scotch. Then he used the telephone. There was no answer. He rang again, later that night, but received only the engaged signal: the phone was apparently off the hook. When the pub closed he rang from a booth on the way home: still the engaged signal.

The next day he rang and Maria answered. 'But,' she said, her voice tiny in the receiver, 'no more do I make appointments. I am sorry.'

'Since when?' he said.

'No more do I make appointments,' she repeated.

'Come now,' he said. 'That's not right. I saw your card only yesterday. You can't do that.'

'Please?'

'You can't do that. It's unfair.'

'Unfair?' she said vaguely.

'I want an appointment tonight,' he said. 'Understand?'

'Please, I do not,' she said.

'Tonight,' he said. 'Expect me.'

'But you cannot,' she said. 'Because you do not know the address.'

'Oh, yes I do,' he said, and went to replace the receiver.

'No more do I—' she appealed, before her voice was silenced. He strode out of the telephone booth, the door banging behind him; he walked a little way, circling a few streets, and then halted in mid-pavement, astonished at himself. He would never look Eleanor in the face again without laughing. He felt a curious excitement.

Someone—a face, a handshake, a voice—led him off the pavement into a coffee-shop and talked to him. About something; it could have been anything. He wasn't listening.

He idled away the time drinking and arrived at the place after eight. He looked up the stairs climbing to Eleanor's room, and then knocked on Maria's door. The door opened partially and Maria peered out. Eleanor's door remained aloof and shut.

Maria, recognizing him suddenly, tried to close the door again. Her eyes were large and luminous with fright. He insinuated himself deftly into the room. 'I made an appointment,' he said.

'You?' she said, her eyes still large.

'Why not?' he said. 'I saw your card. I didn't bring a camera, but that doesn't matter, does it?'

'Please,' she said. 'You must go. You must.' She pushed him back towards the door: she was quite strong.

'Why?'

'You must go,' she said, still pushing at him.

'What's wrong? Don't you want Eleanor to know?'

'Eleanor knows nothing,' she said. 'Now go.'

'But she is suspicious?'

'A little,' she admitted. 'But from yesterday only. From yesterday I am good. For Eleanor. Now please go.'

But he did not go.

Then he flung open the door and shouted up the stairs. Maria watched him silently, sullenly.

'Why don't you come down?' he was calling. He climbed the stairs slowly. 'Why don't you come and see who your friend has for a visitor?' Maria watched silently. She stood in her doorway and drew her kimono tightly about her shoulders. 'Come on down, why don't you?' He rapped sharply on Eleanor's door. 'Come on down. You find real hospitality down here.'

There was silence within.

He paused, and then looked foolishly down at Maria. She was smiling quite distinctly; quite unmistakably. 'Eleanor,' she said, 'is not at home. She is at the theatre.'

'You knew?' he said stupidly.

'But of course. Since it was I who today purchased the ticket for Eleanor tonight. For a play by a Mr O'Neill which she desired much to see.' She paused. 'And I shall tell Eleanor that her friend called.'

'You bitch,' he said. 'You pair of bitches.'

Maria still smiled. He raced past her, down the stairs. '*Adios,*' she called.

It was the end of summer before he called at the old house off Portobello Road again; he found empty rooms, and the landlady. 'They've gone, that pair,' she said. 'Gone. And I can't say I'm sorry. Where did they go? Off to Spain, of course, where that dark one come from. She was no better than she should be, that one; don't think I didn't know. They went off together.'

'Together?' he said.

'That's what I told you. Off to Spain they went. The pair of them.'

'Together,' he said, to himself this time.

The landlady retreated into her dim living room and returned with an envelope. 'You might be the one this is for,' she said. 'That other one left it. She told me someone might turn up to get it.' She handed him the envelope and he saw his name scrawled.

'Thanks,' he said, tearing it open. The landlady, still watching him, regarded the note with curiosity. 'Thanks,' he said again, and left.

Suddenly he was laughing.

He read the note as he walked: he read it and laughed.

Maria told me you called once when I was out. A pity I missed you. I thought you might have called again but you didn't so I guess you must have been busy or something. All I can do is leave this note and hope you get it. Anyway what I really want to do is apologize for being so absolutely disgusting. I said cruel things. I'm sorry. Maria and I are on our way to Spain. She has arranged a place to live in her village. A little fisherman's house by the sea. Maria has not been at all well; but she is recovered now. Poor girl. If I remember right the euphemism is a social disease; a pity all things which could run under that heading cannot be treated so effectively. She needs sunlight and clean air again; as do I. Think of us this grey English winter. Regards, Eleanor.

He might even have read it through again had he not noticed his silence. He had stopped laughing.

THANK YOU GOODBYE

THEY sat in the large-windowed cafe at the corner of the square. Outside, empty tramcars banged, autumn wind scattered coloured leaves over yellow cobbles, strollers dawdled. The pale buildings walling the square were new and austere. Fixed above the tallest building, in the corner directly opposite the cafe, a five-pointed red star rose against evening sky. The couple had only just taken their seats. The man was thin and pale, dressed neatly in charcoal suit and pastel tie. He appeared nervous. Twice as they waited for service he glanced at his watch.

'There is time,' said the girl calmly. 'Much time. More than one hour. A taxi will take only five minutes to the railway station. If that is what worries you.'

'I'm not worried,' he said, without conviction.

'Your suitcases have all gone from the hotel to the station?' she asked. She spoke an unemphatic, almost accentless English.

'They've gone.'

'Good,' she said. 'Then there is nothing to worry about, is there?'

'No,' he said. 'Nothing.'

'You have only to remove yourself to the station now,' she said. 'It is quite perfectly simple. And this time tomorrow where will you be?'

'I don't know. Vienna perhaps. I don't study timetables closely.'

'But you should,' she observed. 'Travel is adventure. I should. I should study timetables all the time I travelled.' She paused. 'But then,' she added wistfully, 'I have never travelled.'

'No.'

'In two days' time,' the girl calculated, 'you will be in Paris. In three days, London. You will be among friends again.'

'Please,' he said suddenly.

She raised her eyebrows.

'Please don't,' he said.

Though there were few customers, service was slow. The girl glanced over her shoulder at the old grey-haired waiter who moved methodically among the tables. She caught his eye presently, and he ambled amiably over to their table.

'*Molya,*' he said. He stood ready to pencil the order.

'Cognac?' the girl said to her friend. 'Or *rakia?*'

'Anything,' he said.

'*Edna malka bofilka cognac, molya,*' the girl requested. The waiter went away.

The man began to drum his fingers on the table. The girl hummed a tune softly to herself; she seemed serene. She was petite, lightly built, with an expressive, delicately-boned Slavic face. She stopped humming suddenly and, as she reached out for his impatient hand, a chunky gold bangle slid down her arm. There was a moment's silence; they could have heard, if they wanted, the rattling of leaves in the street outside.

'Then we will not look into the future,' she said. 'Perhaps the past is the more satisfying. Two hours ago—'

'Not that either,' he said abruptly.

'You are very difficult.' She hesitated. 'And, besides, that reminds me. I left my cigarettes by the bed. Have you—'

He took cigarettes from a pocket and, after she had taken one, he rested the packet between them.

'You are difficult,' she repeated. 'If we cannot discuss the future or the past, then there is only the present.'

'Only the present,' he agreed.

'And the present,' she said, 'is always so difficult to fix. It always escapes before you can discuss it. Is that not so?'

He appeared not to hear.

'Everything escapes,' she observed quietly.

The waiter returned with a small bottle of cognac and two glasses. He set them down on the table, smiled at the girl, and nodded towards her companion.

'*Angliski,*' he said. 'Eng-lish I speak.' He paused impressively. 'How you do,' he said. 'How you do. I love you. Thank you goodbye.'

'You see,' she said. 'He is showing he can speak English.'

'Tell him he speaks well.'

'*Mnogo dobré,*' the girl said to the waiter.

He chuckled, performed a jerky little bow of pleasure, and withdrew. 'How you do. I love you,' he laughed to himself as he went away.

'His vocabulary is limited,' the girl remarked. 'But adequate and effective.'

The man looked at his watch.

'There is still time,' she said.

The sky was darkening. Lights winked about the square. Above the tall building the giant red star was suddenly illuminated. On one side of the square, screened by thinning trees, a theatre opened its doors and a queue formed. Lights picked out the words *Narodna Kultura* and the smaller word *Teatr*. The night came to life; people scuffed past the cafe windows, over the fallen leaves. The girl poured the cognac carefully. They took up their glasses.

'*Nez dravé,*' she said as they drank.

'*Nez dravé.*'

'You learn my language so quickly,' she said jestingly. 'It is a pity you go so soon. A few more weeks and you would be speaking as a native.'

He was silent.

'You are not amused,' she said. 'You are not amused at anything tonight.' She sipped the cognac. 'After all it is I who should be sad. Is that not so? My room will be the same. My streets will be the same. It is your streets which shall be different. It is you who are going away. Is that not correct?'

'I don't want it like this,' he said.

'No?'

'I mean I wish it different.'

'Different?' she said.

'Much different. I wish it weren't necessary.'

'It need not be necessary. You could stay. It would not be impossible to arrange.'

'Please,' he said. 'Be realistic.'

'Ah, yes,' she said. She looked out the window at the lights in the evening. 'We must be realistic. Always.'

'Please,' he said. 'You're just trying to hurt yourself.'

'Trying?' She laughed.

'You're making it worse. For both of us.'

'Can it be so worse?'

'I mean you must see the impossibility of it all.'

'Of course,' she said. 'Naturally.' Without haste, she reached for the bottle and refilled the glasses. 'I must see.'

'We can't persuade ourselves that it could be different.'

'It was not I who was just now wishing it different.'

'It was in a manner of speaking.'

'Naturally. I only suggested that if you meant what you said, it would be possible to arrange for you to stay. But I was not to know that you did not mean what you said, that it was only a manner of speaking.'

'I see you don't understand,' he said.

'There are difficulties. When you talk to me in a manner of speaking.' She studied a speck of ash on the table-cloth and rubbed it away with a finger. She was silent.

'Why does it have to be like this?' he asked.

'I am sorry,' she said. 'If it is I who make it like this.'

'You become so cold,' he said.

'Then you must forgive me,' she said.

'I don't think you really want to understand.'

'I understand you cannot stay. It is quite simple.'

'Besides,' he added, 'I do not belong here.'

'Of course. Now you say what you mean. Now you do not talk in a manner of speaking.'

'It's important,' he said.

'If you wish to make it important, then it is so. But you are not political?'

'If you mean in the shrill sense, no.'

'Then it is perhaps not so important. Many live here who are not political. Like you, they are indifferent.'

'You don't speak of yourself.'

'If I am, it is not important. I am a person.' She paused. 'If you mean— how was it you said it?—in the shrill sense, no.'

'And if I mean any other way?'

'If you mean that it has been necessary, yes. If you mean it has been necessary because otherwise I might have been illiterate and barefoot in my village, yes. For you it has not been necessary.'

'But now?'

'It is necessary also. But that perhaps you would not understand. If one suddenly discovers one is the parent of a bad child, one does not run away. One must take responsibility. Someone must take responsibility. It is necessary.'

'Rhetoric,' he said.

'Rhetoric is sometimes necessary also.'

This time he was silent.

'It seems to me that with all things it is more important to you not being something than being something. Would you not agree?'

'Whatever you say.'

'Please do not be hurt. I mean only that you always make the greatest importance out of not being something.'

'I understand you perfectly.'

'It is nice,' she said, 'to end on such a note.' She saw him glance again at his watch. 'Yes, it is almost time. At the station there will be people waiting to say goodbye. They will wish to shake your hand. You must give them time, and not disappoint them. I will not come to the station. After all, what is one goodbye among many?'

'You won't come?' he said.

'You will observe that there is almost one glass of cognac remaining in this bottle. I shall sit here and perhaps order a plate of peppers to eat with it. Then I shall walk back along the streets to my room. Perhaps I shall listen to the radio, or read a little, and then it will be time for sleep. If I sleep early, then tomorrow I will wake refreshed for work.'

'Are you sure?' he said suddenly. He reached across the table and touched her hand lightly.

'Now go,' she said, not looking at him. 'I will say only the correct things.' She began to recite in a flat voice. 'I hope you have liked my country. I hope you have found much to interest you, and enjoy. I hope you will write pleasant things about us, and that if you must write unpleasant things you will balance them with the pleasant. I hope—' She stopped. 'Politics,' she said suddenly. 'I hate politics.'

'We must write,' he said.

'If you wish,' she said. 'But it is not necessary.'

'I promise,' he said. He looked quickly about the cafe. 'I must pay,' he added. Just at that moment there was no sign of the old waiter. 'Before I—'

'But it does not matter. I will pay the bill.'

'I insist. I mean I—'

'But it is I who am in a position to insist. And after all have you not the saying—in jest, naturally—that it is always the woman who pays?'

He pulled on his coat.

'Now go,' she repeated. 'Go quickly.'

She did not lift her eyes to see his back vanish out of the door of the cafe into the evening. She did not even see if he looked back. She heard his footsteps.

After a while she raised her head. The queue had gone from the front of the theatre; the plate-glass doors were shut against the chill of night. The wind had dwindled, and leaves rustled gently. The lights were cold on the empty square. Above the tall building, above the red star, stars of an older kind were distinct in the sky.

She filled her glass and beckoned the waiter.

'*Piperki—edna chiniya piperki, molya,*' she said.

He looked at the empty chair, then towards the door. '*Zamina li toi?*'

'*Da,*' she said tiredly. '*Zamina.*'

Presently he brought a small plate of peppers. They were red-coloured and covered with a thin film of oil. She ate with a fork, slowly, chunking

150

off the seedy tops and picking stray seeds from the flesh. She ate only a very small portion of flesh at a time. Occasionally she sipped from her glass. When she had finished she beckoned the waiter again.

'*Smetka, molya,*' she asked.

He stood above her to make out the bill, adding two figures in his notebook. He tore out the page and placed it down beside her. She fed out the money from her frayed leather purse carefully, several notes and coins to pay the bill exactly, and beside them a small heap of coins as a tip. He thanked her and helped her into her coat. It was a light, pale-coloured trench coat and she fastened it tightly about her slight figure. Then she went to the door.

'*Dovishdane!*' she called suddenly to the waiter, swinging back on her flat heels as she opened the door.

'*Dovishdane!*' he returned. Then he paused a moment, looked puzzled, and remembered. '*Da,*' he said. 'Thank you goodbye.'

The door closed, feet clipped away, and as he stooped to clear the table he talked to himself, repeating a long-ago lesson. 'How you do. I love you,' he said softly. 'Thank you goodbye.' Now and then, remembering something, he laughed quietly.

THE WATERS OF THE MOON

1

Te Waiotemarama is at the end of a long white road looped through the trees of a kauri forest. Among thick trunks, tangling creeper and spiky foliage, sun reaches feebly into the forest in late afternoon: it is then that the bus, rumbling and jerking, coughs through the dust to Te Waiotemarama.

Bill Waugh, a taciturn man by nature, drove that afternoon with one passenger. They did not converse until Bill stopped the bus in the approximate centre of the forest and, with his thumb, indicated the place where a track rose in umber from the dust of the road and climbed into the forest.

'Get off here if you like,' he said. 'It's a regular stop. There's a monster kauri back there. Hundreds of years old, they say. Worth seeing. Most people have a look on the way through. Please yourself.'

That man's sick, he added mentally.

Bill had been observing the passenger in his mirror. He was a middle-aged man, dry and pale-skinned; he reminded Bill of nothing more nor less than a rabbit. A startled rabbit, with sharp little teeth and rolling white eyes. He was dressed in a suit of indeterminate grey colour, a shirt patchy with dust, and a quiet-coloured tie. He considered the world through thick, hornrimmed spectacles. Watching him, Bill had seen pain twitch the rabbit features. Pain and then bewilderment.

'Yes,' Bill said, ramming a handkerchief on his sweaty forehead, swinging in his scat, cocking back his hat and thumbing a cigarette into his mouth. 'Take a look if you like.'

In the silence of the forest the birds sang.

'Thanks,' said the passenger, groping down the aisle. He lowered himself gently from the bus and walked the track into the forest. His dwindling figure, down a corridor of hundred-foot trees, was lost among fern and shadow.

Bill, who studied mankind with a melancholy compassion, noted that the man was probably sick enough to die. Yet he felt no pity. We all had to face it; sooner or later. For Bill, when the guns of El Alamein lit the desert night, it had almost been sooner. Tomorrow, the next day, each day given to road and dust and forest and beer at the end of the ride, was a gift bestowed. Bill was sorry for no one; and everyone. We all had to die.

Presently the man returned along the track with that same groping step. He lifted himself into the bus and edged down the aisle to his seat. 'Been this way before?' Bill enquired, without interest.

'No,' the man said. 'Not this way.'

'It's a fine trip,' Bill said. 'Pretty. The forest. Then the harbour. We hit the harbour in a minute. She's a great sight. You see.'

The passenger was silent, locked in sickness again. The motor thudded with a crack of exhaust: they climbed to the top of a hill, the forest gone and the harbour unrolled. Heaped yellow sandhills jumbled about it, creeks with twisting mangroves and shining mudbanks, shacks with unpainted weatherboards, white beaches, ragged farmland, tall stands of cabbage trees. The road slid downwards, curled away from the gaunt cliffs at the head of the harbour and ran between rock and hill.

Te Waiotemarama is solitary on that part of the coast.

Contrast clumsy macrocarpas with elegant Norfolk pines along a pleasant white beach. Erect a long jetty on uncertain foundations, so that the slopping waves of a winter storm will see it jerk like a centipede; add a dangerous handrail, a creaking landing stage and a rusty-roofed shed, vacant now the steamboats have gone, and a repository for dead fish and empty fertilizer sacks. Build about the jetty a long patchwork building containing pub, post office, butcher (three times a week) and general store; and a boardwalk on which can be set broken boxes and discarded chairs so that old Maori women sometimes sit and rest. If the place has personality, it is not of a postcard kind.

The bus lurched to a stop outside the pub. The engine clumped once, twice, and was still. 'This is it,' Bill said.

He watched the passenger, weighted with two suitcases, move slowly across the road, up over the verandah, and in through the pub entrance. Then, licking down a rolled cigarette, he shrugged, pocketed the ignition key, and walked to the bar.

2

On the morning of the third day, a Saturday, he met the teacher. The first two mornings he had taken walks in different directions along the sea road. He breathed bright air, found shade to rest, and returned to the pub in time for a pony-beer before lunch. The third morning only one avenue of escape remained, a road which ran inland from the township, above shops and jetty and climbing gently parallel to the sea road until it struck into the hills.

Overlooking the harbour, was a small schoolhouse and a white cottage. The schoolhouse stood empty. The slender, proud-necked woman in cotton frock and sunhat watered the flowers in her half-tropical garden.

'Good morning,' he said, politely.

'Good morning.' She smiled.

He hesitated before walking on.

'I expect you're the stranger,' she said. 'Mr Fail, isn't it?'

'That's right,' he said. 'You know about me already?'

'It would be difficult not to.'

'And I expect you're the schoolteacher?'

'Whom you've no doubt been told you should meet.'

'Yes,' he confessed.

'Everyone new, for some reason, is told they should meet me. I imagine that makes me local colour.' She laughed, and he saw the roll of her tongue behind white teeth. Her arms, legs and face were brown with summer.

'There's colour there,' he said lamely, looking at the garden. About forty, he thought; between forty and fifty. Perhaps a widow.

'Yes,' she said. 'Until summer burns it out.' She smiled ruefully. 'The summer's hot here. Have you been here in summer before?'

'I haven't been in this part of the country before.'

'Well!' she said with delight. 'That's something, isn't it? You've chosen a good time to see it. Early in the season, before the campers come. It's still quiet. Yes, you've made a good choice.'

'Choice?' he said. 'Yes, I suppose it was choice.' And then he added, 'Though there wasn't much. I had to have a holiday now.'

'Oh?' she said. 'Then you've been ill, I take it.'

'Something of the sort,' he said, reticent again. 'Well, I shan't burden you with my company; I'll get on with my constitutional.'

'Please don't feel obliged to go. I was just going to ask if you'd like tea.'

'Well—' He hesitated. He seemed caught in the colour of the garden.

'Please do,' she insisted; and the decision was made. She reached deftly to turn off the tap, disconnect the hose.

Inside the cottage there was colour of a more studied kind. Walls of pale yellow and light blue enclosed contemporary furniture set with sprays of flowers from the garden; paintings of style unfamiliar hung from the walls. Modern art, he thought, without any feeling on the subject. He remembered his landlady informing him that the schoolteacher was something of a poet and sometimes had her name in the papers; perhaps, it appeared, a painter too. The interior of the cottage was filled with light. A surprising place to find in this region of decrepit farmland and crumbling homes. Yet he contained his surprise. 'It's a pleasant place you have here,' he observed mildly.

'I'm glad you like it.'

He turned to the wide windows and the view of the harbour heads; the spray feathering up from the rocks.

'And how do you find Te Waiotemarama?' she added, moving into the kitchen and setting the kettle to boil.

'It has character,' he said with caution.

'But it's quiet.'

'Yes. Quiet.'

'What made you select it? Please do sit down. And tell me.'

He sat awkwardly, looking at his pallid hands. 'Of course I wanted quiet. That was one reason. And I wanted to get away.'

'And other reasons?'

'I wanted to see something of the country I hadn't seen before. I was born here and I've lived most of my life here. But I'm just beginning to realize how little I know about it.'

'Admirable,' she said. She made the tea and poured it.

'So I thought I might take the opportunity while I still had it,' he said. Each movement he made seemed loaded with weariness; he reached to receive his tea. 'To see something new, I mean.'

'And why not?' she said softly. 'This, for me, is the real part of the country. The rest is a confection. This is real.'

'What makes you say that?' he said. He was curious, discerning something passionate.

But her words, her gestures, were casual again. She shrugged. 'Oh,' she said, 'the life, the people, the landscape—everything.'

'It's all vivid enough,' he said. 'But I can't see—'

'Can't you?' she cried; and he saw he had successfully drawn her again. 'Can't you? But look around. You know that this part of the country was the earliest settled—you know that, don't you? Of course you must. It was here that the ship of civilization ran ashore and foundered. And so they tried again, in the south, leaving the big old homes to crumble here. In the south they made their feeble patchwork among other hills, building into it all the rot of older civilization. This they forgot, in time, almost entirely. Here, perhaps only here, with the two races mixed, something new, altogether new, can grow up; only here, given the chance. Like fresh flowers growing from the ruins. Can you see that?'

'Yes,' he said. 'But—'

'Of course it's impossible that you should,' she said. 'One would have to give one's life to this part of the country, and love it, to see that. It's a truth one doesn't stumble across in a day. But you'll see, even if you only stay here a short time— you'll see that this place has a special quality, a special character.' She rose. 'I talk too much. More tea?'

The room rippled with a peculiar yellow light, as if underwater; the serene woman glided through it.

'I'm sorry, Mr Fail,' she said, 'if I bore you.'

'Not at all. Quite the contrary, I assure you.'

'I hardly know a thing about you.'

'There's little enough to know.'

'You might at least tell me that.'

Mr Fail crossed his legs and tried to relax, but found only discomfort. 'I'm a journalist,' he said finally.

'Oh?'

'The rest is detail. There's little more than that to say.'

'Surely not. Tell me more. You've lived here, in this country, all your life?'

'Not all. I worked ten years in England. In Fleet Street.'

'Aha. You see, detail has its interest. And what have you done since you returned?'

'At first I was a sub-editor in the South Island. Since I came north I've been editorial-writing.'

'Aha. Meditating on the state of the country.'

'A country I know nothing about, in the end.'

'You're honest anyway.'

'There's no merit attached to a disease which is honest about itself.'

'I'm not sure. At least, if the symptom is plain, there is greater potential for cure. Wouldn't you say so? Come, now. More tea? After all, Te Waiotemarama is an excellent place to begin a cure.' She paused. 'Even if, in your case, it happens to be a twin cure—mind and body; isn't that so?'

'You could say that.'

'You're married, of course.'

'I was; I left my wife in England. She developed an infatuation for English life.'

'So many do. It's a lack of self-sufficiency and self-assertion in the national character. The surprising thing is that some do return unimpressed; surprising and encouraging. You apparently, for example.'

'You flatter me. There was no intelligence behind it. Only the desire for retreat.'

'Retreat?'

'To safety, if you like—or mediocrity; though that's a word I distrust. Life is lived at an easier pace in these islands. I happen to prefer it.'

'And why not?' she asked rhetorically.

'And so I came back, not impressed or unimpressed; without judgement. I was merely grateful to be back.'

'But you know more than before?'

Mr Fail, on his feet now, walked to the window and studied the view. 'I think I know less,' he said finally. 'And that might mean less than nothing. I don't know.'

That afternoon Mr Fail slept badly. In a dream he floated weightlessly down tunnels of darkness with the sound of wind in his ears. His eyes throbbed in his head as he looked vainly for light. Then he woke to the pain in his side, the cicadas singing in the late afternoon, the shadows crawling across his carpet. He was exhausted and sticky with sweat. He reached for the small bottle of pills on the table beside his bed.

And it was still early summer. The summer was hot, the teacher had reminded him.

He considered the teacher.

He recalled her face with difficulty. Her presence commanded attention; not detail. There was something odd there, something he could not define. If he had met her in other circumstances it would have been easy to dismiss her without further thought. If, for example, he had met her among the people in this country who were so self-consciously sophisticated; among the kind of people he often distrusted and more often despised. A solitary, almost a hermit of her kind, her presence seemed to say: Look at this. Not, as one might have expected in those other circumstances: Look at me.

She had a definite arrogance; there was certainly little humility. And no restlessness, no discontent, no retreat. Only certainty, confidence, assertion.

He hoped they would meet again soon.

Odd, though, that her face blurred so quickly. Next time he must concentrate on it, and not be distracted by delicate hands, swivelling body.

He expected they would meet again soon. After all, when he left, they had been calling each other Isobel and Douglas.

3

Actually her face was not extraordinary. The features were fine enough; the lines firm. There was perhaps a hint of something alien to the Anglo-Saxon in the cheekbones, the slightly lengthened eyes. But really, Mr Fail thought, there was nothing very startling about the face; except its colour. She could almost be Maori.

He had met her again in the schoolyard. He saw her, as he drew near the school, surrounded by children, children in shades from pale coffee to dark chocolate; girls in bright print frocks and boys in check shirts. Looking up from her brood, she saw him. 'Why, hello, Douglas,' she cried, the children still eddying about her, tugging her skirt. Laughing, her teeth flashing, she scattered them homeward and went to the gate to greet him.

'I was hoping I'd see you again today,' she said.

Talking, she led him across the playground, up through her garden, to the cottage. 'I think we might take tea on the verandah this afternoon,' she reflected. 'It's pleasant there, in the shade.'

They took tea there; below, beyond the garden, the land sloped away to the schoolyard and schoolhouse, and then dropped sharply to the rooftops of Te Waiotemarama, the white beach, and the sea. In the sunlit afternoon a fishing launch dawdled down harbour.

'And how are you finding Te Waiotemarama?' she asked, as the cups and saucers chinked.

'I think I'm finding the rhythm,' he said. 'Perhaps, in a day or two, I'll begin fishing off the jetty like the other idlers.'

She laughed. 'I look forward to seeing that.'

'By the way,' he said. 'I don't know Maori. What does it mean?—Te Waiotemarama?'

'The waters of the moon,' she said. 'Rather a pleasant name, don't you think?'

'Tell me,' he said, leaning forward, 'what do people *do* here?'

'Why,' she said, 'they perform essential functions with dignity and non-essentials with difficulty.'

'Take the land as an example. It could be utilized in a much better, much more productive fashion. Thousands of acres, running just a handful of cows when it could run hundreds.'

'But why?' she exclaimed. 'Why hundreds?'

'For money. Just for argument's sake.'

'But if they live a good life already,' she said, 'what's the point?'

'Indeed,' he said. 'In that case, what is the point?' He sighed.

'Poor old Douglas. Things still bewilder you. Perhaps you should go a little south, where you'll find farmers running big herds and dying at sixty.'

'And here?'

'It's different. As you see.'

He shook his head.

'Don't worry,' she said cheerfully. 'You'll get used to it.'

At that point a figure emerged from the schoolhouse. The figure of a tall boy in tight navy shorts and patched flannel shirt; a dusky-skinned boy, with firm brown legs and long arms, lithe and soft-footed with the body of an athlete. He came out across the schoolyard, eyes blinking in the sudden sunlight, and looked up and saw the woman on the verandah; he raised an arm in stiff salute. She waved back, a small fluttering of the hand above the teacups. Then he turned and walked out the gate and down the hill to the town.

'That's Kuru,' she said in explanation. 'My biggest boy. And my star pupil.'

'Oh?'

'He works late, quite often. By himself. After the others have gone home.'

'Conscientious.'

'And conscious of his lack. You see, he didn't begin school till late, for one reason and another. So he's old for his class—a giant among pygmies. He has a remarkably receptive mind and a quite extraordinary intelligence. He could go a long way, given help at the crucial times. He's preparing for a scholarship. If he wins it, he'll be going away next year; rather sad for me, but it can't be helped.'

'You love your work, don't you?'

She didn't answer immediately: he sensed a reluctance to reveal too much. He would never draw her there.

'I do,' she said.

So they did not talk of that again.

'Oh, by the way,' she said. 'I have an invitation for you. To tea on Sunday night at the Hicksons' place.'

'Who are they?'

'You must have noticed their place—that big old pioneer house behind a row of Norfolk pines, all lawned and gardened in front. They're a quaint old couple; you'll like them, once you're used to their idiosyncrasies. And it'll be a chance for you to see inside one of the few original homesteads remaining about here.'

'It sounds interesting.'

'They're quite a scream, the Hicksons. An anachronism. But you'll enjoy them. I visit them regularly, as a rule. Mrs Hickson was, I imagine, quite a cultivated woman once; though she's gone to seed here. Actually she's English in origin; Hickson himself is the one of pioneer stock. He's, well, deteriorating quickly now. He's gone cranky. He seems to sit out on his verandah all day, looking out through a telescope for non-existent steamboats. And, by the way, he's a cripple; some disease of the bone as a child. I think it best to warn people in advance. He's always been a burden, now more so than ever. That's why I visit them so often. It helps her keep her end up. They've one child. He's twenty-three, and a beer-swilling, brawling imbecile. Quite the worst influence around here. It was a relief for us all when he cleared off to the city a month or so ago. But you'll like the old couple. They're quaint. But you'll see, anyway.'

'I expect I shall,' he said.

'Oh,' she said, patting back her corn-coloured hair, 'I know you'll enjoy the Hicksons.'

But he did not enjoy the Hicksons; though he would never have told Isobel. He did not enjoy their gloomy cavern of a house, either; he scented decay rather than history in the rooms cluttered with heavy furniture. He could find no interest in the mahogany desk where administrators of a rough-cast colony had penned dispatches, the bed where eminent missionaries had slept. He wanted escape to clean wind and warm sun. But he was patient and listened quietly as he was led about the house. He could not relax even at the meal. Hickson, misshapen and spidery across the table, fixed him with an idiot eye and talked about the ruin of the country, the calamity of inter-marriage between the races; and about the steamboats, the days that would never return. Mrs Hickson, a prim and plump grey-haired woman, retailed the collected gossip of the week to Isobel; and once, unwinding some frail and tenuous link of memory, led herself back to girlhood, and the neat fields and hedges of the English countryside. While she talked, Mr Fail found himself studying a photograph of the son which squatted, in a heavy gilt frame, on a sideboard. It was a raw, unfinished face, thin with discontent. A face which belonged nowhere.

It was, finally, a relief to escape out the front door; to walk with Isobel down the sea-shelled path through the cool garden and moonlit evening.

'You didn't like it,' Isobel said quietly.

'No,' he lied. 'I liked it. It was pleasant. An experience, you might say. It gives one a perspective on all that one sees here.'

'It does,' she agreed, as they walked.

Not long after the visit to the Hicksons he received something in the post: a thin book which a friend had hunted down through a half dozen city bookstores. Sitting in his room, his french windows open to sea and sunlight while a cool breeze flicked the curtains, he turned the crisp pages slowly, noting passages of interest here and there.

He could not have said he liked her verse. The lines were measured, cautious and exact. Even the images had an austerity. He sensed the supple intelligence lacing them together; and something else, which entirely eluded him. Something odd, tantalizing, erratic. He could not find it, turning and re-turning the pages.

So at length he placed the book beside his bed, dressed, left the pub, and climbed up to the school.

On his way he passed the Hickson place. Behind the trees he glimpsed old Hickson, alone and small on the wide verandah. He seemed to sit there all day, his distorted body in service to the telescope, watching the empty sea, the sky, the seabirds. Mr Fail hailed him, but Hickson did not seem to hear.

He found Isobel that afternoon not at the cottage, but in the schoolhouse, coaching the boy Kuru for his examination. Teacher and pupil sat alone in the dim empty schoolroom, side by side at a ridiculously small desk, among the smell of linseed and chalk. Standing in the leafy shade of the yard, he watched them through the large windows. Patiently she explained; patiently the boy listened. Once she laughed, a high bright sound; and the boy smiled. Then they worked again, Isobel talking and the boy nodding his head in understanding. They worked together in a peaceful intimacy which Mr Fail found beyond him to disturb. He waited until they appeared finished. Then he walked slowly across the yard, into the sunlight, and up to the door of the room.

Isobel gave a small cry of delight on seeing him; she introduced him to Kuru.

'I've heard all about you,' he said. 'I'm very pleased to meet you.'

But the boy greeted him with a suspicion and reluctance near surliness. There was a stiff dignity about the way he shook Mr Fail's hand, gathered his books, and left the room.

'And that's Kuru,' Isobel said, tidying her desk.

They took tea on the verandah again. It seemed to Mr Fail that they were nearer each other that afternoon than they had been before. And for the first time it occurred to him that he was courting Isobel. After all, she was a woman of a kind who could command much more from him than respect and admiration. She was, in fact, a woman of a kind he wished he had met long before. He was relaxed in her company. And entertained by the flash of her wit, the precision of her thought; he seldom wished to broach his own opinions when with her.

The next Sunday they picnicked at the head of the harbour. There was a ruin of a house there, now overgrown with bush, which had once belonged to men who piloted the steamboats over the seething sand-bar into the harbour. They lunched in the shade of a tumbling wall. Salad sandwiches, fishcakes; and a bottle of dry white wine Isobel had packed into the basket.

The day was perfect. Nikau palms framed the harbour, and in the distance the yellow sandhills shone. After lunch Mr Fail remained in the shade while Isobel edged out into the sunlight. Conversation drifted, thinned, and ended; and, as the sun turned her an even deeper brown, Mr Fail discovered himself admiring her long loose body. It might have belonged to a girl of twenty. She seemed so natural there, flung carelessly upon the summer grass.

Why, he thought, she's a regular pagan; a regular little pagan the way she drenches herself in sun. And then he felt the odd, scratching disquiet again; the thing he thought lost when he put aside the book of verse. What was it, he wondered, that disturbed him? What was it about this woman, so relaxed in the sun, that should cry a warning?

She stirred lazily. Raising a hand to shadow her eyes against the brilliance, she looked up at him, her mouth wrinkling into a little-girl's smile. And Mr Fail sat stiffly in the shade.

4

People spoke of the summer. Dry November became hot December. The old Maori men, nodding their heads, observed flowering trees and predicted drought. It was years since the north had known a summer so fierce. Mr Fail, his face colouring with sun, kept more to the shade, and stayed indoors in the heat of noon. When he went out, he always went now in loose open-neck shirt, and sometimes in shorts. He thought sometimes, in moments of weakness, of the mountains and lakes of the south; but in the end did not regret his choice of a place to holiday, not even when tents festooned the sea road and campers crowded the beaches. There was still quietness enough; pleasantness enough. There was the sweep of the harbour beyond his windows in the morning; the brilliant evenings when stars and moon lit the water. There was his chair in the shade of the upstairs verandah, his collection of books arranged neatly beside it; there was the tonic glass of beer at noon, and the siesta after lunch; there were the days when, after sunset, in the falling dusk, he dropped his fishing line off the end of the jetty and yarned with fellow idlers.

And there were the evenings with Isobel.

Sometimes, on these warm evenings, he tried to steer conversations in mid-flight, tried to push them to something more specific, more personal. Why, for example, had she never married? Why had she stayed here? Was she really so content? He met a formidable wall of reticence.

So he began to formulate his disquiet. So at length he told himself: There is something odd about that woman. She didn't play by the rules. She should not be happy and sufficient, alone. Solitary, she should not retain that capacity for delight. So he thought: There is something odd about that woman. Something unnatural.

That they spent so much time together did not go unremarked. The loungers saw it, the idlers, and the publican and his wife; and the Hicksons. They saw it: and made comment. And the boy Kuru saw it, and his eyes made comment.

Summer burned through Christmas into the new year. Mr Fail felt himself stronger, prided himself on his rather weak tan, and walked with more confident step. The nights of the sharp pains in his side were gone; he had not touched the bottle of pills beside his bed for three weeks.

Calling up at the cottage one evening, he discovered a visitor. Someone had come to stay with Isobel.

'Really, Izzy, I just can't understand how you put up with it here, year in and year out. How do you do it? What is it? What makes you stay here? Don't you wish you could go to the theatre sometimes? Or hear good music? Or see a movie? How do you manage it? Tell me—what is it?'

Isobel smiled wryly at Mr Fail. 'These young people,' she said.

The girl pirouetted across to the cabinet and poured herself another drink. She was a startling creature, clad in black, in tight sweater and matador slacks; she clinked and clacked with adornments, beggars' beads from India, beaten gold bracelets, hoop ear-rings. She had long hair, a short boyish figure and a face which, if attractive, was rather shrewd.

'And don't, Izzy, give me any of your stoic philosophy,' she declared, falling on a couch and curling her leg beneath her. She fiddled, drank from her glass, and lit a cigarette. An extraordinarily restless girl, Mr Fail observed; she couldn't sit still for a minute. 'No,' she said. 'Don't tell me. I don't want to hear it all again.' She looked at Mr Fail. 'Do you understand her?' she asked. 'Do you?'

'Sometimes,' said Mr Fail cautiously, 'I imagine I do.'

'Well, then,' the girl said, 'you're a remarkable man, Douglas old boy.' She sipped from her glass. 'Maybe you can give me one or two clues. I've been trying to persuade Izzy down to the city for the last five years. Damn it all, this is no place for her; she needs to be with people like herself. Stimulating people. The kind she never meets here.'

'You forget Douglas,' Isobel pointed out. 'He's been company this summer.'

'But Douglas, after all, is a drop in the bucket,' the girl said. 'If Douglas will forgive the expression.'

'I will,' said Mr Fail gravely.

The girl laughed. 'You know, Douglas, you're a pompous old thing,' she said. 'But I rather love you.'

Mr Fail smiled uncertainly.

'It's really all right,' the girl said provocatively. 'I shan't eat you, you know.' She came to sit on the arm of his chair; and nudged him. 'But you're really terribly lovable. Isn't he, Izzy?'

'Douglas is like me,' Isobel said. 'Impervious to the wiles of the younger generation.'

'You're just a pair of old fogeys,' the girl said, winking at Mr Fail. 'A pair of fogeys meditating in the wilderness. What brought you here anyway, Douglas?'

'Douglas came to spend the summer here for his health,' Isobel interposed. 'Which I think a perfectly good idea.'

'Well, you met Izzy, didn't you?' the girl said, turning to Mr Fail again. 'Don't you think Izzy's rather charming?'

'Please, Cheryl darling,' Isobel pleaded. 'Do leave Douglas alone.'

'But Doug and I are getting on like a house on fire,' she appealed. 'Aren't we, Doug? Of course we are. And Izzy's just an old meanie, spoiling our fun.' Her black arm appeared around Mr Fail's shoulder. 'We could have fun. Couldn't we, Dougie?'

'Really Cheryl,' Isobel said. 'Let Douglas relax a little, darling. You're making him dreadfully uncomfortable.'

Mr Fail felt twice trapped: trapped by this brazen girl and trapped by Isobel's eyes. He must not make it appear he was playing up to the girl; why, at his age, it would look ridiculous. Without thinking, he began to loosen his collar in embarrassment, and then discovered he was already wearing an open-neck shirt. It was suddenly hot: sweat beaded his face.

'But really, Dougie,' the girl insisted, 'don't you think Izzy's charming?'

'Isobel has many fine qualities,' Mr Fail replied. 'Many fine qualities.' The girl was positively like a snake, the way she insinuated herself around him. He mopped his face.

'I think you're so right,' she said. 'I wonder why it is Izzy hasn't married?'

'I think,' said Isobel, rising, 'I am going to make a cup of tea.'

'Apart from the fact that Izzy's a fourth generation New Zealander, she's a perfect Englishwoman,' the girl observed. 'In face of adversity, she makes a cup of tea.'

Mr Fail often saw Isobel and Cheryl together after that evening. But he did not accompany them when they asked him along on their rambles about harbour and coast. It was only partly due to the fact that he preferred to remain indoors in the sticky heat of January; and chiefly because the girl persisted in causing him considerable embarrassment.

He could not understand it.

What could a woman of such fine temperament find in the company of such a cheap little baggage? He could not find one redeeming feature in Cheryl; not one at all. What, exactly, was it?

He met them in various circumstances. Quite often in the village, in the early morning, he saw them as they were starting off for a tramp out to the head of the harbour. Isobel would be carrying picnic basket and swimming costumes; and Cheryl a sketchbook and a box of water-colours. 'Another excursion in the interest of art,' Isobel would protest. 'Cheryl goes crazy over this scenery.'

What, exactly, was it? Mr Fail wondered as he watched them walk away.

This intruder had wrecked the summer. And, waking to the wreckage in empty afternoons, Mr Fail was left with the solitary question.

What, exactly?

5

Towards the end of January there was a patch of cooler weather. The days were still warm, but breezes rose out of the Tasman sea, rattling the bush, rippling dry grass. Mr Fail had for some reason taken to reading the slender book of verse again, with even less success. Restless, he walked again. He walked often in that patch of cooler weather, wondering if it was not time to return to the city. Wondering if after all everything had once again only turned to nothing in his hands.

On one of these walks he met the girl Cheryl by chance. Apparently even Isobel had forsaken her now, for she was alone in a clearing, drawing a tumbledown farmhouse; alone in the light of late afternoon, the cicadas loud around. She sat working on the stump of a tree, clad only in brief sunsuit. He was half-way across the clearing before he saw her; she had not seen him. Even then, at the risk of seeming ridiculous, he was about to retreat. But a dry stick cracked beneath his feet; she looked up and cried out.

'Why, Doug, you are a roamer! Fancy meeting you here.'

His mouth worked dryly; no sound emerged. So he nodded to the girl.

'You didn't follow me, by any chance?' she said cheekily.

'No,' he said. 'I did not.'

'Why, Dougie,' she said. 'I believe you really are frightened of me.'

'Do you think so?' he said steadily. He went to move on. 'Well, I shan't disturb your work.'

'Oh, but you're not. You're not disturbing me at all.'

'I'm sure I must be.'

'Please don't go. I'm finished now. Really I am.' Her voice became oddly wheedling.

He could not help seeing her drawing. Mr Fail knew little about art; but then one only needed to know little to realize that this inexpert piece lacked even elementary graces. He glanced at it only once, and did not look again. Then Cheryl put the sketchbook aside.

'See? I'm really finished.'

'Yes.'

'Really, Doug, you are awfully coy. Please sit down.'

'I prefer to sit in shade.'

Cheryl was another creature of the sun; for a city girl she had gone brown very quickly.

'Well, the shade it is, then.' She gathered her things. 'I don't mind.'

Mr Fail felt despair. 'I should be getting back to the hotel.'

But it was no use. He found himself sitting in the shade of pines at the edge of the clearing while Cheryl chattered beside him.

'We haven't seen much of you lately,' she said.

'No. I've been indoors.'

'I think Izzy misses you.'

'She does?' He tried not to show excitement.

'You're holding out on me, Doug. You do really like Izzy, don't you?'

'Isobel is pleasant company.'

'Oh, come off it. More than that, isn't she?'

'I'm not sure what you mean.'

'Really, Doug, don't give me that.' She laughed, yawned, and stretched herself lazily on warm pine-needles. 'Wouldn't you like to sleep with Izzy?'

'Really, I don't think—'

'Don't be so damn stuffy. Of course you would. Izzy's a marvellous person. Anyone would want to sleep with her.'

'I hardly think it's relevant.'

'Of course it's relevant, damn it all. Why else have you been hanging round this dump so long? Not really for your health, I bet. But really because you want to tumble long-legged Isobel in the hay. Isn't that right?'

'If you'll excuse me—'

But Cheryl grabbed brought him to ground again. 'You don't get away as easy as that. Not from me you don't. Now don't start getting excited;

just relax. There's no need to break out in a sweat just because I ask a perfectly simple question. I believe in honesty; don't you?'

'Up to a point.'

'Well, that's interesting. Honesty up to a point. An interesting comment on the state of journalism. And you were an editor or something, weren't you, Doug? Well, well. So I guess you were only honest up to a point with your readers. Yes. That's most interesting indeed.'

Mr Fail was silent. For some reason he was breathing heavily.

'Come on, now; loosen up. You like Izzy, don't you?'

'Naturally I like Isobel. She's a very attractive person.'

'And you'd like to sleep with her?'

'I told you before; it's not relevant.'

'Of course it's bloody well relevant. I would.'

Mr Fail was not sure he understood. Bewildered, he said, 'Would what?'

'Like to sleep with Isobel.' She paused. 'Really, Doug, I believe you're shocked.'

But Mr Fail was feeling, at that moment, only a great relief. He mopped his face and a sigh escaped him.

'But you don't,' he said quietly.

'Worse luck. No one can say I haven't tried. God knows where she gets her love life. Perhaps she gets it vicariously from the raped landscape or some damn thing. I don't know.'

But Mr Fail scarcely heard a word. His nerves were still settling.

'I've known Izzy five years and sometimes I think I don't know any more about her now than I did at the beginning. She likes having odd kids coming to stay with her from the city. Helps her keep in touch, she says. That's one of the reasons why I've collected the invitation so often. And, as a matter of fact, I like coming up here for the summer with Isobel. But I can't be blamed, can I, if I feel a little frustrated sometimes?'

Mr Fail felt more favourably inclined towards the girl. After all, she was only being frank about herself. He could cope with her now.

'No,' he conceded solemnly. 'You can't.'

'You know,' she said, laughing, 'you're not a bad old stick, Doug. I might have known you had it in you. We understand each other now, don't we?'

'Well,' said Mr Fail, smiling faintly. 'I suppose we do.'

That evening when he visited the cottage, he found himself relaxed there for the first time in weeks; and even discovered himself regarding garish Cheryl with affection. Once or twice Cheryl winked at him when Isobel's back was turned: they were almost fellow-conspirators now.

Cheryl excused herself early, saying she was tired, and so he found himself talking to Isobel till late.

Isobel was excited that night. Her protégé Kuru had passed his examinations and won the scholarship he had worked for; had, in fact, topped the list. It was an evening for congratulation.

The next morning, looking out from his verandah, he saw Isobel walking with the boy near the sea. The campers had begun to leave, and the beach had a deserted appearance now; Te Waiotemarama was shaking off the canvas trimmings of summer. They walked beside the rising tide in the crisp morning. Isobel was explaining something; he saw her lips moving, her hands working vigorously. Even from some distance, he imagined he saw the pride in her face. And the boy walked silently beside her.

In the afternoon Mr Fail happened, not entirely by accident this time, upon the clearing again. Cheryl was there. This time she was lying on the grass, sunbathing nude, her colour so close to that of the sunburned land that he did not see her at first.

When he did see her, he started back. 'Perhaps you'd like to dress,' he said, looking elsewhere.

'Nonsense,' she said. 'I'd only spoil my tan. Sit down there, on that log in the shade, and talk to me.' She was plump and evenly brown the length of her body.

He sat down, as instructed, but could find nowhere comfortable to rest his eyes.

'You're a let-down,' she said. 'An absolute let-down. Hey there, are you so ashamed of yourself you can't even look at me?'

'What do you mean?' he asked, at last looking at her. 'I don't understand.'

'Last night,' Cheryl said. 'I go to pains to leave you alone with Izzy— and what happens? Oh, you don't need to tell me. I listened. You talked to her. My God, man, what's wrong with you? Can't you persuade her out to look at the moon, or something? Instead you say, yes, you will have another cup of tea, thank you. You're a real let-down. Don't talk to me.'

'I think you misunderstand my relationship with Isobel,' he said.

'In that case, I can only conclude you misunderstand yourself. Get her into bed. There's no time like the present.'

'I'm afraid I don't understand why you should be so concerned.'

'My reasons, dear Douglas, are selfish. I'm curious. I want to see if it's possible. I might tell you I'm out of the race now, so you don't need to worry your head about me. You've got a clear field. So what do you do? You bloody well talk.'

He was silent.

'I mean to say,' she added, 'it's not even as if you talk to her about anything interesting. No, it's always about this godforsaken hole, this godforsaken countryside, and the godamn Maoris. Are you really so interested?'

'Isobel makes me interested, as a matter of fact. I like people who are passionate about their interests; her passion is with this country, and its people. She's absorbed in what she's doing here. So I like to hear her talk.'

'Oh God,' Cheryl cried in dismay, rolling over in the grass. 'A bloody great pair of soul-mates.'

'I think you're being rather unfair,' he said.

'What are you trying to tell me now? That you looked after a harem in your youth? That *would* be the unkindest cut of all.'

'I don't think, really, there's any need to be crude. Isobel and I just happen to be very good friends. I'm not sure there's need for more.'

'My God,' she cried, rolling from side to side in the grass again, convulsed with laughter. 'Hark at the man.'

There was a silence. A sea breeze chattered through pines. A tui sang, high and clear, from a flowering flax bush. Mr Fail felt a tickling beneath his chin. Instinctively he slapped at it; and found not a mosquito or sandfly, but a piece of straw. Cheryl held the straw; she sat curled at his feet now.

'I'm trying to wake you up,' she announced.

'Really?'

'Doug, I think you're a very frustrated old thing. And half your trouble is you don't know it. You know that?'

'You seem very concerned.'

'Oh, but I am, really, you see. I'm very concerned about you. You know why? I think you're rather nice.'

'You're flattering.'

'Don't you think I'm nice?' she said pertly, wide eyes blinking.

'Of course I think you're nice,' he said.

'Well,' she said, 'that's fine, isn't it?'

There was a pause.

'Well,' said Cheryl, 'is that all you have to say?' She tugged at his arm like a persistent child, tumbling him off the log. 'Is that all you have to say?' she said again as he floundered on the grass. She insinuated herself against him, so that he felt the gentle pressure of the hard little breasts; a brown arm circled his neck and she fingered his face.

'You're not still frightened of me, are you, Dougie? Don't tell me that. Because we understand each other, don't we? Of course. And we won't be frightened any more, will we?'

'Really, I think—' said Mr Fail, but it was the cry of a drowning man.

'Don't think, Dougie. Thinking's dangerous. Thinking spoils every-thing,' she said as she lifted his spectacles. 'You mustn't think.' There was a considerable pause. 'I'm real, you know. Truly. There's nothing extraordinary about me, really. I'm fitted out the same way as everyone else, only more adaptable than most. There, you see. Touch me. See if I'm real.'

Mr Fail, surrendered. It was astonishing. At a slight touch her head snapped back and her entire body jolted into motion; her mouth drove against him, her tongue flicking. She caught him, pulled him down, he felt the earth peel away.

And then he was no longer drowning. He rose upwards slowly and drifted.

'You see,' she said, 'it wasn't so bad after all, was it?' Her tongue licked his ear as she lay beside him. 'No,' she said presently, 'it wasn't so bad. Only we're just a bit comic, aren't we? Here we are both wanting someone else, and we make do with each other. Sad, isn't it?'

In a little while, kittenish, she added, 'Don't you think I'm nice, Dougie?'

6

Cheryl returned to the city at the beginning of February. Mr Fail was sorry to see her leave; he imagined he felt towards her in a fatherly fashion. Since Mr Fail was childless by his first and only marriage, experience did not contradict him. But certainly he would miss Cheryl. Before she left, she gave him her address in the city; and made him promise to visit her when he too returned. 'But don't get any ideas in your old bonnet,' she said. 'This is friendship from now on.' She laughed. 'This other was summer silliness. But then we understood that, didn't we, Dougie?' Well, he had understood it: up to a point.

She pinched him under the chin and shook his hand. 'And good luck,' she said. 'With Izzy, I mean. I think you'll need it. I hope you make good, anyway. There must be a key to unlock that door, somewhere.'

Mr Fail had tried many keys; and the door remained closed. The first week in February, with school about to begin again, Isobel already slipping into the routine of a new year, he tried more.

Without Cheryl, he felt lost and emptied. The girl, oddly and briefly, had given him confidence of a kind.

Though the sun still fired the rainless days, the long hours of summer were dwindling; soon it would be autumn.

'I hope,' said Isobel one evening, 'that Cheryl didn't pester you too much, Douglas.'

'Not at all.'

'Really? I had the queer notion she completely unnerved you at the beginning. She's a sweet child, but rather hard to take in large doses, don't you think?'

'That's true,' he said.

'Yet after a while you seemed to cope with her quite well,' she observed.

The observation had more truth than was comfortable. But when he looked at her, he detected no knowledge in her eyes. 'Yes,' he said. 'I managed. Young people bewilder me these days. They live by different rules. I imagine it's just a question of getting used to them.' He hesitated. 'Actually, after a while, I found Cheryl entertaining.'

'Well,' said Isobel, smiling, 'I could see you enjoyed each other's company. I must say I was pleasantly surprised the day I saw you come strolling back here with her. For a while I thought she might drive you away.'

'Would that have been so terrible?' he asked quickly.

'Of course. I should have been very sorry indeed, Douglas.' Swiftly she parried him: swiftly she rose and cleared away the tea things. And he remembered it was late; and that tomorrow school began. He rose wearily.

'I shan't keep you up. I'd almost forgotten tomorrow was your big day.'

'There's no need for you to go yet, Douglas,' she said politely. 'The new hordes don't terrify me all that much, you know.'

'But I will go,' he insisted. 'I know you'll be tired.'

He went to the door.

'Oh, Douglas,' she said suddenly.

'Yes?' He turned quickly, expectantly.

'You haven't forgotten the wedding?'

'The wedding?' he said bleakly.

'On Saturday.'

'Oh, yes,' he said. 'The wedding.'

'You do remember, don't you?'

'Yes. of course. I promised to go, didn't I?'

Of course he should have remembered. After all, he was almost a member of the Te Waiotemarama community now.

The wedding was an event in the district. The Hickson boy, having got a girl three months pregnant, had been persuaded by his mother to return from the city and marry the girl to salvage the family honour. The girl was a Maori and the sister of Kuru. Coffee-skinned children would inherit the house of Hickson.

In the days before the wedding, Mr Fail strolling past the school, saw Isobel with her new horde; saw the small hands clutch at her skirt as she led the children in tiny straggling crocodiles across the playground and read them stories in the shade of the cabbage trees. There was a spasm in his throat when he saw her so disposed; she was even more remote behind this new screen of admirers.

One afternoon on his way to take tea with Isobel, he met Kuru emerging from the cottage; the boy, unsmiling and unresponsive as ever, greeted him briefly and continued down the hill.

'I see Kuru hasn't gone yet,' he said.

'No,' Isobel said. 'He should have gone off to his new school last weekend. But he's staying on for his sister's wedding. Then he'll go.'

'You'll miss him,' he observed.

'Naturally,' she said, busying herself, 'I miss all my children as I lose them, one by one.'

The night before the wedding Mr Fail woke with a twinge in his side, and came to the conclusion that he was an idiot. It was an idiot business altogether, proceeding from nowhere to nowhere. All night he had been crushed by heavy dreams. And so he had woken, at this morning hour, with the twinge; and the thought that it had all, in the end, been quite pointless. He swallowed two pills and then walked barefoot across the room and peeled back the curtains from the french windows. It was still dark, with faint moonlight on the harbour.

He could of course finish it quite simply. There was a bus back to the city tomorrow morning, Sunday.

The more he considered it, the more attractive the thought became. He could say something quietly to Isobel, this afternoon, at the wedding. And if he chose his words carefully enough, then it might become the moment for which he had waited so long. Surely then he would be able to prise some response from her; something to put her off guard long enough for him to say what he wanted to say. He padded back to bed and slept till late.

In the afternoon he went to the wedding.

7

Isobel wore white gloves. The Hicksons shuffled in bewilderment through the crush of Maori guests. Hickson grated along on his walking sticks; Mrs Hickson darted glances to right and left like a startled bird. Kuru, surprisingly sleek in a dark suit, guided the clergyman through the guests; and listened attentively to what the sad little man had to tell him.

The ceremony was brief. Kuru's sister was plainly pregnant, though not obtrusively so; young Hickson wore his surliest expression and looked suffocated in suit and tie. The clergyman spoke his solemn words and they, the recipients, bowed their heads; and were joined.

The Hicksons soon escaped the wedding breakfast, before their drunken son began singing bawdy songs with friends. They went meekly down the hall, Hickson hobbling, Mrs Hickson leading gently. They shook hands and vanished.

And Mr Fail felt an unexpected choke of pity.

The cleric was next to leave; and the party raged. Kegs thundered across the wooden floor; feet battered the boards in uninhibited dancing. Voices bellowed and glasses smashed. Occasionally he glimpsed Isobel, unusually elegant, moving lightly and easily through it all, talking to the bride, reproving the groom, chatting to up-country guests; he could not get close to her. Certainly not close enough to talk to her. Perhaps afterwards, he told himself. For urgency possessed him; already he could see the dusty bus rolling out of Te Waiotemarama.

Presently he found the heat and racket of the smoky hall too much to endure. He went out, for a moment, on to the verandah of the hall; and then, feeling a slight palpitation in his side, concluded that he was over-excited and, on reflection, walked down the road to the pub to get his pills. He was away from the hall longer than expected, for when he reached his room he felt need to sit and rest.

When he returned to the hall eventually Isobel was gone. His first thought was that perhaps, like himself, she had merely escaped the place a few minutes; and would return. But with the passing minutes ransacked for sight of her and found empty, he realized she had indeed gone.

Urgency became panic; he hurried out of the hall, up the hill, to the cottage.

The cottage was empty.

He could not imagine where she had gone. Why she had escaped so quickly. He sat, breathless, on the edge of her verandah a minute, shading his eyes against the sunlight, looking down at the harbour, the white beaches among rocks. The clamour of his body settled, leaving a slow burning of mind; he took a deep breath, and found himself watching two figures diminish along the long thin beach which curved around to the harbour heads. One of the pair might be Isobel.

Of course. Her bathing costume was missing from the place where it usually hung to dry. She must have decided, fleeing the heat of the hall, to go swimming. Why not? It was natural. She was not to know he was leaving tomorrow.

Quickly now, he hurried down the hill, through the village. He passed the Hickson house. Hickson was back on his place on the verandah, fastened about his telescope again. He had it trained somewhere in the direction of the heads. As he swivelled it his laughter rang across lawn and garden. He was chortling for no reason plain to Mr Fail.

But that lunatic laughter pursued him out of the village, across the crisp sand. Sometimes he could see the figures ahead; other times he lost sight of them behind dunes and toi-toi. Their direction was obscure. At times they moved inland to no clear purpose, following not the line of the beach, but the straighter line their own feet took them.

When he saw Isobel was walking with Kuru, he knew his time badly chosen. Naturally she would want to have a few words with her pupil before he left. Tomorrow Kuru would leave in the same bus Mr Fail planned to take. Today was the day for goodbye to Kuru: distracted, Isobel would have no time or thought for another. Why hadn't he thought of it? It was too late now; too late. And Mr Fail plodded steadily behind the couple who every now and then receded from sight; receded and then appeared again, even more distant, so that he soon realized his own pace was slowing. He would never catch them at this rate; and they were always too far ahead for him to call across the sound of the sea. They would never hear him.

Then he lost them.

He walked and saw no more of them. And at length he rounded the heads and came to the ocean beach where surf thundered, found it empty, and climbed the sandhills above the beach, through clumps of lupin and marram, to see if height would help. For a time it brought nothing. He saw only long shoreline. Exhausted, he fell to the sand.

He had lost them. It was ridiculous.

He lay there some time. Seagulls wheeled in the sky and wind shook the vegetation. A little while longer and he might have slept.

The voices seemed to swim up from great depth, through layers of wind and sea. At first he thought he imagined them; absurdly he dismissed them.

But they persisted, faint and distant, until they could no longer be ignored. Presently he stood and scanned the shore again.

They were not far away. He found himself looking directly down on them. They were in a place where the sea spilled into the sandhills, a rocky lagoon, circled with toi-toi. They must have only recently arrived, for they had not been there when he looked before; they must have dawdled to this location while he lay among the lupins.

They were swimming, the two, the summer-coloured woman beside her brown companion; swimming and laughing and splashing. Sometimes they spun down into the clear depths, so that there was only the swift flash of underwater flesh as they swam side by side, altogether alone in that remove from the world. Again and again they began to descend, sometimes for so long that it seemed they might never rise at all, and then exploded to the surface, silver water spraying from their bodies.

He called to them. He cried out. They did not hear.

As the pain came beating up his side Mr Fail, sliding in the sand, half-fell to his knees, his hands lifting. Then his hands dropped suddenly, as if to catch the pain, wrench it away. Then they jumped to his eyes, to tug apart the curtains gathering there.

And when he fell, he rolled over once or twice, until stopped by a drift of sand, and lay still.

RIVER, GIRL AND ONION

FOR JENNY BOJILOVA

1

THAT Saturday began badly for Lila.
That Saturday began with the bird. Or, to be exact, without the bird.

The bird was a yellow-green canary which sang from a square wire cage in the courtyard below her window. It was an old courtyard, unevenly paved, with three walls where plaster peeled from bleached brick. At the open end, facing the street, there was an iron railing and a flight of stone steps descending to a dark cellar. Above was a predictably smoky patch of London sky. Five battered garbage cans stood there; and there also, in mild and middling weather, the caged canary sang. Rain would see the old spinster owner of the bird hastening to make safe her pet: the cage would be withdrawn, a window would close, and thin lace would curtain the canary within a dim, drawing-room world. Of that Lila could see little: a cabinet stocked with fragile china, a corner of faded carpet, and two potted plants. Her only contact with that melancholy world was when she flung her window wide on a sunlit morning to hear the canary's song. At that hour Lila preferred joy to melancholy.

In this circumstance, in this receptive mood, Lila one sunny spring noon discovered the absence of the bird. She was alarmed and horrified. For there was the courtyard, painted pale gold, without a song, without a bird; and the spinster's window was fast. Lila shivered in her thin nightdress and distractedly drew a thick woollen dressing-gown over her shoulders.

It seemed a symptom of some tragedy: the bird had escaped and flown; the bird was dead; the spinster was dead; or both, the woman and the pet, were dead. These seemed to Lila the limit of possibilities; but as an omen in Lila's life the event seemed to have unlimited possibilities. Not even the news, which she heard later in the day, that the spinster had merely taken her annual holiday with a sister in Devon, and had given the bird into care of a neighbour, rescued Lila from her intuition of impending disaster. It did, however, jolt her into the realization that she was thinking in Russian; and had, in fact, since she had risen to the songless courtyard, been thinking in Russian. The thoughts coming so darkly had demanded the language. For once, however, she made no effort to revert to English; moodily she tidied her small room and drew the curtains on the afternoon.

When Cecil arrived at five, he found her dramatically arranged upon the bed in a darkened room. This did not surprise him: he was used to what she called her peasant moods. He was used also to dramatic arrangements of her body, and darkened rooms. He shook off his duffle-coat and sat silently on the end of her bed. He lit two cigarettes and handed one to Lila. '*Spaseebo bolshoi,*' she murmured.

'*Pazhahlsta,*' he returned and fell silent, since he had already reached the limit of his Russian. His eyes became accustomed to the dark. She was dressed simply; she wore a loose roll-neck black sweater and her long legs were sheathed in tight slacks. One leg was crooked delicately, while the other cut a straight black line down the pale bedcover. At the head of the bed was an effective arrangement of arms. The pillow was awry, and her head rested crosswise on it; her face was an oval pale and withdrawn in darkly fanning hair. He admired the complete picture and wondered if he should make love to her. He rejected this idea on grounds of expediency, since it was plain that a bout of love-making, however minor in dimension, would delay them over-long in the room; and they had to meet Paul at seven. And it was clear that he would have difficulty getting Lila there on time anyway.

2

Lila was considering Cecil not as a lover; but as an adviser in the matter of love. The fact that Cecil served fitfully as a lover only enhanced his value as an adviser.

Her friendship with Cecil had not been of long duration. They met on a long sea voyage, from New Zealand to Southampton. Lila had lived in that country since infancy; Cecil was a fourth generation New Zealander. His well-connected family included prosperous pastoralists, hard-drinking clerics and unprincipled politicians; its less distinguished side numbered a saint or two. Cecil was of the less distinguished side.

All this Lila learned from Cecil, a vague young man with rumpled clothes and woolly hair, on the long haul up the Pacific to the Panama canal. Her relationship with the islands they were leaving was far less complex. She had simply been taken there as a child after spending her first years in Europe. She had, she once calculated, been conceived in Warsaw, seen out most of gestation in Leipzig, been born in Paris, and then shipped to the Pacific before war or revolution again overtook her family. Life in New

Zealand had a schizophrenic quality; she was always a traveller in a limbo between languages.

The world of her native language was one of wistful evenings at the family fireside, and of bleak old people at Orthodox services praying for the deliverance of Holy Russia; the world of her adopted language was confusingly casual. Though her parents might hold aloof from this world, there was after a while no question but that they must surrender their daughter to this new country.

That was reason for distress; at times cause enough for them to speak of a return to Europe, where there would be a proper respect for traditional values. Sometimes events, the end of the war or the death of Stalin, brought hope and fresh despair. Lila was even more cause for anguish. When she began university, they were happy; when she dropped out they were unhappy. When she announced that her current boy friend was secretary of the university Communist Party, they were unnerved. And when at last she took an interest in drama, their feelings were mixed; they reasoned that it was good that their daughter should find something to enliven her, but their relief was tainted with a long-held suspicion of the theatre, and the fear that their daughter might mix with loose women and homosexuals. They were fortunately not able to see the ease with which their daughter mixed with these people. Rejoicing in her apparent success, they were even able to conceal their squeamishness when she appeared in a Saroyan play as a prostitute, and in a Sartre play as a lesbian; her mother, in fact, conceded that in the latter play she would never have known her little girl, her *malenkaya dyevotchka*.

Actually it was no longer adequate to call Lila even a *bolshoya dyevotchka*. At the unlikely height for a Russian girl of six feet and half an inch (the climate, her parents explained) she had the appearance of a mature woman. Certainly she was afflicted with the discontents of womanhood. Even her parents now seemed to agree that a girl of her age should find the other sex a major preoccupation; indeed they began to seem eager that life should soon bestow the twin blessings of marriage and childbirth upon her. Two boys from the White Russian community became regular visitors, though never at Lila's invitation, to the house; they seemed anxious to co-operate in bestowing blessings. They might have been less anxious had they known, when one or other of them visited the house on a Sunday afternoon, that Lila had the night before drunk whisky and gone to bed with a neurotic but rather brilliant young artist who threw the whisky bottles out of his attic window and sometimes said obscene things to Lila. These polite young men had arrived on the scene altogether too late; their only hope, had they known it, was that Lila might one day tire of having obscene things said to her.

Not that she was fond of hearing these things, or of the artist; it was just that he gave an impression of being human. Also she was not anxious to become the recipient of twin blessings.

Already it seemed to her that she squandered far too much of her dramatic energy upon life. She abandoned the artist and won a scholarship to study in London; and one rainy autumn day found herself waving farewell to her tearful parents from the deck of a ship.

She met Cecil at meal-times; they were at the same table. He was lost and moody among all the strange people; since she was the only one who seemed prepared to listen to him, he followed her about the ship. His sombre face waited for her whenever she came up on deck or turned away from a game. She supposed him brilliant, since he talked about life. After some time, however, it emerged that his regret was that he knew so little about life. 'All the twenty-four years of my life I have been sitting in classrooms and lecture-rooms having things told me,' he explained. 'Nobody gave me a chance to know things.' He had finished university with honours in philosophy; now he was going to Paris. He might study; he might write. Paris seemed the place for a good many things. Two difficulties which he discounted as minor were that he had no money, and spoke no French. But he was confident. 'I read once, in a magazine,' he said, 'about a man who went around the world with twenty pounds and one language.'

After a while he thought fit to say, 'I hope, Lila, you do not think I am pursuing you from some concealed physical motive. My motive is purely intellectual.' Lila was relieved. Presently, however, she felt distinctly dowdy and unattractive; she also began to feel self-conscious and silly. She powdered her nose frequently, studied her clothes carefully, and ensured her head was at the right tilt for a pleasing silhouette when she spoke to him on the deck at night.

At length, the night after Pitcairn, he kissed her, more by accident than design. And the night after Curaçao, where they drank iced beer on a cool white terrace overlooking the sea, there was an incident under a lifeboat on the upper deck. Nevertheless, the voyage between Pitcairn and Curaçao had been a slow one.

After the incident Cecil felt obliged to propose marriage. Lila suggested Cecil have more experience before marriage. 'I am thinking of it only for your sake,' she explained. She added that she believed their affair very Lawrentian; for Cecil's benefit, however, she was unable to specify what she meant since her artist friend, from whom she had acquired the word, had used it in undiscriminating fashion. 'No doubt, Cecil,' she said, 'you will in time understand what I mean. With experience.'

They were in London three days together. After they discovered

Piccadilly Circus small and grubby, St. Paul's pigeon-spattered, and the Thames marvellous, Cecil left for Paris. Two weeks later, when Lila called at New Zealand House for her mail, she found an urgent note from Cecil which informed her that he was back in London. 'I am desperate', the note concluded.

Hoping to save him from suicide, Lila took a taxi to the cheap Bloomsbury hotel where he was staying temporarily. He had no patience with her message that tomorrow the birds would sing. 'It was terrible,' he said. His money dwindling, he was forced to sleep on boulevard benches and slowly nibble long loaves of bread to outwit hunger. He was friendless and alone and twice, while he was sleeping outdoors, it had rained. There had been experiences. Once an incomprehensible gendarme seemed about to arrest him. Another time, in hope that he might glimpse someone famous or perhaps hear English spoken, he recklessly spent sixty francs on a small coffee at the Café de Flore and fell into conversation with a nice young American who bought him two glasses of beer and talked about Gide. Cecil had not stopped running until he found the staid old buildings of London walling him in again, and people speaking a substantially understandable language. He was about to cable a friend for money to return to New Zealand.

Since Lila was at that time lonely in London, disliking her drama school, her fellow students, her landlady and the weather, and most of all the fact that she went alone to the theatre, she was glad to see Cecil and tried to persuade him to stay. After two expensive weeks of coffee, beer, meals and double theatre tickets, she eventually persuaded him; and forgot to be lonely.

After Cecil took a job at eight pounds a week caring for rabbits and guinea pigs in a hospital laboratory, and could pay for his own theatre tickets, Lila suddenly found him a liability. For she met a personable young man at the drama school who seemed more interested in her than in other personable young men, and who took her to cocktails before and after the theatre; consequently she wanted to see less of Cecil.

On lonely Sundays, however, when Cecil trudged bleak streets and tired of looking at the paintings in the galleries, he ended his wandering by knocking at Lila's door. In time Lila began to find this irritating. She suggested Cecil should make other friends in London. 'I am thinking of it only for your sake,' she explained. Cecil tried hard to make friends. At the hospital, though, where he was ordered about by crabby nurses and severe doctors graded in a baffling hierarchy, he only had time to make friends with the cockney boy who swept the floors. This cockney boy, who had a pimply face and a sweet nature, had never heard of Kant or Hegel and privately thought Cecil bloody queer. He took Cecil rock 'n' rolling at the

Palais. Though Cecil escaped with only bruises and abrasions of a minor nature, the evening was sufficiently alarming for the boy not to take Cecil again.

Cecil persevered in his quest for friends. But not until a Sunday when Lila was away, weekending in Somerset with her young man, did he find any. That afternoon, at Speakers' Corner, he found two. He was afterwards grateful to Lila, for had she not so often reminded him of his duty to himself to make friends, he would obviously not have spoken to the two young men with strange accents who seemed to enjoy arguments.

They were students, these two, and shared a room in Gower Street. Jose was from Venezuela and Paul was from Hungary. Jose had been a wanderer ever since he had gone into exile after leading a student strike in Caracas; he had studied in Mexico City, Berlin and Paris. Paul had been in London since late 1956; he also had been some kind of student leader. Both spoke English of an erratic variety. They had only really been speaking it since they had come to England and had evolved a strangely private idiom. Certainly they confused Cecil. They confused him even more with their arguments. Cecil could contribute little since he had so far failed to meet up with the finer points of Marxism.

Jose was handsome, his skin richly coloured by Indian and Negro blood; he had a neat moustache, brilliant teeth, and astonishingly vivid eyes. He wore bright check shirts and a leather jacket. Cecil could imagine a pistol tucked carelessly in Jose's belt; in fact, Jose's personality so much appealed to him that he immediately stopped writing a rather long and complicated story about a young man who looked after rabbits and guinea pigs, and began writing another about a young Latin American revolutionary with wicked eyes. Cecil worked on this story for some months while at the same time, under the guidance of Jose and Paul, studying internal contradictions and dialectical leaps. His difficulty with the story was that he could find no end. He ignored those who advised him that it was no longer necessary for short stories to have ends. Cecil preferred to fly in the face of literary fashion. 'It is cheating to have no ending,' he said.

Paul was a contrast. His face was thick and heavy; he smiled rarely, and dressed darkly. He suffered prolonged moods of depression; and, so Jose once told Cecil, often cried out in his sleep.

Paul's father, a socialist veteran and ally of Bela Kun in 1919, had after the second world war been prominent in the new Hungarian government until arrested and shot as a fascist Titoist-Trotzkyist and imperialist agent. Paul, a student activist, was asked to denounce his father; since he declined to do so, he was expelled from university and went to work in a factory. He was there four years until, after his father's corpse was rehabilitated, he was readmitted to university. When trouble in Hungary began he had spoken with some authority about the nature of the government. He was not able to speak with much clarity about what happened after the tanks blasted into Budapest. His last clear memory was of participating in a radio broadcast before some of his remaining friends, fearing for his safety, pushed him into a fast car headed for the border.

He was tumbled about from bed to bed, place to place; people kept trying to make him say things he didn't want to say. He wanted to say different things, but when he said different things, no one seemed to be listening. Naturally, because of his father's name, a large number of journalists wanted to talk to him. He should have been a gift for any journalist; instead of a gift, he was a problem. For example, when asked to outline his disillusionment with Communism, he unreasonably persisted in saying he was still a Communist, and that Rakosi, Krushchev, Stalin and the rest were not Communists at all; and the journalists fiddled, talked among themselves, and lit cigarettes. In the end, then, he began to say nothing and the journalists lost interest. When he reached London he met Jose, with whom he had corresponded since Jose visited Budapest for a youth festival. He was ill for a while, and Jose looked after him. Jose would listen to what he wanted to say. Jose could sometimes even make Paul smile.

Jose entertained Paul by persuading him to laugh at the English. Jose once said he hoped Cecil didn't mind them laughing at the English. 'You are English colonial, no?' he said.

'Please do not worry,' Cecil said. 'I feel my inherited English blood must have undergone some change under the South Pacific sun. It is probably something dialectical. For I have no longer anything in common with this tribe of strange castes and rituals. I am not an Englishman of the colonial variety. I am a Polynesian of the pale-skinned variety.'

'You are an angry young man, yes?' said Paul.

'No,' said Cecil. 'I am an unhappy young man.'

Lila, while Cecil dutifully developed new friendships, had begun to give herself to twilights of the soul, and wandered at dusk through streets and parks. Her young man had left her for a baronet's daughter who would one day inherit a fine estate and several large companies. Lila could have competed against this girl, who was actually a silly creature, but she could not compete against the fine estate and large companies. She was also disillusioned with the theatre. Her height made her unfit for consideration in any serious dramatic role. Plainly a woman with such difficult statistics could only hope, at best, to play comedy. Also she objected to the methods of tuition at the school. These seemed more concerned with displaying the body than displaying the soul. She deduced that the school was more a slavemarket than a school for the theatre. Lonely and depressed, she resented the fact that Cecil no longer came to see her. 'He is mean and disloyal,' she told herself sulkily, 'after all I have done for him. But I have my pride. I will not seek him out.'

They met again by accident in a book shop in the Charing Cross Road. Lila was reading a life of Stanislavsky, and Cecil a novel well reviewed in the Sunday papers. Cecil often did this. After a study of the Sunday papers he selected the novel most favourably reviewed and read it on Saturday afternoons all the way down the Charing Cross Road. He read an average of forty pages in each shop; then moved on to the next.

On that afternoon, when he met Lila, he ignored his cool reception and took her to an espresso bar where he gave her a long and detailed appraisal of the contemporary literary scene and assailed a prominent new writer. 'He ignores the role of the cash nexus,' he said. Lila, with the memory of the baronet's daughter still fresh, was inclined to agree with Cecil's view of the cash nexus but, preserving her frigid front, did not say. Instead she burst into tears. This blunted the point Cecil was making about the definitive nature of the Hungarian revolution.

Cecil was embarrassed. When they left the espresso bar he perceived the most obvious way of ridding himself of his embarrassment. 'I will take you home,' he said. Lila sprinkled fresh tears on the busy footpath. 'You are only trying to dispose of me,' she claimed. Lila wanted not to be disposed of; but to be loved. 'I have a suggestion to make,' Cecil said finally. Lila was by this time relieved to know Cecil was capable of making any suggestion whatsoever. 'I will take you to meet two good friends of mine,' he said. 'The company may do you good.'

They ate that night in a little Italian restaurant just off the Tottenham Court Road. This became a habit; every Saturday the four met to eat in the same place. Afterwards they walked Soho or went to a Thames-side pub. Sometimes, though rarely, their number was increased by a stray Latin American, Hungarian or New Zealander. One feature of their group, however, was that there was never an Englishman. They all regretted this. 'Maybe,' said Paul, 'we should better know England if we knew just one Englishman.' Lila said she knew an Englishman once and didn't like him anyway; but Lila was prejudiced. Each week they exchanged stories gathered from observation of the native population of London. For example, Lila once reported, 'Today I saw a bowler-hat kissing a girl.' This story, however, was disbelieved.

Lila departed stormily from her drama school. It was the result of a tutor describing Russian character so that the students might better involve themselves in a Chekhov play. Lila quarrelled with this description as superficial, and indeed stupid; but the tutor countered with the remark that Lila could scarcely profess to know a great deal about Russian character since she had never lived in Russia. Lila, who felt the truth of this keenly, was dismayed and angry. 'If I am not a Russian,' she demanded, 'then what am I?' 'Very probably,' replied the tutor coolly, before proceeding with evaluation of the Russian character, 'you are a New Zealander.' Lila walked out of the class. 'I am a woman without a country,' she told them sadly the following Saturday. 'I am a lonely voyager on a strange sea.'

'We are all voyagers,' Paul observed. 'All lonely voyagers on strange seas. Even,' he added significantly, 'even Cecil.' This was to reassure Cecil and include him in their company since, though Cecil was the only one of them who felt free to return to his own country, he still lacked money to do so.

'What can I do?' Lila appealed. 'Where will it end?' She tried to get work in repertory; she finished working as a waitress. She received a large number of tips and propositions from the customers she served. Lila took the tips and ignored the propositions; they nevertheless disturbed her. 'I am sliding down,' she declared. 'I shall be on the street in a few weeks.' However, Jose, Paul and Cecil promised to save her; they would, they said, keep her as collective mistress. Lila did not think this idea amusing. 'Where will it end?' she said.

One Sunday afternoon she walked with Jose through Kensington Gardens; afterwards they passed along the street which held the Soviet embassy. Up and down the street small children played, jabbering in Russian; their parents promenaded and gossiped in the sunlight. Lila was excited; she had never heard so many talking Russian around her before. She began to shiver. 'I feel queer,' she said. 'Quickly, I must sit down.' Jose was alarmed and attentive. 'Have you one ache in the head?' he said uncertainly. No, said Lila. It was not a headache. 'It is nothing,' she added. 'It will go away soon.'

It did not go away soon. Some days later Lila returned to the street and talked to a cultural attaché at the embassy about going to Russia and working in the Soviet theatre. The attaché discussed socialist realism. This upset Lila. 'I am an unsocially realist person,' she said the following Saturday. 'There is no place for me.'

Lila, who was a head taller than chunky Jose, had fallen in love with him. This presented difficulty. Lila liked to give the impression of being a loose woman. She gave a good impression of being a loose woman. Also she liked to leave the impression of being in love with everyone; in this she was successful too. That was the difficulty. For when she told Jose she loved him, Jose presumed she told Cecil and Paul the same thing; and felt no urgent or personal concern.

Lila on principle disapproved of revolutions. Yet she managed to listen without protest when Jose announced, in a fit of frustration, that instead of studying philosophy, it would be far better if he learned to use a tommy-gun. Lila soothed him; and he told her about his father, a colonel in the Venezuelan army who, since late adolescence, had had a pouched pistol swinging against his thigh. When a disagreement with the current dictator sent him into exile in Mexico, his father, without his pistol for the first time in twenty years, felt naked, and constantly slapped his unadorned thigh in bewilderment. He stayed indoors, fearful of open streets in daylight and dark streets at night. With such a father it was not surprising that Jose should have begun life a pacifist. But now he was convinced pacifism was useless. 'I have dead pacifist friends,' he said, to clinch his argument. 'Maybe,' he added presently, 'I am no right to say the tommy-gun is superior to philosophy. Combining the tommy-gun and philosophy is one big problem.'

Lila was alarmed when Jose spoke of returning to Venezuela. 'What will become of you?' she cried. Jose answered the question coolly. 'Maybe for me only more exile,' he said. 'I think I will no be dead. They make dead only big men. I am one little man.' Lila was not reassured. When she said 'What will become of you?' she meant 'What will become of me?' Jose appeared to think revolution risky enough without marriage too. Lila displayed affection for Paul and Cecil in hope of making Jose jealous; since Jose had not minded this situation at the beginning he saw no reason why he should dislike it now. It was also less demanding.

Lila became despondent. To console her, Jose read her Lorca as they lay in her room, or sat in the pale sunshine among the falling autumn leaves. Lila listened with impatience; she liked the sound of Spanish, she explained, but she couldn't understand the words. Jose bought her a book of English translations and she followed him through the *Romancero Gitano*. 'Is beautiful, no?' said Jose. 'I like much the poem of the gypsy and the woman who was no a maiden.' 'It was a very ephemeral affair,' said Lila. 'Russians do not have ephemeral affairs. They love with the soul.' Jose was silent and thoughtful.

'Jose, darling,' Lila said, 'why don't you take me away somewhere?'

'I will take you to Brighton,' Jose said. Jose had heard of the English custom of weekends at Brighton. But Lila really wanted to be taken to Paris. When they went to Paris Lila found herself miserable; Jose insisted on visiting all his exile friends and discussing, in rapid Spanish, the political situation up and down the Americas while Lila sat dismayed in corners of crowded, smoky little Latin Quarter rooms. Jose's friends all seemed to find

Lila, and her height, very amusing; she became tired of hearing them refer to her, when they talked to Jose, as *su amiga alta* and *su amiga loca*. 'I wish we had gone to Brighton,' Lila said after three days. Jose concluded that she was impossible to please.

Paul and Cecil saw each other often. Paul was still unhappy about people trying to make him say things he didn't want to say. One friend of his had gone back to Hungary safely by saying all the things they wanted said there; another had made himself prosperous, writing and lecturing in America, saying what they wanted said there. Both had written him letters. One called him a traitorous counter-revolutionary; the other called him a traitorous stooge. 'I want only to be left alone,' Paul said.

Cecil was persevering with literature. He had found no end for the story about a character like Jose; and returned to his story about the young man who looked after rabbits and guinea pigs in a hospital. After some deliberation he attached an end to this story; it showed the young man being taken to a mental hospital and, in his cell, proclaiming himself a guinea pig. Cecil thought this story ironic and symbolic of the human condition. He read the story to Paul. He explained that the young man in the story had only a passing resemblance to his own character. Paul said he understood perfectly; but suggested the end of the story sounded contrived. Cecil began writing a new, rather bitter story about a Hungarian.

On New Year's Eve Jose and Paul gave a party. Their room had been conscientiously tidied: coloured streamers tangled from their ceiling: the table was set with wine and beer, bright paper hats, salt biscuits and potato crisps. When they arrived, Lila received flowers and kisses, and Cecil a large glass of beer. They sang away the time before midnight. The landlady came upstairs to complain about the noise. Jose, with Latin charm, pacified her and sent her downstairs with a gin and tonic.

At midnight, wearing their bright party hats, they stood holding hands in the centre of the room. Cecil and Lila taught Jose and Paul to sing *Auld Lang Syne*. After midnight, separate again, Jose revealed he was returning to Venezuela. Since everyone had been drinking, and everyone spoke frequently of returning home, only Paul, who knew already, took the announcement seriously at first. But when Jose went on to explain that he had received a letter from Caracas which told him a movement was afoot against the regime, and which urged him to return as soon as he could, Lila, who wanted to hear no more, rose to her feet with a stricken face. 'This room is stuffy,' she said. 'I want to open a window.' Jose said he hoped to get a post lecturing at Caracas university; it would be a good cover for clandestine political activity. 'Even with the window open,' Lila said, 'this room is still stuffy. Why don't we go for a walk?' The other three, drowsy with drink and chilled by the rush of frosty air into the room, were not enthusiastic. When Lila became insistent they pulled on their coats and followed her down into the street.

At Piccadilly the crowds were thinning in the cold evening, leaving the Circus webbed with streamers and strewn with confetti. There was a man being sick on the footpath; another asking passers-by if they were Irish.

By the time they found coffee in a dimmed Soho, they were miserable. 'In New Zealand,' Cecil said, 'it is summer. After midnight we go swimming.' Paul said he was going to bed. 'That,' said Cecil, 'is the most sensible idea I have heard for a full hour.'

Jose took Lila home. When they were alone together, walking lifeless streets, Lila said, 'It is terrible. The new year is two hours old already.' Jose was silent. 'When are you going?' she said finally. He was not sure. 'But soon,' he added. She took his arm tightly. 'Will you remember me?' she said. Yes, he would remember her; and Paul, and Cecil. But her particularly? Yes, her particularly. 'How could I forget?' Jose sighed. And—who knew?—maybe after the revolution she would come to Venezuela, he said; she, and Paul, and Cecil.

But Lila only said, 'Wouldn't it be a wonderful thing if we could just go on walking like this, arm in arm, on and on, for ever?' Jose, who thought the night too cold to enjoy walking, failed to embrace the notion with conviction.

At the airport, the morning he left, there were gifts and tears. They would all, he said, have to visit Venezuela soon. Jose embraced all three dispassionately and strutted jauntily across the tarmac to the waiting aircraft. '*Salud!*' he cried before a door sealed him from sight. A hand waved at a window and the aircraft rose up into a cloudless sky. Lila, in the restaurant, said she wouldn't have coffee. 'I want English tea,' she said. 'Very weak, with milk and sugar.' The next morning, opening her newspaper, she read about tanks racketing through the streets of Caracas.

3

'It is getting late,' Cecil said. To verify this he rose from the bed, crossed the room, and peeled back the curtains to reveal the darkening courtyard.

'Of course,' said Lila. 'It is always late.'

Cecil let the curtains fall with a swish. The courtyard depressed him. He turned to Lila; and discovered she depressed him too. 'We shall keep Paul waiting,' he said.

'We are always waiting,' Lila said. 'In our different ways. All of us are waiting.'

'Lila,' said Cecil gravely, resuming his place on the edge of the bed, 'you generalize too much from particulars.' He paused and sighed. 'But I know,' he added, 'that you are miserable just now. I mean about Jose and everything.'

'It is more than eight weeks,' Lila said. She meant since she, Paul and Cecil had received postcards which showed Caracas in colour, and told them Jose had arrived. 'And I have written sixteen letters, and there is still no answer. After all, he can't be busy now, can he? The revolution was over almost as soon as he arrived.'

'Perhaps,' said Cecil, 'they are consolidating. And preparing against the counter-revolution. Who knows?'

'God knows,' Lila said firmly. 'He could have sent another postcard at least. Don't sixteen letters deserve something?'

Cecil allowed that they did; and shrugged. Presently he took Lila's long slender hand and rested it gently on his palm, as if measuring it for weight and size. He spoke carefully. 'You must bear in mind, Lila, that Jose may have a girl friend, or a fiancée, or even a wife, in Venezuela.'

'Impossible,' Lila said with vigour. 'He hasn't been there for years.'

'Nevertheless,' Cecil said, shrugging again, 'such things are not unknown.' He was content to leave it at that. He meant, however, no cruelty; he wanted Lila to become herself again. She was playing her present role with too much verve.

'I want to ask your advice,' she said at last. 'Do you think I should go to Venezuela? There are planes flying all week, and I have almost enough money. It is perfectly safe now there is no revolution.'

'I think it would be unwise,' Cecil said. 'To say the least. Apart from all the more obvious reasons, if you spent all your money flying to Venezuela, you would have none left to pay your fare back to New Zealand.'

Lila abruptly withdrew her hand from Cecil. 'Who said I was going back to New Zealand? I didn't.'

'I was coming to that,' Cecil said quietly.

'Anyway,' Lila continued, 'why New Zealand? The world is my country.'

'No one has said that seriously since Thomas Paine,' Cecil observed. 'He also said mankind was his religion. But that is, of course, beside the point.'

'You annoy me,' Lila said. 'How can I go back? To go back would be to admit the world has defeated me.'

'See it as a tactical movement to the rear.' Cecil suggested.

'I don't understand why you should talk about New Zealand.'

'I was coming to that,' Cecil repeated patiently.

'Then I wish you would come to it. And stop—what is it?— beating about the bush.'

Cecil took Lila's hand again. 'Lila, why don't you come back to New Zealand with me?'

'Is this another proposal?'

'You might consider it one.'

'Very well. You astonish me, Cecil. But I have just one question to ask: how can you possibly expect to keep me in the manner to which I am accustomed?'

Cecil made a thoughtful survey of the room, the meagre collection of belongings within it. 'It should not be too difficult,' he said.

'How can you understand?' she cried. 'How could you possibly understand?' She pointed an accusing finger at him. 'You are a materialist. So you can think only in material terms.'

Cecil felt helpless.

'And when,' Lila continued, 'I asked if you could keep me in the manner to which I am accustomed, it would not occur to you that I meant in a manner quite other than material: that I meant in the manner of inner life.'

'I am aware,' said Cecil, 'of your spiritual inclination.'

'Do you seriously expect me, Cecil, to surrender my rich inner life to become the wife of a New Zealand petit bourgeois?'

'On the contrary,' Cecil said indignantly. 'My background is working-class. My father is a truck-driver and very proletarian. I am not petit bourgeois.'

'In New Zealand even the bourgeoisie is petit bourgeois,' Lila said, rising from the bed. 'Now, shall we go?'

They met Paul a little after seven in the restaurant. His face was no more grave than usual; but he was strangely quiet during the meal. When coffee came he revealed the cause. He had a letter from Venezuela.

'Why,' Lila protested, 'haven't I got one?'

Probably because, Paul said, she had not taken the precaution of writing her return address on the back of her letters. In any case, the letter had not been from Jose, and was written in Spanish. Since Paul knew little Spanish, he had been forced that morning to go out and purchase a Spanish-English dictionary and a grammar. He had spent the rest of the day preparing a translation.

'Well?' Lila said.

The letter was from Jose's wife. It appeared that Jose and some other students had been involved in a skirmish with militia during the closing stage of the uprising; because they were poorly armed, most of the students, including Jose, had been killed. The concluding part of the letter expressed some moral and religious sentiments which were idiomatic in expression and too difficult for Paul to translate.

After a time Paul suggested they walk. Lila, confessing a headache, agreed. Cecil, saying nothing at all, followed them out of the steamy restaurant into the cool night.

They wandered in no direction, through bright streets and dark, streets crowded and streets empty, until a late hour found them on the embankment. Nearby was a pub; noise came to them faintly. Lila watched the river and shivered. Lights criss-crossed the dark water.

'We shall be philosophical,' Lila said.

'Yes,' Cecil said.

'We shall,' Lila said, 'smoke cigarettes and look out upon the river. If we wish to be philosophical, we may reflect on how life is like a river, lazily twisting and sharply plunging, a river of many currents interwoven. If the image is too tired and outworn, forgive me. It is convenient and near at hand. Sometimes good images are hard to find. We have not yet learned to package them in plastic and put them into deep-freeze so that they may be purchased fresh and ready-made—though that day too may come. However,' she finished, shivering again, 'I think we could find a better place to spend the evening.'

Cecil and Paul watched Lila with curiosity. It occurred to Cecil, as they began walking again, that he had an end for at least one story.

Presently they found more coffee. It was in a gloomy little cave of a place with shiny espresso machine, juke-box jazz, and bare wooden tables. At the next table a number of bearded young men swarmed about a girl with long yellow hair, black sweater and corduroy slacks; the girl's face, while not particularly pretty, had a very serene expression. There was a perfect stillness in the way she sat at the centre of the bubbling young men.

'What are you watching her for?' Lila asked Cecil. 'Am I not so interesting?'

'I was just thinking,' he said. 'There; if you still want one, is your image. But I will not elaborate.'

'Nonsense,' Lila said. 'You want to make it glamorous suddenly. Young men flirting with a fair muse. But there is nothing glamorous. Life is about as glamorous as an onion. Peel it down, skin after skin, and what have you got in the end? Nothing. Only tears. Only the tears.'

'You are being very brave,' Paul said, reaching for her hand.

'We are all being brave,' Lila said. 'Or trying to be. And who knows? Perhaps we are.'

After a long silence, they all at once began to talk. Paul thought that, after all, he might return to Hungary soon. Perhaps he could escape having to say anything; perhaps not. Perhaps he could escape prison; perhaps not. 'There is no longer profit in running away,' he said. 'Countries are much like suits of clothes. I think it is better to wear only the dirty suit of one's own country than to keep covering it with the dirty suits of other countries. Eventually one could suffocate in such dirt.' He shrugged, turned his empty palms upwards, and smiled sadly.

It was late. The music had subsided, and the girl with yellow hair had left with one of the bearded young men. Cecil talked about return to New Zealand, where life was less intemperate. Lila also confessed that her ambitions were now on the modest side.

When the shop closed, they went into the night and found a slender moon risen. A peace had descended on the city, the murky river, the old buildings.

Cecil was telling Paul that in New Zealand there were no revolutions. 'Sometimes,' he added, 'I think that it is a good thing, and sometimes I think it is a bad thing.'

Lila took their arms and fell into step between them.

'And sometimes,' she said, 'you don't know what you are saying.'